Praise for **You Are Here**

An *Oprah Daily* Best Book
An *Elle* Best New Book
A *Library Journal* and *Zibby Mag* Most Anticipated Book
A Goodreads Buzziest Debut Novel

"A novel about a dying suburban mall sounds . . . well . . . depressing. Instead, Lin-Greenberg creates an uplifting story about the people who depend on it: the hairdresser renting a chair at the salon, the teenager working at a fried chicken stand, the floundering bookstore manager, the boy who befriends them all. Toward the end, the plot takes an unexpected turn. But it's the generosity that the writer lavishes on this hardworking, diverse community that makes this book so special. A standout." —LEIGH NEWMAN

"Saying *You Are Here* is about a mall closing in a small town is like saying *Moby-Dick* is about a whale. The commonplace happening is merely a tool to explore both how human beings are intimately connected and how others are fully unknowable. This books reminds me of early Celeste Ng—in the best way." —SARAH GELMAN, A Sarah Selects Pick

"Absolutely irresistible." —*People*

"Karin Lin-Greenberg's thoughtful, empathic *You Are Here* [is] such a bittersweet treat." —*Elle*, a Most Anticipated Title of the Year

"Lin-Greenberg's web of characters illustrate the complex lives of ordinary people." —LAURA ZORNOSA, *Time*

"Like Elizabeth Strout's *Olive Kitteridge*, the charm of Lin-Greenberg's engaging story lies in the sweetness of the characters' everyday lives." —BECKY MELOAN, *The Washington Post*

"Charming . . . The small lies woven into a lifelong marriage, the petty resentments harbored by polite neighbors and, above all, the comic discrepancy between a character's outer and inner life—all emerge unforced and unadorned in this multifaceted narrative . . . But the everyday reality that Ms. Lin-Greenberg so memorably creates is not easily eclipsed. Compassion and wry understatement remain her strengths, and in *You Are Here* she captures not only the frayed texture of suburban existence but also the turbulent emotions, immediate and long buried, of protagonists who are ultimately far more than stereotypes."
—ANNA MUNDOW, *The Wall Street Journal*

"Beautifully written and radically sympathetic . . . Among its achievements, *You Are Here* is a breathtaking depiction of a community—even one at the mall." —JEFFREY CONDRAN, *Pittsburgh Post-Gazette*

"This poignant novel by Karin Lin-Greenberg movingly portrays a community of people whose local mall is shutting down. Rich and nuanced in her descriptions of her characters, Lin-Greenberg illustrates both the humanity of their private lives and the layered entanglements of their relationships." —KARLA J. STRAND, *Ms.*

"The novel is entertaining and incisive, and Lin-Greenberg captures a range of human experiences, with a reminder that no one ever knows what another person is experiencing." —KATIE TAMOLA, *Shondaland*

"Lin-Greenberg weaves together . . . individual stories with skill and nuance. The small details of each character's experience provide a kaleidoscopic portrayal in this heartfelt exploration of what makes up a life: secret hopes and dreams, human interactions, moments of kindness and care." —KERRY MCHUGH, *Shelf Awareness*

"With Lin-Greenberg's in-depth character development, *You Are Here* shows both the unexpected connections between strangers and the unshakeable assumptions we have about one another. Lin-Greenberg mines the spectacular within everyday life, whether that is a moment of public violence or intense beauty. Similarly, she highlights how mall culture functions simultaneously as a dying part of suburbia, a symbol of lost dreams, and—perhaps surprisingly—a form of controlled community."

—JAEYEON YOO, *Electric Literature*

"Stunning . . . Among the extraordinary aspects of *You Are Here* is that it encompasses so many different points of view . . . The imaginary community Lin-Greenberg offers us in *You Are Here* is filled with people who have their hopes dashed—who face irrelevance, desolation, and despair. And yet the author's vision is hopeful: in each other, we find humanity."

—LEIGH HABER, *Publishers Weekly*

"Exceptional . . . This is a remarkable study of ordinary people's extraordinary inner lives." —*Publishers Weekly* (starred review)

"Lin-Greenberg's masterful and understated debut novel is an engrossing, character-driven story that will delight fans of Liane Moriarty and Celeste Ng . . . At its heart, this is a story about our ties to and interactions with others and how our communities impact our actions, influence our aspirations, and shape our identities. Lin-Greenberg beautifully translates the lives of an ordinary group of people into an extraordinary, even triumphant novel. *You Are Here* is sure to be a book-club favorite."

—*Booklist*

"This novel is a community and a tour-de-force account of small-town America. How do we survive ourselves and each other? How can we thrive instead of simply coexist? Lin-Greenberg brings her imperfect yet perfect cast of characters to answer this very question and shows us a way. A magical book, brimming with soul."

—WEIKE WANG, author of *Joan Is Okay*

"A boy, a beauty, an elderly gardener, a failed PhD, and an artist with scissors: Where else could all of these characters meet but at the mall?

"In Karin Lin-Greenberg's clear-eyed and heartfelt *You Are Here*, the failing Greenways Mall makes community out of a group of characters so fractious and real, you feel like you're hanging out with them at the food court." —ALEXANDRA LANGE, author of *Meet Me by the Fountain: An Inside History of the Mall*

"A charming and witty work that will also break your heart—a story about America, set in that most American of places: the dying shopping mall." —MARIE MYUNG-OK LEE, author of *The Evening Hero*

"With great insight and care, Lin-Greenberg chronicles the daily lives of neighbors connected to a local mall that's soon closing. *You Are Here* shows that times keep changing but the American Dream persists."
—SARAH LANGAN, acclaimed author of *Good Neighbors*

"In her gorgeous debut novel *You Are Here*, Karin Lin-Greenberg shines her magical light on ordinary characters whose lives intersect at the local mall—the most ordinary place in America—to show how remarkable and singular those lives actually are. Every page carries the author's trademark fusion of poignancy, humor, insight, and yearning, along with the powerful reminder of how the seemingly random connections among us can lead to unexpected grace."
—JESSICA TREADWAY, author of *Lacy Eye* and *Infinite Dimensions*

"In this beautifully affecting novel, Karin Lin-Greenberg creates a chorus of characters so fully human they come to feel like friends and neighbors. In lucid, graceful prose, she illuminates how these lives—brought together in the most banal of places, an upstate New York shopping mall—touch each other in unexpected, lasting ways. We become confidantes to their private hopes, fears, and biases, as we watch their intersecting stories blossom into something rich, complex, and larger than the sum of its parts. I'll be thinking of these people, and this book, for a long time."
—LAUREN ACAMPORA, author of *The Hundred Waters*

YOU
ARE
HERE

ALSO BY KARIN LIN-GREENBERG

Faulty Predictions: Stories

Vanished: Stories

YOU ARE HERE

A Novel

KARIN LIN-GREENBERG

Counterpoint | Berkeley

This is a work of fiction. All of the characters, organizations, and events portrayed in this novel are either products of the author's imagination or are used fictitiously.

Copyright © 2023 by Karin Lin-Greenberg

All rights reserved under domestic and international copyright. Outside of fair use (such as quoting within a book review), no part of this publication may be reproduced, stored in a retrieval system, or transmitted in any form or by any means, electronic, mechanical, photocopying, recording, or otherwise, without the written permission of the publisher. For permissions, please contact the publisher.

First Counterpoint edition: 2023
First paperback edition: 2024

The Library of Congress has cataloged the hardcover edition as follows:
Names: Lin-Greenberg, Karin, author.
Title: You are here : a novel / Karin Lin-Greenberg.
Description: First Counterpoint edition. | Berkeley : Counterpoint, 2023.
Identifiers: LCCN 2022047268 | ISBN 9781640095434 (hardcover) | ISBN 9781640095441 (ebook)
Subjects: LCGFT: Novels.
Classification: LCC PS3612.I52 Y68 2023 | DDC 813/.6—dc23/eng/20221012
LC record available at https://lccn.loc.gov/2022047268

Paperback ISBN: 978-1-64009-643-1

Cover design by Jaya Miceli
Cover images: lemon tree © Natallia Novik / Shutterstock; woman on escalator © Yaorusheng / Getty images
Book design by Laura Berry

COUNTERPOINT
2560 Ninth Street, Suite 318
Berkeley, CA 94710
www.counterpointpress.com

Printed in the United States of America
10 9 8 7 6 5 4 3 2 1

For Jeff

PART I

September

The Sweeper of Hair

Jackson Huang's mother arranged for the school bus to drop him off outside the mall every weekday afternoon because she works at the salon until nine. After he finishes his homework, which he does sitting in one of the stylists' chairs with a book balanced on his lap, he helps his mother. He sweeps the hair that falls around her chair. He also sweeps the entire salon, from one end to the other, because hairs swirl in the breeze created by the air-conditioning and heat. When someone walks quickly through the salon, they stir up the hairs on the floor, which then land all over the place, and this leaves Jackson more to sweep too.

A year ago the salon was more fun because there were other stylists working there, and Jackson could talk to them when they weren't busy. There was Irma, with her bright orange hair piled high on her head, her dangly earrings, her loud laugh that filled the entire space. There was Missy, who was young with a small diamond stud in her nose and saw every single movie shown in the mall's theater. There was Jack, with his snakeskin boots, who would tease Jackson, saying he was named after him, even though Jackson knows he was named after Michael Jackson who was his mother's favorite singer when she was growing up, and because he was born on the same day in 2009 Michael Jackson died. But they are all gone, off to salons where business is better, and there is a row of empty chairs now. Jackson's mother is the only stylist left.

Today Belinda, who manages the salon, is here. She pops in a few times a month to see how things are going, but she doesn't cut hair anymore. She used to, but now the arthritis in her hands is too painful. Jackson's mother rents her chair from Belinda, who walks with a limp and wears long flowered shirts and sighs a lot. Jackson's mother dyes Belinda's hair the color of eggplants. Belinda is always saying she's not sure how long the salon can stay open. "There's rumors the whole mall will be shutting down soon," Belinda says, sitting in the chair next to Jackson's mother's station.

Jackson is sweeping and pretending not to listen, but he always listens to everything people say to his mother. He's very good at what she calls multitasking. He can sweep and eavesdrop. He can do math homework and eavesdrop. He can fold towels and eavesdrop. Eavesdropping is one of his top skills.

"They've been saying that for years," says Jackson's mom. "I'll believe it when they turn out the lights and lock the doors."

Belinda points to a bucket in the hallway next to a yellow sign that says WET FLOOR and features a silhouette of a man slipping. Water from the leaky roof has been dripping into the bucket for the past week. "They've stopped fixing things, Tina." Belinda opens a grease-stained paper bag from Burgerville in the food court and gestures for Jackson to come over. "Fries for you," she says, holding out a carton. "And fries for me too," she adds, taking another carton out of the bag. "Who knows if Hank's dinner will even be edible. He never cooked a meal in the forty-five years we've been married, then he retires and suddenly thinks he's Gordon Ramsay. It's ridiculous to think you can go from an accountant to a gourmet chef, you know?"

"Thank you," Jackson says. He's not sure if he's supposed to say something about Belinda's husband, but he knows Belinda will be satisfied with his thanks. Adults always act so impressed when kids say *thank you*, as if just saying these words is something big and difficult to do. At school, his teachers always tell him he's so polite, even though he doesn't do anything special, just follows directions, doesn't run in the halls, doesn't cut in line for the water fountain after gym class, says *please* and *thank you* when people help him. He just does what he's supposed to do.

Jackson sets the broom against the wall and takes the fries from Belinda. He thinks Belinda feels sorry for him for having to come here every day, so she brings him treats when she visits. His mother always tells Belinda it's unnecessary, but she doesn't stop Jackson from eating the junk food. He tilts the carton of fries toward his mother, and she shakes her head. She's folding the clean black capes the customers wear when she cuts their hair and stacking them on a metal shelf.

Belinda eats a fry, rummages in the paper bag, pulls out a napkin, and wipes her lips. Her cherry-red lipstick comes off on the napkin. "I'm telling you, it might be time to retire. Hank wants to go down to Florida, and I'm starting to think it's not such a bad idea. Warm air might do me good."

"You're not old enough to retire," says Jackson's mom, and Jackson is unsure whether she's saying it because she really means it or because—as Jackson has learned from listening in on conversations in the salon—women sometimes lie about their age. Jackson wonders how old Belinda is. It's hard to tell with her eggplant-colored hair and her makeup and her bright clothes. If she had white hair and clothes that weren't splashed in color, maybe she would look ready for retirement.

"I don't look old because you keep me looking good," says Belinda, patting her hair. She finishes her fries and sticks the empty carton in the bag. "I better go," she says. "I've got to make sure Hank doesn't burn down the kitchen."

After Belinda leaves, Jackson's mother flips through a stack of papers on the receptionist's desk. There's no longer a receptionist. There aren't enough clients to need one.

"How old is Belinda?" Jackson asks.

"Seventy-one," says his mother. She looks up from the messy desk and says, "Old enough to retire."

"Does she have white hair?" Jackson says.

"A stylist can never reveal these things," his mother says, and Jackson thinks about the advice he's read about keeping secrets in his books on magic. Jackson has been practicing saying, "A magician cannot reveal his secrets," in front of the bathroom mirror while attempting to lift one eyebrow in a way that looks mysterious. He has been studying magic—in books borrowed from the library and in videos on YouTube—for the past three months. His mother doesn't know about this new hobby. He won't tell her until he's good enough to perform ten minutes worth of magic tricks for her.

"Why do so many women like dyeing their hair purple?" Jackson has noticed a lot of women ask for purple streaks or for entire heads the color of eggplants or plums or red grapes. "Isn't dyeing hair a trick?"

"A trick?" says his mother.

"An illusion," says Jackson. "Like magic. The illusion that someone doesn't have white hair, even though they really do."

"I guess it is," says his mother. "Here!" she shouts, as she pulls a piece of paper out from beneath a Thai takeout menu. "Found it."

Jackson peers at the paper and sees the number for the scissor sharpeners. They are a husband and wife—both with gray hair, the husband with a big gray mustache that hangs over his upper lip—and come to the salon twice a year.

"But if it's an illusion, why don't people dye their hair real hair colors? Like brown or blond?" Wouldn't the point be to look like they *weren't* dyeing their hair?

"Because they want to feel different from everyone else. Maybe a little dangerous. They want to show the world they're not growing old."

Why, Jackson wonders, is it bad to be old? He doesn't like being nine. He doesn't like not being able to drive or pay for things or own a dog or make decisions about his life. All he wants is to be older.

"Why is purple hair dangerous?" Jackson says.

"It's not," says his mother. "Not really. But I think it lets people believe they're doing something daring, something outside of what's expected. And it's not so out-there, not like a Mohawk or something, so people with boring office jobs can get away with a few purple streaks." She picks up the phone at the reception desk, and Jackson can hear the dial tone. At home, they don't have a landline, just his mother's cell phone. That's another thing he wants—a cell phone—but his mother says he's too young. He mostly wants a phone so he can take pictures, but his mother thinks kids who have phones can get themselves in trouble by talking and texting with strangers.

Jackson's mother punches in the number for the scissor sharpeners, and Jackson can hear music that sounds like it should be played on a carousel coming out of the earpiece. "I'm on hold," she says. "Hold! It's not like they're some big corporation."

"But you don't dye your hair," Jackson says.

His mother lifts a finger, telling him to be patient, but Jackson still hears that carousel music and knows no one is talking to her on the other end of the line.

"And you're forty." He has heard other women complain about being forty; last week a woman getting her hair dyed told his mother that once she turned forty, white hairs started sprouting, and her thighs seemed to get lumpier overnight. Jackson is not sure what it means to have lumpy thighs, but it seems like not a terrible trade-off: white hairs and lumpy thighs for the ability to drive and to have a cell phone and to own whatever kind of dog—preferably a corgi—you want. "You don't have gray hair," Jackson says.

"I'm lucky," says his mother. "Good genes."

"What does that mean?" says Jackson.

"Hello?" says his mother. The other end of the phone is silent.

"Shit," she says, slamming the receiver back into its cradle. "I got cut off." She looks up at Jackson and says, "Don't curse. I shouldn't curse, but you especially shouldn't, okay?"

Jackson nods, and his mother picks up the receiver and punches in the number for the scissor sharpeners again. "Do I have good genes?" Jackson says. The carousel music comes on again and floats out of the part of the phone Jackson's mother holds to her ear. She reaches into her pocket and hands him five dollars. "Food court," she says.

"But I just ate fries."

"Then could you get me a Diet Coke?"

"Diet Cokes are cheaper at Dollar General than at the food court," says Jackson.

"Hello?" says his mother. "Yes, hello, this is Tina Huang at—" and before she can say the name of the salon, she looks up at him and says, "I finally got to a real person and they put me on hold again." The carousel music starts once more.

"Genes?" says Jackson.

His mother sighs. "It just means what's passed down to you by your parents. What you're made of. And I got to forty without gray hair, so you should too."

But Jackson knows this isn't the whole equation. His mother is only half of things. He has never met his father, and his mother won't talk about him. Maybe his father's hair has turned completely white. Maybe his father dyes his hair purple so he can pretend to be younger and cooler than he is. And even though Jackson knows his mother doesn't like to talk about his father, he says, "But what about my dad? What's his hair like?"

"I don't know," says his mother. "I haven't seen him in a long time." She pounds her fist on the desk. "These people know they have a monopoly on this business. They're the only ones who still come to salons. If they don't come, I have to send my scissors back to the manufacturer for sharpening, and that means they go all the way to Japan, and you know how long that takes?"

Jackson shakes his head. "But what was his hair like when you knew him?" He knows it's a risky question to ask, knows his mom might get mad, but she's already mad at the scissor sharpeners, so maybe she's distracted enough to tell him more.

"He's Chinese too, so his hair is probably still dark."

"What does being Chinese have to do with it?"

"Because Asian don't raisin," says his mom. She picks up the Thai menu and slaps it again and again on the reception desk as the carousel music plays.

"Doesn't," says Jackson, who is good at grammar, who always gets 100 percent on grammar quizzes in school. But he has no idea what his mother means. "What are you talking about?"

"It's just a saying, Jackson. Like 'Black don't crack.'"

"What does that mean?"

"Shit," says his mother again. She hangs up the phone. "Don't curse, okay? It's bad to curse. And don't go around saying those things I just said."

"But what do they mean?"

"I can't keep up with your questions," she says, pawing through the pile of papers on the desk. "I can't answer them and try to schedule a scissor sharpening and do everything on my own." She sits down in the receptionist's chair, and a sigh of air comes out of the cushion.

"You have to tell me what they mean," Jackson says.

"You have to promise never to repeat them at school."

"But they're not bad words," says Jackson. He goes over the words in his mind—*Asian, raisin, black, crack*—none of them are curses.

"All they mean is that people who are Black or Asian tend to look much younger than they are."

"But that's a good thing," says Jackson. Aren't his mother's clients always talking about wanting to look younger? He's confused. The words aren't bad, and their meaning isn't bad either.

"Jackson," says his mother, shaking her head. "Will you get me a Diet Coke? Please?"

"Would I really get in trouble if I said those things in school?"

"I don't know. Maybe. But you're nine. You and your friends shouldn't even be thinking or talking about getting old."

Jackson doesn't really have friends at school. People who have friends do stuff after the school day ends, play on sports teams or join clubs, but he's at the salon every afternoon. Suddenly, he has a thought. "What about Michael Jackson?"

"What about him?"

"He cracked," says Jackson, pointing to his own nose. He's seen the pictures, the ones that look like Michael Jackson's nose is almost falling off. "And he was Black."

His mother puts her head in her hands. "I don't know whether to laugh or cry," she says.

"Do you feel bittersweet?" says Jackson. *Bittersweet* was one of his vocabulary words last week, and it means something that's both good and sad.

His mother looks up at him. "I guess I do," she says.

Jackson pauses a moment, then he laughs. He's figured it out. Raisins are wrinkled. Old people are wrinkled. "Asian don't raisin," he says. He likes the incorrect grammar of the sentence.

"No," says his mother, standing up. She puts her hands on his shoulders. "Please don't go around saying that. And don't say the other thing either."

"Why?"

"Because you're not Black. And there are certain things you can only say if you belong to a certain group."

"But then why can't I say the Asian one? I'm Asian."

His mother takes her hands off his shoulders, covers her own eyes.

"Would you please take a walk to the food court while I call the scissor sharpeners again? You can use the change to buy yourself something." She puts her hands on his shoulders again, turns him around, so he is facing the entrance of the salon. She pushes him forward and says, "And while you're gone, I'll work on not saying things I shouldn't."

JACKSON PASSES THROUGH the food court on his way to the dollar store. If he buys his mother a bottle of Diet Coke there, he will have almost four dollars left over for whatever he wants. He wants to buy a Bite Coin, which costs eleven dollars at Game World, which is at the far end of the mall next to Boscov's. Bite Coin is a trick quarter that looks like a bite has been taken out of it, so a magician can ask an audience member for a quarter, pretend to take a bite, hide the original, and then hold up the trick quarter with the tooth marks. With the change from his mother's Diet Coke he will have almost nine dollars saved up, and he'll be able to get the Bite Coin soon. Most people go to Game World to buy video games, but Jackson's mother won't let him play them. She says they make people forget about the world outside, and once they start playing all they want to do is stare at their screen and pretend to be elves or dragons or race car drivers.

He walks past Pizza Perfecto and Taco Bell and Panda Wok, and then he thinks he sees a familiar puff of white hair in line at Hot Dog Charlie's. He gets a sample of teriyaki chicken from Didi at Panda Wok who is handing out samples speared on toothpicks. He doesn't really want the sample, but it allows him to get closer to the man with the puff of hair and to see that he is, in fact, exactly who Jackson suspected. It's Larry Bornstein, a magician who used to be famous enough to do shows all across America and now posts videos on YouTube explaining how to do tricks. Other magicians hate him for giving away secrets and call him a traitor in the comments. He's known for being rude and grumpy, but Jackson isn't sure if that's just part of his act.

"Kid, take a picture. It lasts longer," says Larry.

Jackson swallows his bite of teriyaki chicken. "I wasn't staring."

"You were. Your mom ever tell you staring is rude? You from around here?"

"My mom works at Sunshine Clips," Jackson says, pointing to the salon.

"I didn't ask where your mom works. You live in the area?"

Jackson wonders what's going to happen, whether Larry Bornstein is planning to kidnap him. His mother has told him not to talk to anyone he doesn't know when he walks around the mall. But he does sort of know Larry Bornstein.

"Yes," Jackson says. "I live eight miles from here."

"How do these hot dogs work?" says Larry, pointing to the menu. "I'm from Vegas. We don't have these baby hot dogs there."

"How do they work?" says Jackson. They work like any other hot dog. They go in a bun and you eat them, so he's not sure what sort of information Larry Bornstein wants.

"Like how many of them should a grown man order?"

"For dinner?"

Larry shrugs. "Maybe. It depends if I get fed after my show. I want to be full for the next four hours. How many hot dogs do I order?"

Jackson looks at Larry's belly swelling over the waistband of his black pants, at his shiny purple shirt, the buttons ready to pop. He calculates that Larry weighs at least three times as much as he does. After school, he sometimes has two hot dogs for a snack. So if Larry weighs three times as much as Jackson, he should eat six hot dogs. But he wants more than a snack, so maybe he should add on a few more.

"Eight," says Jackson. "With the works. That means yellow mustard, onions, and chili."

"I can read," says Larry, pointing to the description on the menu. "Eight? You sure?"

Jackson nods, even though he's not sure and thinks Larry will be mad at him if he's not able to finish his food. "They're pretty small."

A teenage boy in a gray denim jacket and gray pants in line in front of Larry moves to the other end of the counter to pick up his food. Larry steps up and places his order for eight hot dogs. Then he looks down at Jackson and says, "You want anything? I can buy you something. I'm not going to kidnap you or anything." Jackson shakes his head because it seems impolite to ask someone he just met to buy him something, but then he says, "A Diet Coke. Please." If Larry Bornstein buys him a Diet Coke, he can keep the entire five dollars his mother gave him and buy the Bite Coin sooner.

"You watching your weight?" says Larry, and Jackson isn't sure how to respond, so he doesn't. Larry reaches into his pocket and takes out his wallet. His hands shake, and he has trouble taking out a twenty-dollar bill. When the woman at the register gives Larry his change, the coins jingle in his hand and keep clanging together until he shoves them in his pocket.

After they move down to the end of the counter to wait for Larry's hot dogs, Jackson says, "I know you're a magician. I watch a lot of magicians on YouTube."

"Then you don't know me as a magician. You know me as a secret giver-awayer."

"Where's your show?"

"In the theater here. Chuckles, where the washed-up comedians usually do their shows."

"I didn't see any posters for it," says Jackson. He isn't exactly sure what *washed-up comedian* means, but then he thinks about the trip to Maine he took with his mother last summer and how dried seaweed and shells and a few empty plastic bottles and even a fish skeleton washed up on the shore. He thinks he understands: these things were once useful or full of life and no longer are.

Larry shakes his head. "Of course not. I'll be playing to another empty theater. You want a ticket?"

"I only have five dollars."

"I can get you in for free."

Jackson considers the offer. Would his mother let him go to a magic show? Would she be suspicious of Larry Bornstein?

"As I said, I'm not trying to kidnap you or anything," says Larry. "I'm a magician. If I wanted you to disappear, I could just make you go poof, right?"

The worker at Hot Dog Charlie's slides a tray toward Larry with two small Styrofoam plates filled with eight hot dogs, a Coke for Larry, and a Diet Coke for Jackson. Larry looks at the tray for a second, then says, "Give me a hand?"

Jackson takes the tray and holds it steadily, careful not to drop it, and follows Larry to a table. "You want to join me while you have your drink?" says Larry.

"The Diet Coke is for my mom."

"God dammit. Now I'm buying drinks for women I haven't even met."

Jackson looks back at the salon. His mother has a client now, Mrs. Goodson, a very old woman with white hair. She doesn't dye it, just lets it be white. His mother won't mind if he's gone for a little longer. She'll probably assume he's looking around some of the stores, which is what he usually does when she sends him to buy her something.

"I can keep you company," Jackson says.

"Do I look like I need company?"

"I can leave."

"Sit down. Here, eat a hot dog. I think seven is my limit." Larry Bornstein pushes one of the Styrofoam plates toward Jackson and the hot dogs on it wobble from side to side. Then Larry reaches into his pocket, takes out two tickets, slaps them down on the table. "One for you and one for your mom. Show's at eight."

"My mom works until nine."

"Take 'em or leave 'em. I don't care." He takes a large bite of his hot dog and looks toward Panda Wok.

Jackson takes the tickets, folds them in half, and slips them into the pocket of his jeans. "Thank you," he says. He wonders if his mother would let him go alone. He wonders if she'd be willing to close the salon early and go with him. He wonders what his mother thinks about magic.

"What are you doing watching my videos anyway? You want to be a magician?"

"Maybe," says Jackson. He takes a bite of his hot dog and wishes it didn't have onions on it. He looks at Larry's face while he chews and notices deep wrinkles and the way his eyes look foggy. How old is Larry Bornstein? Would he look younger if he were Asian or Black? What would Larry Bornstein look like with purple hair? Or a different hairdo? He's always had this puff of frizzy hair, even in the old videos where he has brown hair and is performing, not just telling people the secrets behind magic tricks.

Larry laughs. "Not a career path I'd recommend. You'll end up playing kids' birthday parties and shitty malls." He gestures toward the salon and says, "No offense to your mom."

Jackson says nothing, just finishes his hot dog and watches the pieces of onion fall off the top of Larry's hot dog as he moves it to his mouth.

"What's your backup plan if magic doesn't work out?" says Larry with his mouth full.

"Right now I'm the sweeper of hair. At the salon."

"And there are excellent career options for hair sweepers?"

Jackson shrugs. "I'm good at it."

"Well, good for you," says Larry, but he says it in a mean way.

But then he adds, "It's nice to be good at something," and his voice is softer, quieter.

Again, Jackson doesn't know how to respond, so he says, "I should get the Diet Coke to my mom."

Larry nods. He finishes his seventh hot dog. "See you later, kid," he says. "Or not. Whatever. Do whatever you want."

JACKSON SETS THE cup of Diet Coke on the receptionist's desk and waves at Mrs. Goodson, whose hair his mother has set. She is wearing one of the salon's black capes and sitting under the dome of the dryer chair reading a magazine about home decorating. She waves back at Jackson and then returns to her magazine.

"I met a magician," Jackson says to his mother. "He gave me tickets to his show tonight. Can we go?" He takes the tickets out of his pocket, unfolds them, and hands them to her.

"I told you not to talk to strangers. And for God's sake, don't take things from them." She reaches for the Diet Coke and takes a long sip from the straw. Jackson decides not to tell his mother Larry Bornstein bought the drink.

"I know him. I've seen videos of him before. Can we go to the show?"

"It's a school night. And I have to work until nine. And since when have you been interested in magic?"

"Please?" says Jackson.

"Is this some magician you really like?"

"Not really, but I've never been to a magic show."

His mother looks at the tickets. Then she picks up her phone, and Jackson can see her googling Larry. "People say he's a hack. They don't like his show." She holds up the phone to Jackson, and he takes it from her.

"He used to be more famous," says Jackson. "People used to like him."

"Well, no one must like him now if he's giving away his tickets for free in a mall food court," says his mother. She goes over to Mrs. Goodson, lifts the dome of the dryer, and leads her back to her styling chair, where she'll take the curlers out.

Jackson clicks on another site and reads more comments about Larry. "It's Parkinson's," says one of the comments. "It's too bad," writes another commenter. "A magician needs his hands." Jackson finds the website for Larry Bornstein's show tonight at Chuckles. During the show, he projects old videos of himself doing tricks. Then he tells the audience how the tricks were done. Reviews of the show are terrible.

Jackson gives the phone to his mother, and she slips it into the back pocket of her jeans. She sprays Mrs. Goodson's hair with hairspray, then turns the chair around and gives her a hand mirror so she can see the back. Mrs. Goodson nods, and Jackson's mother unbuttons the black cape and takes it off. When Mrs. Goodson stands up, Jackson notices the curve of her back, how it looks almost like a question mark. There is a pile of white hair under his mother's chair, and Jackson goes to the corner of the salon to fetch the broom and dustpan. He sweeps up Mrs. Goodson's white hairs. Then he walks the dustpan to the garbage can and empties it.

Mrs. Goodson pays and says, "See you next week," and Jackson's mother says, "Same time, same place." Mrs. Goodson is now one of the salon's only regular clients. Jackson's mother has told him she thinks Mrs. Goodson comes in so often because she's lonely.

His mother walks over to him. "Look," she says, "if it's important to you, we can go to the show. I can close early."

But Jackson doesn't want to go to the show anymore. He doesn't want to see those videos of how Larry Bornstein used to be able to perform. He wishes he didn't know Larry can't do tricks anymore because of his shaky hands. He wishes he'd never met Larry, that he'd just gone straight to Dollar General for his mother's Diet Coke.

"No," he says, "that's okay. I have to work on my essay about bald eagles. And I have to study for my grammar quiz."

"You're a good boy, you know that?"

He does know it, and he's glad—so glad—that he's still a boy and that he'll be a boy for a long time to come. He doesn't want lumpy thighs or white hair or a back shaped like a question mark. He doesn't want the day to come when he's no longer good at the things he can do now without even thinking. He can barely imagine it, but years and years from now, the day will come when his skin will have raisined, and even something as simple as sweeping the floor will no longer be easy. He leans the broom and dustpan against the wall and examines the floor for more hair to sweep, but there is none. The floor is perfectly clean.

October

Neighborhood Watch

Here is Kevin tromping across the backyard in a white beekeeping suit, looking like a space explorer. How he managed to shove his enormous orange beard into the veil that hangs from his hat, Ro doesn't know. He's holding something that looks like a silver coffee pot with bellows attached to it, and each time he squeezes the bellows, a puff of smoke emerges from a spout and floats over the two wooden hives that have appeared in his backyard.

Can Ro call some authority on him? Is it illegal to raise bees in a suburban backyard? What if swarms of angry bees escape from the hives and chase the residents of Willowbrook Drive screaming and panicked into the street? If Ro hadn't seen the hives Kevin put in the backyard, she might have thought this was another of his ridiculous costumes. When she goes to the mall to get her hair done, she sees him in the bookstore, where he's the manager, leading story hour dressed sometimes as a giant rabbit, sometimes as a wizard, sometimes as a chef. And lately he's been dressed as a gnome, wearing green clogs and a pointy red hat as he sits on a small stool that looks like a mushroom and reads to children. But this beekeeper getup is no costume; the fool is actually tending to bees. Ro stares for a few moments out the kitchen window at Kevin in his beekeeper suit and then stomps to the front door and goes outside.

Kevin stops squeezing his smoking contraption when Ro reaches his yard, says, "Hello, Mrs. Goodson. Your hair looks nice today."

Ro raises a hand to her hair then quickly drops it. She just had her hair done yesterday, and she slept on a silk pillowcase to ensure the style would keep, but she's not going to let Kevin compliment away her annoyance. "What's the meaning of all this?" she says, gesturing up and down at the two large hives that sit fifty feet from her home. The hives had not been there yesterday.

"The meaning?" says Kevin. His voice is muffled beneath his veil.

"Can you take that hat off?" says Ro. Between the veil and the overgrown beard, she can barely hear him.

"I guess so," says Kevin. "I think there's enough smoke now that the bees should be drowsy." He pulls the hat off and holds it under one arm.

"Are these bees going to bother my flowers?" Ro's house is surrounded by rosebushes, hydrangeas, oleander, rhododendron.

Kevin shakes his big, fuzzy head. "I mean, only in the best way. Bees pollinate, Mrs. Goodson. They'll help your flowers grow."

Of course she knows bees pollinate. Everyone knows this. Kevin has a way of overexplaining. He's working on a PhD in English, so he thinks he's more intelligent than everyone else, goes on too long without seeming to notice when others are getting bored. But this is because he doesn't have a teaching job, couldn't get one, even after all those years of schooling. He doesn't have students to spout off to, so he must subject others to his blathering. He's lucky parents bring their children to story hour in the bookstore because toddlers seem to be the only people willing to listen to him. When Ro waits for her hair to set at Sunshine Clips, she looks into the bookstore and, aside from story hour, it's usually empty, no one seeking out Kevin's help, no one engaging with him at all.

"Did you know bees are in crisis mode?" says Kevin. "The decline of bees is significantly impacting food production."

"And you're going to solve this problem single-handedly? You're going to repopulate the United States with bees?"

"Well, no. Gwen and I are thinking of starting a honey business. We could supply local restaurants, maybe sell honey at the farmers market, stuff like that."

Gwen, Kevin's wife, is another overeducated young person. She went to graduate school to study poetry and she gets to teach, but just one or two classes a semester and sometimes even those get canceled because of low enrollment. Ro knows she is named after the poet Gwendolyn Brooks; Gwen's parents, Joan and Earl, went on and on about how she was their daughter's namesake when she was born thirty-three years ago. They were so proud, as if simply naming her after a well-known poet would ensure their daughter's future literary greatness. How Kevin and Gwen are supporting two children on their salaries, Ro has no idea. Ro knows about their jobs from talking to Joan. Joan used to be Ro's only neighbor on the right side of her house, but now Kevin and Gwen have moved in with their six-year-old twins. "Moving in" isn't the right phrase to use, though, because they haven't moved *into* Joan's house. They've parked themselves in her backyard, where they've built something called a tiny house, and now they've also set up beehives as if four people and a house aren't enough extra occupants for the backyard.

"Would you like some bee pollen?" Kevin asks.

"Why would I like some bee pollen?"

"It can help with allergies. You're supposed to get pollen from local bees because they're consuming local plants, and then you can build up immunity to allergens in the area. So pollen collected from my hives would be hyperlocal."

"Hyperlocal," echoes Ro. She wonders if this is a real word.

"I'll leave some outside your door. Some pollen and some honey once I've harvested it. As a thank-you for letting the bees be your neighbors."

Ro thinks Kevin is smiling, but she's unsure because of that beard. For all she knows, he could be sticking his tongue out at her.

"I should be going," says Ro. "I have something boiling on the stove."

"Oh, you came outside just to talk to me?" says Kevin. "I thought you had something else to do out here."

"I did, but I forgot what." This is, of course, a lie, but she'd rather be thought of as the forgetful old lady than as someone who finds Kevin important enough to leave the house to speak to.

RO IS ASHAMED to admit it, but she has recently become addicted to a television program called *Tiny House Hunters*. She watches a new episode every week, and she even scans the *TV Guide* for reruns, which she also watches. She'd never heard of tiny houses before Kevin set up shop on Joan's lawn with a truckload of lumber and built his tiny house over the course of the spring. At first, Ro thought it was just a shed, but Joan explained that Kevin and Gwen intended to live in it.

"They're struggling financially," Joan said, when she was in her side yard putting up Japanese beetle traps and Ro was weeding around her rosebushes. Joan sighed. "I suppose this makes them feel independent. I keep telling them there's plenty of room inside the house."

"It must be a big change to suddenly have so many people living with you. Or near you," said Ro. Joan's husband, Earl, died two years ago, and she's been alone since.

"It's nice to have Gwen home again," said Joan. "It's been quiet around here."

It was hard for Ro, at first, when the Walkers moved next door in the mid-seventies because they were the first Black family in the neighborhood. Ro wondered why the Walkers moved to this neighborhood—there were other places in Albany, like Arbor Hill or Rapp Road—where maybe they would be more comfortable, and she said this to her husband, Lawrence. "How would you like it if someone told you where you should live, Rosie?" he asked.

Before the Walkers moved in, Ro heard from other neighbors that Earl was a poet, hired to teach in the English Department at the university. After they moved in, Ro learned Joan was a librarian at the university. The Walkers were about twenty years younger than Ro and Lawrence, and it was hard to believe the young man who liked to spend his Saturday mornings kicking a soccer ball into a net Joan inexplicably allowed him to keep on the lawn was old enough and serious enough to be a professor.

Throughout the years, the Walkers were a source of contention between Ro and Lawrence. Lawrence thought Ro should be more welcoming. He made a joke of it sometimes, said because he was an ophthalmologist, he could help people see things more clearly. "I'm not *not* nice to them," Ro said. "I let them be, and they should let me be."

"Maybe you could bring a basket of muffins over?" said Lawrence, right after the Walkers moved to the neighborhood in August. "We could make an effort."

"It's too hot to bake muffins," said Ro, and then time passed and it became too late to welcome the new neighbors because they were no longer new. And anyway, why was it always the woman's job to make an effort? Maybe Lawrence had some progressive views about the races, but he certainly had what would now be called old-fashioned views about the role of women. He could have baked his own damn muffins.

And now, over forty years later, Lawrence is gone and Earl is gone, but Ro and Joan are still neighbors, still cordial. Sometimes Ro thinks she and Joan could have been friends. When they bump into each other outside, they can talk for a long time without running out of things to say. But Ro has never been inside Joan's house, and Joan has never been inside Ro's house. Maybe forty years ago she wouldn't have invited a Black woman into her home, but today she would. If Joan were a new neighbor, she could invite her over, but they've settled into a pattern, they do things a certain way. Even back then, she was sure she wasn't a racist, just someone who followed the established way of doing things. And nowadays, she certainly isn't a racist. Just look at all the people Ro has in her life. The woman who cuts her hair is Chinese, José, who mows her lawn every Wednesday morning, is Mexican, the neighbors down the street are from Pakistan, and the neighbors in the other direction at the end of the street are from Iran. At the block party in August, Ro even ate the biryani the Agarwals made and the fesenjan cooked by the Farzans, and, if she's being honest, she liked both of those dishes. A young lesbian couple, Dawn and Amy, live four houses down from Ro, and they have a rainbow flag flapping from their front porch. Ro smiles and says hello when they pass by while she's working in her garden, even though they put their three-legged pug in a stroller and roll the dog around the neighborhood, which she doesn't approve of. And this is not her being homophobic, but rather being practical because dogs are supposed to walk, even if they only have three legs, which is more than enough legs. So look at her and look at these neighbors and look how they all live here on Willowbrook Drive peacefully. She's come a long way from who she once was; she is not someone whose mind cannot be changed.

But there's one thing she won't budge about: these tiny houses—they are appalling. *Tiny House Hunters* only confirms this. Tonight's episode features a woman who sold her colonial in Greensboro, North Carolina, after she got a divorce and her son went off to college. Ro takes a sip of her Sleepytime tea and watches as this woman divests herself of everything except what can fit into the trunk of her Subaru Outback. This woman has to climb a ladder in her tiny house to reach a loft for sleeping. She owns one bowl, one mug, one pan for cooking, one spoon, and one fork. What will she do when her son comes to visit? Will she tell him to steal silverware from the dining hall to bring home?

"It's so freeing," says the woman. "It makes you realize how much things own you."

Ro snorts. Soon, this woman is going to miss her spatulas and colander and couch cushions. She wonders what the inside of Kevin's tiny house looks like, the size of their toilet, whether they have enough silverware, whether there's a comfortable spot for sitting.

The woman on TV pushes a button on the wall and a plank comes down, and this is her dining table. "I can push it back up, and look at all the room I have!" the woman declares, holding her arms out. Her fingers touch the walls on both sides of the house.

Ro surveys her own living room, looks at the floor lamps and the brown sectional sofa and the paintings of mountains and trees she and Lawrence bought at an estate sale in 1982 for twenty-three dollars. She looks at the beige carpet, which is plush under her slippers. She looks at the pine coffee table Lawrence made forty-seven years ago. Her eyes land on the fireplace, which needs to be cleaned by the Russian chimney sweep, whom she forgot to call at the end of last winter. She hasn't built a fire in ages, but if she wanted to, she could. Ro thinks about Lawrence's model trains in the basement. There is an entire miniature world—houses, stores, a town, mountains—built around the trains, and she has not touched a single thing in the layout since Lawrence's death. She looks around at all that she has, and looks at the poor woman with just her one spoon, and thinks what a sad life the woman leads. How can she stand a life that small?

THE NEXT WEEK, after she has her hair styled, Ro picks up a fluorescent green flyer from a pile on the reception desk at the salon. "We're looking for models!" the flyer declares. "Ages 3-12! Come audition for our scouts on October 14, 2-5, main pavilion, Greenways Mall. Be in print and television commercials!!!"

Tina Huang glances at the flyer as she's making change. "Someone dropped off a bunch of those the other day."

"Are you going to bring Jackson to audition?" Ro looks at Tina's son, who is sitting in one of the stylists' chairs, absorbed in a book, which features a painting of a weasel wearing a maroon ascot on the cover. Ro notices his cowlick, which his mother should be able to control if she cared to do so. With a better haircut and clothes that aren't so baggy, Jackson could be a pleasant-looking child.

"Aren't these things always scams? Don't they just want you to buy a bunch of photos and they promise you all sorts of things and then nothing ever happens?" Tina says.

"But what if something *could* happen?" Ro is thinking of the well-being of both Jackson and Tina. It's no secret that the mall is falling apart, that stores are closing and no new ones are replacing them, the metal gates in the doorways permanently down and locked. There's been a bucket outside the salon for two months now, catching drips from the leaking ceiling, and a yellow WET FLOOR sign has taken up permanent residence in the hallway. It would behoove Tina to have another plan for making money.

"You could ask if he's interested, but my guess is he's not," says Tina.

Ro waves the flyer in the air until Jackson looks up from his book. "Did you see this flyer?"

"About being a model?"

She nods. "What do you think?"

"I don't think that's a flyer."

"Of course it's a flyer." What is wrong with the boy?

"It's a *portal*. To another world," says Jackson. He splays the fingers on both hands, and holds them up around his face like some deranged magician.

"I'll be back in a minute," says Tina. "I just need to see if someone at the food court can break this twenty."

Ro debates being generous, telling Tina to keep the twenty, but she doesn't want to get into the habit of overtipping. "That's fine," she says.

After Tina leaves, Jackson says, "Will you please bring that portal over here?" and since Ro has nothing else to do, she brings the flyer to him.

He pops up from his seat, plucks a pair of scissors out of the container of blue Barbicide disinfectant on his mother's station, then wipes the scissors dry on his jeans. He folds the flyer in half and cuts halfway through the page six times, moving the scissors an inch to the right before each cut. Then he pulls on the edges of the paper, and it unfolds into a large, jagged circle, which he steps through dramatically. "A portal!" says Jackson.

"Aren't you still here in the salon? A portal would take you to another world."

Jackson looks disappointed, rubs his hand on his forehead, crinkles his brow. "It would be a better trick if I made myself disappear once I stepped through the portal, wouldn't it?"

"If it were a real portal, you wouldn't have to *make* yourself disappear. You'd just be somewhere else. And you haven't answered my question about modeling." She knows she should pretend to be amazed that with a few cuts, Jackson was able to make the paper big enough to step through, but, really, there wasn't much impressive about it.

"If I was forced to do something with modeling, I would want to be a photographer," says Jackson. He returns his mother's scissors to the jar of blue fluid and crumples the cut-up paper in his hand. "But if I had to be a photographer, I would want to photograph wildlife instead of humans."

Tina returns with change. "You're not bothering Mrs. Goodson, are you?"

"No," says Jackson. "We were talking about photography."

"Next time I come, I'll bring you a camera. An old one that uses real film, not that digital business," Ro says. Lawrence's camera—a Pentax—has sat on a shelf in her basement for years. "And I'll bring you some film. Then you can take pictures of wildlife."

"Oh, that's kind of you but not necessary," says Tina. "Please don't go out of your way."

"Nonsense," says Ro. "It's not getting any use otherwise."

She feels good, benevolent, thinks Lawrence would be proud of her. Not only will his camera get some use, but she's giving it to a little Chinese boy. A little Chinese boy who seems to not have a father and whose mother certainly can't be making much money in the salon where Ro is often the only customer. Tina has been Ro's stylist for the past nine years. Ro chose her while walking by the salon on her way to buy a pair of black Easy Spirits at Boscov's to wear to a funeral. When she looked into the salon and saw that Tina was Asian, Ro decided to give her some business. It was a decision Ro thought Lawrence would have supported. *Asian* is a word Lawrence taught her to use. He'd told her she wasn't supposed to say *Oriental* unless it had to do with a carpet.

Before she leaves the salon, Ro slips the top flyer off the pile and slides it into her purse. "I'll see you next week," she says. Then she exits the salon and walks across the way to Book Nook, where Kevin is slumped over the register working on a crossword puzzle. He is wearing a T-shirt that says *Star Wars*, with some character holding a light-up sword. Perhaps Ro should just be grateful Kevin is dressed as a human being and not a giant rabbit or a gnome. He is wearing a crooked name tag, and above his name is the word *Manager*. In her day, a manager dressed in respectable clothes, an ironed shirt, a tie, a blazer, clothes that let customers know this person was in charge. But nowadays no one dresses up at the mall, except for the employees at Kay Jewelers so they can convince people their chintzy mall jewelry is something exclusive and special.

Ro has something she needs to tell Kevin: Kevin and Gwen's twins should audition to be models. She sees mixed children in ads all the time now. She doesn't exactly approve of Samuel's long curls—they make him look like a girl—but she suspects the model scouts will like them, will like how he looks halfway between Black and white, halfway between boy and girl.

"Kevin!" barks Ro when he doesn't look up after she's approached the register. She pulls the flyer out of her purse.

"Oh, hello!" he says, surprise in his voice. He caresses his beard. Ro has never gone into the bookstore, even though she passes by it every time she gets her hair done. "Can I help you find a book? Maybe something about gardening?"

"No, no books," she says. "Not today." She says it as if on another day she might purchase a book from him, but she will never buy a book from Kevin. He'd probably want to give her a lecture on whatever topic the book was about, and Ro has no patience for that.

"Did you just get your hair done? It looks nice."

Can Kevin say anything else complimentary besides "nice hair"? She is not here for compliments. She has an idea, a good one. If Simone and Samuel can get hired as models, then they can make money, and their parents can have enough to put down a deposit on a real house and they can move themselves and their bees out of Joan's yard. What's going to happen if the mall closes and Kevin loses his job? Is he going to get another job if he wears *Star Wars* T-shirts to interviews? Or, God forbid, his gnome clogs?

"Look," Ro says, sliding the flyer closer to Kevin.

"Oh, yeah," he says. "Some people came by last week with a pile, but I recycled them. We aren't allowed to post flyers in our store. Corporate policy."

"Did you read it?" Ro says. She refrains from asking if corporate policy also forbids a person in a managerial position from dressing up as an enormous bunny.

Kevin reads the flyer, puts it back down. "Good," he says.

"Good?"

"If they're holding auditions in the mall, it means more foot traffic. And with more foot traffic, people buy more things. Even books."

"That's not what I mean," says Ro. "You should bring the twins to audition."

Kevin laughs; his laugh is raucous and fills the entire store. It's as if Ro has just told a hilarious joke.

"Modeling can be quite lucrative."

"I want my kids to be kids," says Kevin, "not part of some filthy capitalist system."

Ro takes a deep breath. "Don't you think working in this bookstore, this *chain* bookstore, is also being part of a filthy capitalist system?"

Kevin seems to shrink right before her eyes. Even his orange beard looks to be deflating, though Ro knows this is impossible. "This is just temporary," he says. "I'm working on my book. It's about the poet Horchester Glinton. Have you heard of him? No one reads his poetry anymore, but I think they should. Once my book gets published, I'll get a teaching job."

Ro ignores Kevin's question about the ridiculously named poet because she hasn't heard of him, even though long, long ago, she'd studied poetry in college. "Just imagine if your children could be on television or in ads in magazines. You wouldn't have to live in that tiny house anymore."

"It was an intentional decision," he says. "We've chosen to live simply."

Ro snorts, because this is what all the people on *Tiny House Hunters* say, when it is so obvious there's something wrong with their lives that has driven them to tiny houses. Before Ro can say anything else, Gwen enters the store with Simone and Samuel, who are both licking ice cream cones. "Dad!" says Samuel. "They had bubble gum." He holds up his cone, which is filled with pink and blue swirled ice cream.

"Bubble gum ice cream?" says Ro. It sounds vile.

"Yeah," says Samuel. "Bubble gum–tasting ice cream with bubble gum in it."

"How do you chew the gum and eat the ice cream at the same time?" Ro asks.

"You eat the ice cream now and save the gum for later," says Samuel.

"Where do you save the gum?" says Ro.

"This is where it gets unappetizing," says Gwen, who holds out a paper napkin filled with goopy-looking gumballs that have been plucked from either Samuel's cone or from his mouth. The gumballs stick to the napkin.

"What flavor did you get?" Ro asks Simone.

"Strawberry."

Ro nods. "A good choice." Perhaps it is only this little girl who is reasonable in this family. "That's my favorite flavor."

"Nice to see you here, Mrs. Goodson," says Gwen. "We were just coming by to visit Kev."

It is four o'clock on Wednesday afternoon. Ro wonders if Gwen is teaching at all this semester. Maybe if you don't pay rent and siphon electricity from your mother's house, you don't have to have a job and you still have money for ice cream.

"Are you here to get a book?" asks Gwen.

"I just got my hair styled," says Ro, pointing toward Sunshine Clips. "And then I brought this flyer over, but Kevin's not interested."

Gwen looks at the flyer, then she laughs. "I don't know," she says. "This kind of thing enforces the idea of appearance as a commodity, you know?"

Ro sighs. "Your children are *adorable*." Ro realizes this comes out of her mouth like an attack, not a compliment.

Gwen says, "They're also smart and kind and thoughtful. Why can't there be auditions for those things?"

Ro sighs again. Why are Gwen and Kevin so unreasonable? "Smart and kind and thoughtful do less to get you ahead in the world than beautiful. It's just how the world works."

Simone takes the flyer and holds it with one hand while bringing her ice cream up to her mouth with the other. Ro watches as Simone's eyes scan the flyer. The twins are six, in first grade. Can Simone read all the words on the flyer? Samuel digs in his mouth, pulls out a saliva-drenched gumball, and deposits it into the napkin Gwen is holding. It is now abundantly clear which is the smarter twin.

"Can I go to the audition?" says Simone.

"You want to be a model?" says Kevin. "You understand what a model is?"

Simone nods. Ro likes Simone more and more.

"Models are judged on their appearance, not on their smarts," says Kevin, pointing a finger to his temple. Ro knows he's trying to show Simone where her brain is housed, but instead he looks as if he's shooting himself in the head.

"Kevin," says Gwen, "if this is something she wants to pursue, maybe we shouldn't stand in her way."

"Is this because you were a model when you were a kid?" says Kevin. There is an edge of irritation in his voice.

"It was a one-time thing!"

"You were a model, Mom?" says Samuel. Ro is as shocked as Samuel sounds. How had she not known little Gwen Walker next door was a model? Why hadn't Joan told her?

"I was on a diaper box. My mom sent in a picture for a contest, and I was one of the faces of Squeakies Diapers for a year, and my parents used the Squeakies money to start a college fund. The end."

"You want your butt on a box of diapers?" Samuel asks Simone. He has a ring of ice cream around his mouth.

Simone shrugs then takes a bite of her cone. "I'm not a baby."

"It was my face, not my butt, on the box," says Gwen.

"Can we go to the audition?" says Simone.

Kevin stares wide-eyed at Gwen, as if he's trying to communicate with her telepathically. Gwen seems to miss his look, takes the flyer from Simone, and studies it. "I guess we can go if you want to."

"Excellent!" exclaims Ro, and everyone turns and looks at her in surprise, and it's abundantly clear they'd forgotten she was still there.

On Friday, Ro watches Joan's house. The upstairs bedroom window allows her a good view for surveillance, lets her observe Joan's front door and the driveway and the tiny house. At seven forty-five, the school bus stops in front of Joan's house, and Simone and Samuel leave the tiny house and get on. At eight thirty Joan heads off to work at the university library. Neither Gwen nor Kevin leave the tiny house all day. At three twelve, the school bus drops off Simone and Samuel. They clatter off the bus with their oversize backpacks, a rolled piece of poster board under Samuel's arm, a pair of pink sneakers dangling by the shoelaces from Simone's hand, a purple water bottle hanging from the other. The auditions run until five. The children need to hurry to the mall. Ro paces in her bedroom. What if they've decided not to go to the auditions? What if Kevin has convinced Simone that modeling is silly?

But a few minutes later Gwen and Simone emerge from the tiny house. Simone looks pretty, in a nice blue dress and shiny patent leather Mary Janes, her hair neatly tied back with a pink ribbon. Ro is glad Simone still has a dress to wear, that Kevin and Gwen didn't give away all her clothes before they moved into their three-hundred-square-foot home. They get in the old silver Yaris Gwen and Kevin share and pull out of the driveway.

Ro needs to occupy herself until Gwen and Simone come home. She needs to be at the window where she can see the Yaris puttering down the street, and then she can casually go outside and pretend she has pruning or weeding to do. Her garden, which she first planted decades ago because she wanted bright and beautiful flowers to grow around her house, has proven remarkably useful in terms of keeping a watch on the neighborhood.

Ro settles herself in the threadbare olive-green armchair a handyman moved from the living room into the bedroom after Lawrence's death. It was the chair Lawrence sat in to watch television in the evenings. Now, twenty years later, she sits near the bedroom window and reads—or pretends to read—and keeps watch on what's going on below. She opens a book about growing prize-winning roses, but she's unable to pay attention to the words on the page. She imagines Gwen and Simone driving on the Northway, taking the exit to the mall, Gwen guiding Simone through the parking lot, walking in the doors near JCPenney. She imagines them lining up with the other children—mostly girls—who are wearing their nicest dresses and their shiniest shoes. She imagines Gwen promising Simone strawberry ice cream after this is over, after the scouts have signed the papers, after they've told Simone she has just the look they've been searching for. She imagines Gwen sighing with relief, knowing her daughter's good looks will lead to financial security for the family, even if the mall shuts down and the bookstore closes, even if Gwen doesn't get any classes to teach next semester. Ro is proud of herself, and she thinks Lawrence would be too if he were here to see what she has set in motion.

The doorbell rings, a series of quick peals, which startles Ro. The rings continue furiously. She is not expecting anyone, and she curses the fact that she can't see the front door from her perch in the bedroom. "Coming! Hold your horses!" she yells, slamming her book shut and standing up. She ordered two bottles of fish emulsion to fertilize her roses last week, but they weren't supposed to come for another few days. But maybe her package has arrived early, and maybe this is some new, overeager deliveryman. She heads down the stairs while the rings continue, and she wonders if this might be a prank, a neighborhood troublemaker ringing with urgency and then sprinting away once she nears the door. She gets closer to the door, and the ringing does not stop. She looks out the glass pane in the door and sees it is Samuel, and he is weeping.

"Samuel?" she says, opening the door.

"Sammy. No one calls me Samuel," he says, as he continues to cry.

Ro resists telling him that Samuel is a good, strong name, and Sammy is the name of a fourteen-year-old girl who pops her bubble gum loudly and refuses to do her algebra homework.

"Are you upset that your mom and sister went to the audition without you?"

He shakes his head hard. "Ow, no," he says. "The audition is stupid."

"Well," says Ro, "then how can I help you?"

Samuel steps into Ro's house, even though she hasn't invited him in.

"I got stung," he gasps. "A lot."

"By the bees? By your father's bees?"

Samuel nods, the tears continuing to stream down his cheeks, and now mucus is running out of his nose.

"Are you allergic to bees? Should I call an ambulance?"

"I don't know." He jumps up and down and howls, as if this might somehow resolve his issues.

"You don't look swollen to me. You would swell up if you're allergic."

"I really hurt," Samuel wails. He holds his arms up, and Ro can see a half dozen stings on each arm. He also has several stings on his face.

Samuel whimpers as he trails Ro to the kitchen.

"Is your tongue swollen?" says Ro. "If your tongue is swollen, it means your throat is going to close up, and we should call an ambulance immediately."

Samuel sticks his tongue out, wiggles it, draws it back into his mouth. "My tongue is normal," he says. "Am I going to die?"

"You are not going to die," says Ro. "Not for a long time."

In the kitchen, she seats him at a wooden chair next to the small table where she and Lawrence used to eat dinner. She takes two ice cubes out of the freezer, wraps each in a paper towel, and hands them to Samuel. He takes them, holds them in each hand, and looks up at her with wet eyes.

"Put them on the stings," says Ro. "It'll help the pain."

"Which stings?"

"Start with the ones that hurt the most." Ro leaves him in the kitchen and gets a box of tissues from the living room and puts it on the table next to Samuel.

"What are those for?" asks Samuel. He has calmed down some, the gasping has stopped, but his cheeks are still tear stained, and there is still mucus below his nose.

"To wipe your face."

"But my hands are busy." Samuel's hands are each holding an ice cube on the opposite arm.

"Well, it's for when you get the chance."

"Can you wipe my face?"

It is not the type of thing she does. She is not a tear wiper, a hugger, a consoler. She is a problem solver. If the leaves on her oleander yellow, she waters the plants less. If there is fungus on her rosebushes, she makes a concoction of water, baking soda, and dish soap and sprays it on the leaves. If a boy has been stung by bees, she offers him ice. If *any* boy had been stung, she would offer him ice. It wouldn't matter if a little white boy came into her kitchen crying; she wouldn't wipe his tears either. She wouldn't.

"Can you?" says Samuel.

"You could put down the ice for a moment and wipe your own tears." It is the only practical solution unless Samuel intends to grow two more arms.

Samuel puts the wet clumps of paper towels and ice on the table, and Ro watches the liquid seep into the wood. Every night, she and Lawrence ate dinner on place mats so as not to leave water stains on the table. "Here," says Ro, grabbing the box of tissues. "Put the paper towels back on your arms."

Samuel does as he's told, and Ro crumples two tissues together and pats Samuel's face, as if she's blotting a stain from the carpet. She never had children and is not sure how to touch one, unsure whether she's pressing too hard. Her dabbing manages to get the tears and most of the mucus off his face. Ro bends down to look more closely at Samuel's face to see if there's any swelling.

"Are you sure you're not allergic to bees?" she asks.

"I don't know."

"Does your throat feel like it's closing up?"

"What does that feel like?"

"Like you can't breathe. Take a deep breath."

He does, and then he puckers his lips and blows a long stream of air out. The air hits Ro in the face.

Ro stands up, takes the dirty tissues to the garbage. "How did you come to get stung so many times?"

"I wanted honey."

Ro waits for him to elaborate, but he does not. "Did you get any honey?"

"No."

"So you bothered the bees?"

"I got a stool and climbed up and tried to take out one of the frames from the beehive, but I didn't know how to do it right."

Ro gets two fresh ice cubes from the freezer, wraps each in a dry paper towel, then swaps the new ice cubes for the old ones.

"Who's supposed to be watching you?" Ro asks.

"No one is watching me. I'm not a baby."

"What I mean is, who's home with you? Your father?"

Samuel nods.

"Why didn't he stop you from trying to get honey?"

"He was busy."

"Doing what?"

"Writing his book. He told me if I didn't bother him, we could get soft serve later."

"And do you still think you'll get soft serve? You bothered his bees."

"But I didn't bother *him*."

"And this is why you came to my house?"

"I was supposed to go to the big house and watch TV because he was working in the tiny house, but then I got stung and Grandma is still at work and I couldn't bother Dad so I came to your house."

"And what would you have done if I wasn't at home?" Ro is offended. She is only involved in all of this because Samuel is afraid of losing the opportunity to get soft serve.

Samuel stares at Ro without speaking and then begins to cry again.

"Why are you crying?"

"You're mad at me. And everything hurts."

"I'm not mad at you, Samuel."

"Sammy."

Ro takes another tissue from the box and wipes Samuel's face again. Should Ro offer him a Tylenol? Should she give him a Benadryl? Should she march him back to his father? Or maybe she should do nothing. Samuel's breathing is fine, not labored. His tears have stopped now. And it's nice to have someone in her kitchen. She likes having company, even if it's a child who doesn't follow directions, didn't audition to be a model, and likes bubble gum ice cream.

"Who lived here first? You or my grandma and grandpa?" asks Samuel.

"I did. I moved into this house one year after I got married. In 1954."

Samuel appears to be doing some sort of calculation in his head, but the math is likely too much for someone his age, and he says, "How old are you?"

"Didn't anyone tell you never to ask a lady her age?" Ro is eighty-nine; she knows she is twenty-three years older than Joan. It strikes her that she might be the oldest person Samuel has ever met.

"Why is it bad to tell your age? I'm six."

"I know that."

"So how old are *you*?"

"Guess," says Ro.

"My dad says you're a million years old and you grew up with the dinosaurs and that's why you're a racist person."

Ro can feel the drumming of her heart in her ears. So this is how it is. All that politeness, all those compliments about her hair, and this is what Kevin is really thinking.

"You tell your father I grew up with Jesus, not the dinosaurs. Will you tell him that? Tell him Jesus was my lab partner in biology and we dissected a frog together."

"You know Jesus?"

"I used to. We had a falling out. He asked another girl to the homecoming dance."

Through her outrage, Ro feels a small flicker of delight when she imagines the conversation Samuel will have with Kevin later about dinosaurs and Jesus.

"I'll be back," Ro says. She walks to the bathroom, where she finds a half-empty tube of hydrocortisone cream. She returns to the kitchen and says, "Here," placing the tube on the table. "Put this cream on your bites. It'll make them feel better."

Samuel stares at the tube. "What time is it?" he asks.

"Five twenty-five."

"That's after five fifteen?"

Ro nods.

"My dad said he'd be done writing at five fifteen and then we could get soft serve."

"So go, then. Go home." Ro knows she's saying it in a rough way, as if she's shooing a rabbit from her garden. What did she expect? That she and Samuel would sit in the kitchen together all day? That they would become friends and Samuel would come visit every afternoon? Samuel doesn't move, so Ro says, "Go home. Your dad is probably wondering where you are. Take the cream with you."

"Okay." Samuel picks the tube up from the table.

"Here, let me get you fresh ice cubes before you go," says Ro, taking the soggy paper towels he's placed on her table and throwing them into the trash. They've left water stains on the wood. She wraps up two new cubes and hands them to him. "Put the cream in your pocket. You don't have three hands, so you can't hold both ice cubes and the cream."

Ro walks Samuel to the front door. She opens the door and Kevin is outside, and he looks frantic, running toward the street. "Here!" she yells, waving him over, and Kevin turns his head.

Kevin races toward Ro's house, his beard flapping as he sprints. Samuel leaves the house, walks down the steps, and Kevin kneels at the foot of the stairs, pulls his son into his arms, clutches him tight. "Are you okay?" Kevin asks.

"Yeah," says Samuel. "She gave me ice," he says, pointing to Ro.

Kevin looks up at Ro from his crouch, says, "Thank you."

But there is something dark in his eyes. Ro realizes what he's seeing: she's not the woman who gives cameras to Chinese boys, or the woman who encourages half-Black-half-white children to be models, or the woman who eats food from around the world at block parties and waves to lesbians as they roll their three-legged dog around the block. It all comes into sharp focus, as if she's slipped on a pair of glasses for the first time: she is the old, bigoted woman next door, someone from whom Samuel and Simone need to be protected.

Kevin pulls Samuel closer to his chest, hugs him tightly, as if he's afraid Ro will do something terrible if he loosens his grip. Ro stands in her doorway and desperately wishes she had a portal she could step through and be transported to a place where she could be someone different. Or a time machine would do, a contraption to bring her back to those first days after Joan and Earl moved in. She would ignore the August heat and bake muffins and as she handed the muffins to Joan, she'd invite the Walkers to dinner and then Joan and Earl would have stepped foot into her house all those decades ago and things would have been different and it wouldn't have been so strange and terrifying for Kevin to learn that his son has come to her house. But of course time machines and portals to other worlds do not exist. All that exists is Ro and her house and the top step she's moved onto as she watches Kevin pick up his son and carry him away.

November

Solitaire

Tina thinks Kevin is absurd. He's had plenty of opportunities in life, and yet he, like Tina, is working at the mall. Tina knows he wishes he could do something else because he spills all his plans—his ridiculous, money-sucking plans—to everyone he meets. Why can't he see if his ideas pan out before he goes around squawking about them? Today Tina is trapped listening to Kevin because she's cutting his hair. He's a paying customer, so she is a captive audience. She stares down at his wet orange hair, which he really should condition regularly, says "Mmm hmmm" every once in a while, and restrains herself from poking him behind the ear with the point of her scissors—just a little stick, small enough to seem like a slip of the hand—while he yammers on. He has left a gold paper crown on her station, which reminds her of the crowns given out at Burger King when she was a child. The crown left an indentation in Kevin's hair that Tina had to wash out.

Kevin is talking about dogs, specifically border collies. Tina doesn't know much about dogs in general and border collies in particular, but her son, Jackson, insisted she watch a dog agility competition on TV with him last week, and the border collies kicked most of the other dogs' asses as they snaked around weave poles, ascended and descended A-frames, and dashed through tunnels with speed and precision. "If I were to get a dog, I would probably get one of those," Tina said as she gestured toward a border collie on the screen named

Verb, who the announcers said won first place in agility several years in a row.

"I would get an all-American dog," said Jackson.

Tina pictured a dog wearing a red, white, and blue bandana snarfing down a slice of apple pie. "What breed is that?" she asked, and Jackson said, "It's not a breed. It's another name for mutt. A nicer name."

Tina runs a comb through Kevin's hair and stares down at all the split ends on the side of his head. She wants to tell him maybe he shouldn't wait four or five months between haircuts, but she can't say that because it would seem as if she's telling him to spend more money at the salon.

"Kevin, who are you supposed to be?" She pokes at a bunched-up lump of fabric below his neck, where she shoved a hood with attached bunny ears under the cape she draped around him.

"Max," Kevin says, as if Tina should know exactly who this is.

"Max who?" Maybe this is a character in some new children's book. It's been three or four years since she's read picture books to Jackson and maybe a new book has come out featuring a rabbit king. Kevin dresses up to read to children on Tuesday and Thursday afternoons. Usually he reads *Goodnight Moon* in the rabbit costume. He pairs the costume with a blue-and-white-striped sweatshirt, and Tina guesses he's supposed to be the little bunny falling asleep in the green room, not the adult bunny, although his big orange beard kind of gets in the way of him appearing to be a child of any sort.

"*Where the Wild Things Are?*" says Kevin.

"Isn't Max supposed to be dressed like a wolf?" She remembers the pointy ears and the puffy dark tail on Max's costume.

Kevin sighs. "I mean, yes, but I don't have a wolf costume. So the rabbit costume is close enough as long as I roll up the ears and hide them inside the crown."

"Book Nook won't get you a wolf costume?"

Kevin laughs. "Book Nook doesn't buy any of these costumes. They're all mine."

Tina is floored. Has Kevin actually *decided* to dress in these costumes for story hour? She always assumed it was some sort of corporate mandate, something he suffered through because it brought in customers. On more than one occasion, sitting in the empty salon and watching Kevin dressed up and parents and children flooding into the bookstore, she's wondered if she could get more clients by putting on some sort of costume. Maybe if she dressed as a haircut fairy, maybe with a purple wig and sparkly tights and a tutu, parents would bring their children into Sunshine Clips after they finished with story hour. But no, she is not the costume type. It takes a special kind of adult—special in the arrested development, too naive, happy-to-look-like-a-fool way—to dress in costumes twice a week. To *voluntarily* dress in costumes twice a week.

"So you went out and bought all these costumes?" Tina says.

"No, of course not," Kevin says, as if Tina's question is the most preposterous thing he's ever heard. "I had the costumes. Ever since grad school, my wife and I were known for throwing really elaborate Halloween parties. We had these parties for years, until we got too busy with the kids. This rabbit costume was for an *Alice in Wonderland*–themed party. I was the White Rabbit. My wife was Alice." Kevin shifts a bit in the seat, and Tina looks down and notices the puffy round rabbit's tail the size of a grapefruit that Kevin is sitting on; it must be making him uncomfortable. Why, she wonders now, didn't he take off the bunny costume before coming to get his hair cut? And then she has a horrifying thought: maybe he's not wearing anything underneath it.

Tina cannot help herself. "Kevin, are you wearing clothes under the rabbit outfit?"

Kevin bursts out laughing. "Of course!"

"Then why would you wear the outfit to get your hair cut? It can't be comfortable to be sitting on that tail."

Kevin shakes his head. "You're right, it's not. It's just that my wife is bringing my kids by this afternoon and they wanted to see the costume, and I just thought taking it on and off would be a lot of effort. It's a little tight, and the zipper is in the back. It takes like ten minutes to get the thing on, and I basically become a contortionist to get the zipper all the way up."

Tina softens. He is wearing the costume for his children. She can understand this, can understand doing things that are maybe not logical, maybe uncomfortable, maybe considered weird, for the sake of your child. She often thinks of Kevin as foolish, but can a man who gets dressed up every week—for his own children and for other people's children—really be that awful? She feels a little guilty about contemplating poking him behind the ear with her scissors, so she asks him to tell her more about the dogs he was talking about earlier, the border collies he wants to buy.

Kevin says, "I'm not usually a proponent of purchasing purebred dogs since there are plenty of good dogs in shelters who need homes, but these would be working dogs. I'm thinking of getting two border collies to start out."

"What kind of work can border collies do? Stock brokers? Air-conditioning repair? Personal chefs?" Tina asks.

Kevin laughs. "Can you imagine training dogs to be chefs? You come home from work and there they are, wearing white jackets and chef's hats, chopping vegetables."

Tina cannot imagine something so absurd. She picks up her thinning shears and works on blending the hair on the left side of Kevin's head. "That would be quite the sight," she says, because if the years she's spent cutting hair have taught her anything, it's how to be a good audience for everyone's stories and jokes.

"The business would be geese chasing," Kevin says. "They'd chase the geese off golf courses and college campuses and parks and soccer and football fields. Even cemeteries. Border collies have an amazing herding instinct, and they love to work. And it's all totally humane. They don't bite or harm the geese. They just chase them and the geese fly away. Have you ever been somewhere with nice, green grass, and there are goose droppings all over?"

Tina nods. There's a park she and Jackson like with a big pond filled with ducks, but aggressive geese often surround the pond, proud and puffy, as if they're lackeys protecting a mafia don. There are goose droppings all over the park, and they wedge into the grooves in Tina's sneakers if she's not careful where she steps.

Once, when he was a toddler, Jackson was chased by a goose, who hissed and angrily flapped its ugly feet on the blacktop around the pond. Jackson refused to go to the park for weeks, certain he'd be mauled by the goose, its powerful wings knocking him over. Tina told Jackson a story her own mother told her about how in ancient China scrolls were attached to the feet of geese to carry messages. And there was another story Tina wanted to tell Jackson, one Tina's mother told her about Su Wu, a diplomat during the Han Dynasty, who was captured and held by enemies for many years. He told his captors he'd attached a message to the foot of a goose, revealing where he was being held. Not wanting to be found, his captors released him before the goose could deliver the message. Tina couldn't remember all the details of this story, knew she only remembered it halfway and maybe got some details wrong, but by that point her mother was no longer speaking to her, and she couldn't call home to ask. She knew she could look up the story online, but she didn't want to. Having to turn to Google and Wikipedia instead of calling her mother would only make her estrangement from her family feel more profound.

Kevin says, "For a few weeks, you bring the dogs a couple times a day to the park or cemetery or wherever, and then the geese start to know they'll be chased away and stop coming back. And in the long run it saves a lot of money because maintenance crews or gardeners don't have to spend time cleaning up goose droppings."

Then how will the business continue? If the geese don't come back, there's no more need to hire Kevin and the dogs. This is why Tina is grateful that long ago she'd bumbled into her line of work; generally, people's hair will always keep growing, will always need cutting. The work might not be particularly fulfilling, but it pays the bills. How many colleges and parks and golf courses are in the area that would be willing to pay for dogs to chase away geese? And if the business fails, what will Kevin do with the dogs? They'll be two more mouths to feed. Kevin can't be making that much at Book Nook, especially not if his paycheck depends on sales, since aside from the children's story hour the store is generally empty. And if the rumors are to be believed, the mall might not even stay open much longer, which might leave Kevin without a job at all.

"Amazing, right?" Kevin says.

Tina looks at Kevin's reflection in the mirror and he's smiling widely, like a child reaching into a full bag of Halloween candy, and Tina wonders how life hasn't stomped the enthusiasm out of him yet. He's maybe five years younger than her, in his mid-thirties, and it seems that by his age it makes little sense to dream big, especially if your day-to-day life involves coming to the mall and working while the smell of french fries from the food court wafts into your store every time a basket of them is plunged into hot oil. Plus, Tina knows Kevin's real dream is to work as an English professor. Wouldn't he feel like shit—like a shriveled green tube of goose shit—if he had to go to a beautiful campus and stand outside the humanities building while professors inside lecture about great works of literature as his dogs chase geese across the lawn?

"I just read an article about how border collies are being used in Chile after a wildfire destroyed a forest. They've been trained to run through burn areas with backpacks that release seeds so the forest can be repopulated with native foliage."

"They seem useful," Tina says, and she knows it's an understatement, but she can't muster up enthusiasm for these dogs or for a business venture that will likely be an expensive failure. She wishes Jackson were here, but he's still at school. Jackson loves animals and would be delighted to hear about these worker dogs, and he'd respond to Kevin with enthusiasm so Tina wouldn't have to.

"What happens if the business doesn't take off? Won't your kids get upset if you have to give the dogs away?"

"I'm trying not to think about failure," Kevin says. "If I start out by thinking of the ways I could fail, I'd never do anything, you know?"

"Right," says Tina, and she does know. She indulges in thoughts of failure all the time. She loves to draw—has always loved art—but knows it's not a practical thing to pursue, so she's pushed aside any fantasies about being an artist. If she could have any job in the world—and be able to make money at it—she'd illustrate children's books. She's studied Jackson's old books, copied the drawings in them. Maybe she remembered Max from *Where the Wild Things Are* was a wolf because she tried to draw him with a black ballpoint pen, attempting to match Maurice Sendak's ink strokes in the tail, before becoming frustrated. She couldn't get it right, even though she attempted to draw that tail three or four times, and finally concluded that Sendak probably used a different type of pen, probably a dip pen and a pot of dark black ink. She gave up on drawing Max. It wasn't worth it to spend money on a special pen that she'd only use for drawing. It would be a waste. Anyway, writing and illustrating children's books isn't her job, never will be.

Tina is different from Kevin because he could have been something else, could have pursued a different career. He was a student at the university, on his way to getting his PhD. He told her many times he's ABD, which means "all but dissertation." He's taken all his classes, completed the coursework, but never finished writing his dissertation. But why not finish? Why do all this work and then give up? It's like signing up for a marathon and quitting three miles short of the finish line. Kevin must have teachers and advisers who could help him become a professor. If he finished his PhD, something could happen for him career-wise. Tina, on the other hand, knows no one that can help her with art, no one who can offer guidance.

"God, I'd love to get out of here if I can just make some other business take off," Kevin says. He waves a hand toward Book Nook.

Tina nods and looks into the bookstore, which is empty except for an employee in a purple sweatshirt reading *Us Weekly* behind the register.

"I don't mean there's anything wrong with working here," Kevin says, looking guilty, and Tina wonders if he feels sorry for her. What she knows, what is unspoken, is that Kevin has, for some unfathomable reason, chosen this life. She, on the other hand, is stuck. "It's just that I don't know how much longer my job will even exist if the mall closes."

"Yeah, me too."

"What would you do? Move to another salon?"

"I guess so. This is really the only thing I know how to do." What else can she say? She knows illustrating children's books is not a realistic goal, and it would be silly to mention it to Kevin. It's a secret fantasy that gets her through the day; sometimes she imagines her customers as the protagonists of children's books. Sometimes things they say give her ideas for plots of books.

Later, after Kevin leaves the salon, Tina plans to find a scrap of paper and sketch a goose and a border collie. She'll jot down notes for a story about these two animals. Maybe they start out as enemies and become unexpected coconspirators. Maybe they spend most of the story playing tricks on the dog's orange-haired owner. Tina has so many scraps of paper covered in sketches tucked into unused spots in the salon. She only draws on scrap paper—old receipts, the backs of flyers, greasy fast food bags—not on good, thick paper purchased at art supply stores. Buying real paper would make drawing feel too official, and there's nothing official about her sketches.

Tina unbuttons and removes the black cape, then sweeps the hairs off Kevin's collar and neck with a duster brush. Many of his hairs fall into the hood of the rabbit costume, but there's nothing she can do about that. "Have you heard anything official about the mall closing?" she asks.

"No," says Kevin, standing up. "But look at this place. It's only a matter of time. How long can we keep going?" He reaches into a pocket of the rabbit costume and takes out his wallet. Tina wants to laugh about the costume having pockets but a quiet sadness has settled into the air with their talk of the mall's possible closing. Kevin hands Tina twenty dollars for a fifteen-dollar haircut and tells her to keep the change. She knows he likely can't afford the tip, but she doesn't want to embarrass him by giving the money back, so she just takes the twenty-dollar bill, thanks him, and says, "I guess we just keep going until someone tells us to stop."

At night, after Jackson has gone to sleep, Tina brings her laptop to the kitchen table and watches videos about drawing and painting, takes notes in a composition book with a speckled black-and-white cover, and tries to replicate some of the artwork she sees on the screen. She's amazed at how much material exists online for free. This is good because at her age there's no way she's going back to school. She doesn't need a degree to prove she can draw. She knows she has a short fuse, and she doesn't think she'd be able to handle four years in classrooms with students half her age. She can control her tongue with her clients because they're paying her, and the nicer she is, the better her tips are. But there would be nothing to stop her from saying something inappropriate to one of her classmates. Tina is old enough to be annoyed by everything, but not old enough to allow herself to act annoyed in public, not old enough to have her behavior excused as grumpy-old-lady behavior. She's jealous of Ro Goodson, who must be nearing ninety. She's cantankerous and mean, and no one ever calls her out for it. Sometimes Ro snaps at Tina, but Tina lets it go because Ro, for some unknown reason, has a soft spot for Jackson. And Jackson likes Ro, so Tina just brushes off any rude comments Ro makes. Tina can't wait for the day when she's ninety and can get away with voicing any thought that crosses her mind.

Tina can mostly tolerate the people on YouTube who post videos about drawing or watercolor techniques or reviews of different brands of pastels. A lot of times they're know-it-alls or seem like aggressive salespeople even though all they're pushing is the concept that constant practice will lead to improvement. Tina figures she can tolerate their annoying personalities—it's not like she has to hang out with them—if they offer her some useful information. But last week, Tina discovered something that greatly irritated her, yet she couldn't stop watching. She spent hours in the middle of the night watching videos of teenagers—mostly girls—holding up their artwork, showing viewers the contents of their portfolios that got them accepted at prestigious art schools. Tina hadn't been searching for these videos; they popped up as suggested videos because of all the art instruction videos she watched.

Tina viewed one seventeen-minute video four times, two with sound, two without. It featured an Asian girl, Chinese, Tina could tell, with the screen name ArtyAnnieAmazing, who planned to apply to RISD, SCAD, Yale, Cooper Union, Carnegie Mellon, CalArts, and MICA. Annie was so smug, so certain of her talent, so willing to reveal where she planned to apply because it was clear she thought she'd be accepted everywhere. Annie obviously knew her artwork was, for lack of a better word, amazing, and Tina had been stunned by both the girl's arrogance and her skill.

In the video, Annie Amazing held up still lifes in oil paint, charcoal self-portraits, nudes in deep, rich graphite, and even work she said she did in Adobe Illustrator in a graphic design class at school. There are other videos by Annie that show her working on a variety of paintings and drawings. Tina watches them, one after another, and she's jealous of the easy way Annie sketches, of the control she has over her materials. "My goal is basically to get out of Albany," said Annie in one video, and Tina felt a sharp pain in her chest learning this awful and talented girl lives in the same city she does. "It's so lame here. No one cares about art. No one's good at art. It'll be nice to be somewhere more serious, where people actually have talent."

Imagine if Tina got into art school and encountered someone like this girl. Or had to endure an entire class full of Annie Amazings. It would be awful. Tina wonders if Annie ever acts like a regular seventeen-year-old, whether she ever wanders aimlessly around the mall eating fries and trying on clothing she has no intention of buying, attempting to burn off the hours of the day between the end of school and bedtime. No, Annie Amazing would never squander her time like that. Annie is probably far too good to ever step foot in a mall; she likely thinks the saddest thing in the world would be working in a mall, coming to a run-down place day after day, its eventual shuttering offering the only possible escape from such a sad and pathetic life.

THE NEXT DAY Ro arrives for her weekly appointment. Tina washes her hair and puts in curlers to recreate the style Ro prefers. Tina is certain Ro has been wearing her hair in the same style since before Tina was born. Ro seems sullen, much quieter than usual, and Tina wonders if she's feeling okay. Ro is usually not short for words.

"I heard a rumor," says Ro, as Tina walks her over to the hooded dryer, "that the mall might be closing."

"That's the rumor." Tina settles Ro under the dryer and looks to make sure there are magazines on the nearby table.

"What will you do if the mall closes?"

"Everyone keeps asking that."

"Well, do you have a plan?"

Tina shakes her head. She's wearing boots with thick and heavy soles, and she thinks it would be satisfying to clomp away loudly, leaving Ro and her questions behind.

"Maybe you could go back to school. You didn't go to college, did you?"

"Why would you assume that?" says Tina. She points across the hall toward Book Nook. "Kevin went all the way through a PhD program and he works at the mall."

"Well, Kevin is a different sort than you are," says Ro, and Tina wonders if Ro is implying something racist. Then Ro says, "It's just that, well, I can tell he's on the lazy side and you, you're a hard worker. I think you could do just about anything if you set your mind to it."

Tina is both surprised and irritated by Ro's brief pep talk. She doesn't like being told that she can do anything if she only works hard enough. Doesn't Ro understand that not everyone is in a position to pursue their dreams? "My parents wanted me to be a doctor."

Tina will not tell Ro she fantasizes about being an artist. In high school, Tina dreamed of attending art school, but her parents told her it was a waste of money and would not lead to a real job the way medical school would. She always got As in math and science classes, and her parents kept asking why a smart girl would waste all her brainpower on art. They had owned a furniture store in China and moved to New York City right before Tina was born in order to provide her with more opportunities. They found jobs that didn't require them to speak much English, her father taking the subway to the Bronx every evening and working overnight as a loader at UPS, hefting packages onto the trucks, her mother working in a Chinatown Laundromat, a job that mortified Tina because it was the most clichéd job a Chinese immigrant could have. Tina was their only child, and she didn't like all the pressure her parents put on her. In a great act of defiance, she didn't apply to any colleges her senior year, but she lied and told her parents she'd applied to the schools with the best premed programs in the country. It was a misguided decision made with teenage stupidity and lack of foresight. She thought she was being daring, believed she would prove something to her parents about her independent and free-thinking nature.

When her friends got their letters of acceptance from colleges, she profoundly regretted not applying anywhere. Her mother was furious but told her to go to community college for a year and then transfer. Tina told her mother community college was for losers, and she enrolled in cosmetology school, even though, at the time, she thought cosmetology school was just for losers who liked to play with hair and makeup. She liked doing neither of these things, but it was a quick way to gain a skill, to plunge right into the working world after only a year. Right after she was certified and licensed, she got a job and even though the hours were long and her feet were sore at the end of the day, she was making good money. It was hard to think about giving up that money to enroll in college, to pay tuition and be forced to take classes like Freshman Literature or Introduction to Philosophy, which would serve her in no practical way. She thought she'd work for a few years, save money, then apply to art schools. She certainly hadn't envisioned she'd still be cutting hair over twenty years later.

"You could still be a doctor," says Ro. "It would be a lot of hard work for you to finish all the necessary schooling, but you could do it."

"But it's not a matter of whether I *could* do it. It's a matter of whether I *want* to do it, and it was never something I was interested in."

"Then what do you want to do?" says Ro.

"Why do you assume I'm not doing what I want to do?"

"Are you?"

"I didn't say that either."

What Tina won't say is that she's stuck. She has one marketable skill and not a lot of money and a son to take care of. And she's got no one to turn to for support. Her parents' disappointment was obvious when she didn't go to college, but Tina was certain she would go back to school, so she told them not to worry, said her goal was to pay for college on her own. She didn't tell them she still intended to go to art school. Although they never said anything about their finances, she knew they didn't have money to pay for her tuition. Her mother washed Ziploc bags and reused them, draped wet paper towels on the dish rack so they could dry and be reused. Her father wore his shoes until the soles were paper-thin and refused to let Tina pay to get them resoled. After working for three years in a salon near NYU, Tina moved upstate when she was twenty-two and bought a small house. She wanted to move away from the city, build something for herself in a place she could afford. Her parents thought the purchase of a house was an adult and responsible decision. And so they entered into a truce for many years, but her parents kept asking about college, reminding her that the sooner she finished, the sooner she could go to medical school, and the sooner she could become a doctor. "Maybe next year," she told them again and again. "But business is good. I can't just leave."

The years tumbled by and business was good until a few years ago, but by then she was already in her late thirties, too old, in her mind, to go back to school. And even if she wanted to, how can she just quit her job and go to school—and pay tuition—when she has a child to care for? When she got pregnant, her parents told her she'd gone too far. Jackson's father was someone she dated for a few months. He was a good man—nice and smart and hardworking at his job as an auditor—but as the months went on, she realized she did not want a serious future with him, didn't want him as her companion for the rest of her life. The pregnancy wasn't planned, but once she found out, she embraced the idea of being a mother. It would be a family life do-over.

"What do I tell everyone at church?" her mother asked when Tina told her she was pregnant.

"How about you tell them it's none of their business?" Tina said. After all, Tina no longer attended the Chinese Christian Church, hadn't since her junior year in high school. She didn't want to hear how Mrs. Liang's daughter, Lily, was doing so well in the PhD program in neuroscience at Princeton or how Dr. Zheng's son, Simon, was top of his class at Stanford's medical school. Often, she wondered what her parents said when their church friends asked about her. She wondered if they told people she never went to college, that she cut hair. She wondered if they pretended she no longer existed. Maybe they now went to a different church, where no one knew they once had a daughter smart enough to be a doctor but who squandered all her potential.

Right after she learned she was pregnant, Jackson's father was offered a job in Australia, and Tina decided it was best not to tell him about her pregnancy and allow him to start a new life abroad. She would raise her child alone, and she wouldn't have to deal with anyone else's ideas and opinions about parenting. When it became clear to her parents that Tina was not planning to marry Jackson's father and that she intended to raise her son as a single mother, her parents stopped speaking to her. She vowed to raise Jackson differently than she'd been raised and would support whatever decisions he made. She wonders sometimes what her parents would think of her monkish life, one filled with only work and caring for her son, with no time for dating or socializing. Would they approve? Would they think she got what she deserved?

"If you could be anything in the world, what would it be?" says

Ro. She picks up a copy of *Good Housekeeping* from the table next to her, but she doesn't open it.

Tina's not going to tell Ro any more. Revealing your fantasies makes you vulnerable to mockery and judgment.

"I don't know," says Tina. "What about you? Did you get to do everything you wanted?" She is good at deflecting, at being the one who asks the questions, who elicits the secrets.

"Why are you talking like my life is over? I'm alive and well."

"I didn't mean to imply you weren't. But what did you want to be when you were a little girl?"

"I wanted to be a poet," says Ro.

"Really?" says Tina, stunned. She can't imagine crusty, cranky Ro ever harbored such a romantic notion.

"Really."

In all the years Tina's been doing Ro's hair, she's learned very little about her life. All she knows is Ro's a widow and cares very much about her garden. "So, wait, *are* you a poet?"

"Of course not. I grew up and realized it was a silly idea. But you asked me what I wanted to be when I was a little girl and so I told you the truth. It hasn't escaped me that you haven't yet told me the truth about your own career aspirations."

Tina needs to end this conversation about hopes and dreams. It can go nowhere good. "What do you think of border collies?" Tina asks. She knows Ro is smart enough to understand she is changing the subject, but she'd rather talk about dogs than about herself right now.

"I think nothing of them. Why should I?"

"Because they're very smart and agile dogs," says Tina. She tells Ro all the things Kevin told her about border collies and how they can chase geese and replant forests after wildfires, and she is suddenly thankful for Kevin because now she can talk and talk and fill the rest of Ro's appointment and not reveal a single thing about herself.

A FEW WEEKS ago Tina discovered a series of figure drawing videos on YouTube from an art academy featuring nude models holding poses for a minute, three minutes, five minutes, ten minutes. She knows artists need to learn human anatomy, so she's working through the videos, seeing what she can do in each of these time blocks, trying to indicate the shapes of bodies and limbs with quick, sweeping movements. She draws on the insides of brown grocery bags from Trader Joe's. She cuts the bags open, the way she used to decades before, when she used them to cover her textbooks in middle and high school. But now she draws on the insides of the bags, then brings her nightly efforts to the garage and dumps them into the recycling bin. The drawing is an exercise, just something to do to fill the late-night hours.

Although her nightly drawing usually calms her, tonight she's on edge. Earlier, she made a discovery. When she searched YouTube for art instruction videos, she found URLs for videos Jackson had watched on the drop-down menu of her web browser. She told herself not to click on any of these links. They were his business. Clicking on them would be something her parents would have done if YouTube existed when she was young. But curiosity got the best of her, and she clicked and saw the videos all featured magicians. Many were fuzzy, taken by audience members during their stage shows. Some were of magicians on a TV variety show called *Talent Abounds!* making themselves disappear onstage and then reappear in the audience or conjuring a deck of cards out of thin air. Some videos revealed how tricks were done. Several months ago, Jackson showed her a pair of complimentary tickets to a magic show in Chuckles, the run-down comedy club in the mall. He hadn't acted particularly interested in the show, so Tina encouraged him to do his homework instead. Why hadn't he told her he liked magic and wanted to go to the show?

"Mom!" Jackson says. "There's a naked person on your screen."

Jackson has wandered into the kitchen in his sleepwear, a T-shirt with a dolphin on it and a pair of gray sweatpants. It's after midnight, and Jackson is usually a sound sleeper.

On her computer, an unclothed woman stands with both arms folded over her head, a clock ticking down from three minutes in the corner of the screen.

"Are you drawing?" Jackson looks down at the cut-open grocery bag covered with pencil sketches. "Why are you drawing on a grocery bag? Do you want me to get you some printer paper?"

How will Tina explain this? The clock ticks down to zero, and then another model pops onto the screen, this time a man who is sitting, his knees pulled up to his chest.

"We saw some paintings with nudes when my class went on that field trip to the Albany Institute of History and Art," says Jackson. "And some sculptures too. The tour guide said when you're talking about art you're supposed to say nude and not naked. Nudity is on purpose and the model knows they're being drawn, but naked could be an accident, like if you saw someone changing their clothes."

Tina feels immensely grateful toward this tour guide who has educated her son about nudity in art. "I'm glad you were listening so carefully," Tina says. Jackson is always listening, always absorbing everything around him, and sometimes she wishes Jackson were one of those kids who constantly has their ears plugged with headphones, oblivious to the world around them.

"Why are you up?" Tina closes the laptop.

"I'm thirsty."

"I just put a new box of Dixie cups in the bathroom."

"I wanted ice in my water. And I wanted to drink out of a glass made out of glass."

Tina gets up, takes a pint glass out of the cabinet, and hands it to Jackson, who fills it with ice cubes and water from the door of the refrigerator. He takes a sip, surveying Tina's drawings.

"You can draw," Jackson says.

"Oh, I can't, not really." Tina always hides her drawings from Jackson, draws only when he's asleep or not around, but this time she can't deny what she's been doing, so she makes up a lie to explain it away. "The thing is, I read in a magazine that some stylists use drawing as a way to improve their hand-eye coordination. So I thought I'd try it out."

"Like how some football players do ballet so they can be more flexible and have better balance? My gym teacher told my class about that."

"Exactly," says Tina. "Exactly like that."

Jackson paws through a stack of magazines and newspapers on the kitchen table, searching for something. He pulls a catalog from the Art Center from the pile.

"I thought I recycled that," Tina says.

"You could take an art class." Jackson holds up the catalog. "Then you could have a real model to draw and you'd probably get to use an easel too. And you wouldn't have to draw on a bag."

"Oh, I'm too old to be a student."

"No," says Jackson, putting his glass on the kitchen table, flipping open the catalog, and pointing to a photograph of three white-haired women painting still lifes of a vase of flowers surrounded by three apples and a lemon. "These ladies are *much* older than you are."

And here it is: education is for the young or for the retired or the wealthy, for people who have time on their hands, for people without children to care for. If she wanted to take a class, she'd have to pay for the class and she'd have to pay for a babysitter. These are not expenses she needs to take on. Tina sees there is a life drawing class on Tuesday nights. A class at the Art Center with other adults is more appealing than an undergraduate class, but there's still the babysitter issue. "It might be fun, but it's not practical," Tina says.

"You mean because you need to find a babysitter?" Jackson says.

Sometimes Tina wishes Jackson wasn't so easily able to connect the dots. But she nods, says, "That's right. It's a lot of money, you know, paying a babysitter and also paying for the class."

Jackson looks thoughtful for a moment, rubs his chin, then says, "Let me see what I can figure out," and Tina wants to laugh because he sounds like a middle-aged CEO trying to manage limited resources.

"Okay," Tina says, "but for now, back to bed." She picks up his glass and leads him to his bedroom and hopes by morning Jackson will have forgotten about all of this.

A FEW DAYS later, there are no clients in the afternoon, so Tina looks up images of geese on her phone and sketches one on the back of a receipt. She is so absorbed in her drawing that she doesn't hear anyone enter the salon and startles when she hears a loud, obviously fake cough.

"Oh, hello!" Tina says, looking up from the reception desk to see Maria, who works at Chickety Chix in the food court. Maria helps Tina out with change when she's forgotten to go to the bank to exchange larger bills for an envelope of fives and ones. Tina slides her half-finished drawing beneath a pile of mail. "Are you here for a haircut?"

"No, I'm here to talk about the deal," Maria says.

"The deal?"

"The one Jackson mentioned yesterday?"

When Tina sends Jackson out on errands in the mall, he lingers in the food court talking to Maria. Maria is seventeen and beautiful, even though she has to wear bright yellow overalls and a hat shaped like the head of a chicken, complete with a red comb made of felt.

Tina has no idea what Maria is talking about. "I've been distracted lately," Tina says. "Remind me."

"Oh," says Maria, "It sounded too good to be true. I'm sorry." Maria shakes her head, and the comb on her chicken hat wobbles.

"It sounds like Jackson's the one who should be sorry if he's going around making deals. What did he say?"

"He said I could trade babysitting for free hair styling and you could do my makeup too before any shows or auditions. I'm auditioning in a few weeks for *West Side Story* at the high school and I'm trying out for the role of Maria, which I know is ironic since, you know, that's my name."

Maria sounds anxious, and Tina wonders if, for some reason, she makes Maria nervous. Why does Jackson think he needs to do this sort of bartering on her behalf? Just so Tina can go to an art class? Does he want more time away from her? Is he getting to the age where so many hours a day spent with his mother is too much for him?

"I know, it's stupid," says Maria. "You're too busy and it would cost a lot to get those things done, and you'd lose money. I shouldn't have mentioned it."

Tina realizes she hasn't said anything about the deal, and that Maria is not nervous but embarrassed.

"No, no, it's okay. It's just that Jackson didn't mention it, but I'm happy to do your hair and makeup for free for auditions. And maybe one day you can babysit. It'll all even out. And look, I'm never busy," she says, gesturing with both hands around the empty salon. "It would be fun." Maybe when she's doing Maria's hair, she can ask if she knows a Chinese girl from YouTube named Annie who is good at art. Maybe Maria and Annie go to the same school. Maybe Maria will say, "Oh, yeah, Annie. You know she nicknamed herself Arty Annie Amazing, but behind her back everyone calls her Annie Annoying Asshole."

Maria says, "Jackson said you'd need me to babysit on Tuesday nights for the next six weeks."

"Tuesday would be a school night. I'm sure you have homework to do." Tina can't figure out why it's so important to Jackson that she go to the art class. And then Tina has a thought that makes her head feel like it's swirling: What if Jackson is embarrassed she's a hair stylist? What if he wishes she did something else, something he can be proud of? What if he's feeling the same embarrassment she felt about her parents' jobs? Would he like being able to tell people his mother is an artist? Doesn't Jackson know that one class at the local Art Center isn't going to transform her into an artist?

"I have study hall second period on Wednesday, so if there was any homework that I hadn't finished, I could do it then," says Maria. "Plus, it would give us time to practice our act."

"Your act?"

"Yeah, I'm his magician's assistant for the school talent show in February. This would give us a chance to practice."

Tina knows nothing about a school talent show, nothing about Jackson's act, nothing about a magician's assistant. Was he ever going to tell her? Was he planning on inviting her to the show? "Of course," Tina says, "the talent show."

"So do you want me to babysit on Tuesday? I have my license, so I can drive to your house. And if you want references, I can give them to you. I used to babysit a lot, before I got the job at Chickety Chix."

"I believe you're a good babysitter." Any teenager who would dress like a chicken and work at a mall where other high schoolers might see her is likely not going to be a troublemaker. "But Jackson's wrong about my needing to go out on Tuesday nights."

"Oh," says Maria, "okay."

Tina sees disappointment wash over Maria's face, so she says, "But how about this Friday or Saturday? And let's make an appointment so you can come in before your audition." Tina will go to the movies by herself on the night Maria babysits, enjoy a rare evening out, eat an entire box of Junior Mints she won't have to share. She'll see a movie with dinosaurs or aliens or vampires, something so different from the mundane and ordinary world she inhabits. Jackson doesn't need Maria to come over six times to practice magic. Is he expecting Maria to leave the high school in the middle of the day to be his assistant at the elementary school talent show? For a smart boy, Jackson doesn't always think things through.

"I can do Friday," says Maria. "And if you want to do Tuesdays in the future, that's cool too."

Tina nods, but she knows she's not going to take the art class. What's the point? She's forty years old, she has a nine-year-old son, the mall where she works might shut down soon. Paying to take an art class is frivolous. There are limits to her irresponsibility and right now it is allowing herself to buy one full-priced movie ticket and one box of candy at the concession stand. That is enough.

TINA IS WAITING for her teriyaki chicken and noodles at Panda Wok when Jackson arrives at the mall. His backpack looks full and heavy. He trudges past Old Navy and Kay Jewelers, then passes Book Nook and heads toward the yellow WET FLOOR sign outside of Sunshine Clips. Tina waves at Jackson, but he doesn't see her.

"Sorry, need to cut more zucchinis," says the cook behind the counter, as he uses a spatula to move the greasy noodles around the flat-top grill.

"No rush," says Tina. There are no customers waiting at the salon, and Jackson is settling down at the reception desk. She sees Jackson's found the small package of Oreos she left for him. He opens it, twists the top off one cookie, and takes a small bite of the half of the Oreo that doesn't have cream on it. Then he reaches into his backpack and takes out a deck of playing cards. Where did he get those cards? He clears some room on the desk, then puts a handful of cards facedown on the open space. His right hand hovers over the cards, lingers a few seconds over each card, and then he finally flips one over and Tina sees him smile. Then he picks up the cards, splays them out in one hand, and then reaches into the pocket of his button-down shirt and extracts another card. He smiles again. Tina understands he's practicing magic.

"Sorry for the wait. Very hot." The cook pushes Tina's box of noodles and vegetables and chicken toward her. She grabs a plastic fork and a handful of napkins and brings her food back to the salon. When she enters, Jackson looks startled, and he quickly gathers his cards.

"Hey," says Tina. "What are you up to?"

"Nothing," says Jackson. He lays down cards across the desk; some of the cards land on top of papers and pens and napkins from the food court.

"You were doing *something*," says Tina. "Want any noodles?"

Jackson shakes his head. "I was playing solitaire. I'm playing again now."

"Really?" Why is he lying to her? Why won't he tell her he's been practicing magic tricks?

"Yeah," says Jackson. "Solitaire is good when you're bored."

"I haven't seen anyone play it with real cards for a long time. Only on the phone."

"I don't have a phone. That's why I have to use real cards. You can have my seat," says Jackson, collecting the cards, pushing them back into their box. "So you can eat at the desk."

"Okay, thanks," says Tina. She sits down and opens the box of noodles, and steam drifts up. Jackson slips the deck of cards into his backpack and moves to one of the stylists' chairs.

"You know," says Tina, "if you ever want to show me what you can do with cards, I'd like that."

Jackson takes a book out of his backpack, opens it to the page where his bookmark rests. "I don't know how to do anything with cards," he says.

Tina nods, winds noodles around her plastic fork, but she's lost her appetite. The flimsy tines wobble as she spins them around the greasy noodles, and Tina sets the fork down in the cover of the takeout container. Why is her son lying to her? Why won't he show her his trick? Why hasn't he told her about the talent show at his school? She'd be supportive, even if he told her his biggest goal in life is to become a professional magician, which is quite possibly the most ridiculous job a person could want.

Jackson is reading, head down, his bangs too long, hanging into his face, and Tina can't remember when she last cut his hair. She stares at her son, willing him to look at her and tell her about the magic tricks he's been practicing. She wants him to invite her to his school talent show. She wants him to tell her about the videos he's been watching. But he just keeps reading. Tina looks down at the desk, sees her sketch of the goose peeking out from under some menus Jackson shuffled around, and she grabs the sketch, balls it up, and drops it into the garbage can beneath the desk. As the crumpled paper falls from her hand, she thinks it's not just that Jackson is hiding something from her; it's that he is imitating her. He's keeping secret something that's important to him, maybe because he's afraid he's no good or it's silly or she'd be disappointed to know he cares about such a thing. She feels certain he has learned to be quiet and secretive and to not allow himself to talk about impractical dreams from her.

Tina sees movement out of the corner of her eye and looks across the hall and sees Kevin waving at her. He's standing behind the register at Book Nook. Today he is dressed normally, in jeans and a blue-and-white-striped sweatshirt. But then Tina realizes that's the sweatshirt he wears when pretending to be the little bunny from *Goodnight Moon*. Today there is no bunny suit beneath the sweatshirt and his hair still looks neat from his recent haircut. He holds up a hardcover book with a border collie on the cover, points to the dog, grins. Tina pauses for a few seconds, then does something she never does: she gives him a quick thumbs-up, a small sign of encouragement. Maybe he should try out this dog business, even if the odds of it succeeding are minuscule. Maybe people who aren't at Annie Amazing levels of amazingness should pursue the things they like to do without worrying they're being foolish. Maybe Kevin is not so absurd after all. Tina reaches into the garbage can, extracts the crumpled drawing of a goose, and smooths it out on the desk. Then she says, "Hey, Jackson, want to see something I drew?"

December

The Eyes of Men

Maria's eyes burn and her vision blurs as she stares at the cast list thumbtacked to the corkboard outside the music classroom. It isn't fair. She should have been cast as Maria in *West Side Story*. She's a senior, she's been in the high school musicals for the last three years, getting bigger and bigger parts, and, for God's sake, her name—her real, on-the-birth-certificate name—is Maria. What role could be more perfect for her? She's improved, working on her vocals and practicing her acting in front of a mirror. And Maria is half Puerto Rican, which would lend authenticity to the role. Madison Olafsson, who has been cast as Maria, is zero percent Puerto Rican and one hundred percent blond and blue-eyed and already got the starring role in *Alice in Wonderland* last year while Maria had to play the hookah-smoking caterpillar. Maria subjected herself to that inanity, and now, as she is putting together her college applications and needs stellar extracurriculars, her name appears under the word *Chorus*. The chorus is for tone-deaf kids who belong in clumps in the background while the talented students belt out solos under spotlights. Maria glares at the cast list, makes a fist, and punches Madison's name.

"Sucks," says a voice behind her. She turns around, rubbing her stinging knuckles, and sees a pale boy with stringy brown hair falling into his eyes. He looks vaguely familiar. The high school isn't so big—only 850 students total—and even though she doesn't know everyone by name, she at least recognizes them. So why does this kid only look a little familiar, like someone who occasionally bags her family's groceries at the supermarket, and not someone she passes daily in the hall?

"What sucks?" says Maria. She isn't sure whether he's chastising her, telling her it's sucky behavior to punch the corkboard, or if he thinks it sucks she didn't get a speaking part in the musical. She shakes out her hand, but it doesn't feel any better.

"You're too good for the chorus," says the boy. "And you should get some ice on your hand soon. Otherwise it'll bruise and swell up."

The boy sounds hoarse, like he was screaming before talking to her. But his words calm Maria: the indignation coursing through her veins suddenly mellows because of his flattery. Maria wants to ask his name, ask how he knows she's too good for the chorus.

"I do lighting for most of the shows," he says, as if he knows what she's thinking. "I'm on the stage crew."

"Oh, right," says Maria. So this is where she's seen him, blending into the shadows while she was onstage.

"I would quit if I were you," the boy says. He reaches a hand up and swipes the hair out of his eyes. "It's disrespectful."

"For me to be in the chorus?" Maria says. She rubs her unwounded hand over her throbbing knuckles, but this just makes them feel worse.

"You know the rumors, right? Madison Olafsson takes private voice lessons with Mrs. Wilder. She basically bought the part." The boy has pale gray irises, so light they almost blend into the whites of his eyes. Maria has never seen anyone with eyes this color before.

"I didn't know that," Maria says. It seems unethical for the director of the musicals to give private lessons. "Who told you?"

The boy shrugs. "You hear stuff when a lot of your job is done in the dark and people forget you're there. Your hand is turning red."

Maria feels creeped out, a chill running down her arms, and she wonders how many times this boy listened to her chatting with her castmates during rehearsal breaks over the last three years.

"You should march in there and quit," the boy says, pointing toward Mrs. Wilder's office, and Maria is shocked by how forcefully he says it. "I'll quit stage crew too in solidarity."

"Oh no, don't do that." Maria doesn't want this strange boy to do anything on her behalf.

"Well," says the boy, taking a step backward, "if I were as good at singing and acting as you, I'd be pretty pissed off. You should get some ice for that hand." He turns and scurries down the hall, leaving Maria to stand and stare at the list, the fury about being relegated to the chorus churning again in her belly, acid swirling up into her throat, her hand throbbing.

At lunch, Maria describes the boy to her best friend, Chloe. Chloe dunks a crinkle-cut fry into a small paper cup of ketchup and shakes her head. "Are you sure you weren't so filled with rage you blacked out and dreamed up this guy telling you to quit? Or maybe he's your bad angel. You know, good angel on one shoulder, bad on the other. Like in the cartoons."

"He looked a little familiar. Said he was on the stage crew." Maria is holding a plastic bag of ice on her hand, even though it's been a few hours since she punched the board.

"Wait, was it Creepy Chester? Like gray denim jacket, greasy hair?"

"Is that his name? Chester?" Maria asks.

"I don't know if that's his real name, but that's what people call him. He's always just, like, lurking around. That's a weird word, isn't it, *lurk*?"

Lurking is the perfect way to describe the boy, Maria thinks. Always there in the dark, always watching and listening.

"Do you think you should go to the nurse?" Chloe says, pointing to Maria's hand. "Or maybe show Mrs. Wilder and tell her you want to be one of the Jets or Sharks. Tell her you beat someone up to prove your toughness."

"Hilarious," says Maria, lifting the bag of ice on her knuckles and seeing that her whole hand has turned bright pink from the cold. "I'm not going to the nurse because she's going to ask me how I hurt my hand, and I don't want to tell her. You're the only one who's allowed to know."

"Well, me and Creepy Chester. Do you think he lives in the underground tunnels?" Chloe asks. "Do you think that's why his skin is so pale?"

"There are no underground tunnels."

"That's what they want us to think!"

Maria knows students at Greenways High have been talking for decades about the tunnels that are supposed to crisscross the length of the school. Underground tunnels could be practical for the frigid upstate New York winters, yet no one has ever seen them. Many students spend time looking for hidden entrances to the fabled belowground world, although nothing has ever been uncovered as far as Maria knows. But if the tunnels exist, and if there is a secret society living there, the boy would fit in perfectly with his pale skin and gray eyes and crackly voice.

"So are you going to take Creepy Chester's advice?"

Chilly water drips out of the bag of melting ice and pools on the table. Maria puts the bag on Chloe's tray. The boy's idea has been spinning around her mind all day. If she quits the musical, she'll have more free time. She can put in extra hours at Chickety Chix. This will allow her to save more money for college. But college! She wants to study theater, and she thought she'd get a starring role in *West Side Story* and be able to send in a video of her performance with her college applications. And now what? Is she supposed to send in a video of her in the chorus, surrounded by out-of-tune freshmen?

"We can make a pros and cons list," says Chloe, taking a notebook out of her backpack and ripping out a piece of paper. She plucks a pencil out of a cloth case that looks like a wiener dog and draws a line down the middle of the page. "Pros?" Chloe says.

"I could get more hours at Chickety Chix."

Chloe's pen hovers over the page. "That's a positive? You have to dress up in a chicken costume!"

"I like working at the mall. It's a great place to study humanity."

Chloe snorts when Maria says this, but she sketches a cartoon chicken in the "Pros" column. Then she writes "More time with Seth" under the chicken.

"I don't know what's going on with Seth," says Maria. Seth is maybe her boyfriend, maybe not her boyfriend. She hardly sees him at school because they're in different classes and have different lunch periods. Sometimes he comes to the mall to hang out in the food court, but she can't talk to him when it gets busy. She has kissed him five times in the past two months, all in a dark corner of the parking lot of the theater after seeing movies with a pack of friends. They have never been on a date alone. Last Saturday night, Seth took a necklace out of the pocket of his jeans. A small fried egg, about the size of a quarter, hung on a silver chain.

"My mom dragged me to this craft fair and I saw this and I thought of you," he said. The fried egg seemed to be made of glass, the yolk shiny and runny-looking. She put the necklace on because what else could she do? What about Maria reminded Seth of a fried egg?

"Thank you," she said, and Seth seemed pleased with himself, smiling and nodding at the necklace, which hung over the collar of Maria's fleece jacket.

"It would be extra funny if you wore it to work with your chicken outfit," said Seth. "Like chicken, egg, chicken, egg, chicken, egg."

She stared at Seth and contemplated whether his handsomeness was his most positive quality. He had broad shoulders, and long eyelashes that made Maria a little jealous the first time she saw them up close, and a jawline that made her think of Superman. He was muscular, not someone to mess with, not because he was scary, but because he was strong. His appearance, both the handsomeness and strength, would likely be enough to get him through life, and it probably wouldn't matter if he was not smart enough to know that an egg necklace wasn't a romantic gift.

"Can you put Seth in the middle of the two columns? Not a pro, not a con," says Maria, pointing to the line Chloe drew down the page. "I'm currently neutral on him."

"He looks like a model. You shouldn't be neutral on male models. I wish he had the same lunch period as us. You should spend more time with him."

Maria thinks of that egg necklace, which is in the little clay bowl on her desk where she keeps paperclips and thumbtacks, the chain tangled now. She has not worn it since the night Seth gave it to her. It's not just the necklace that has her confused about Seth. Her older sister, Julia, told her not to get too involved with boys in high school. Julia dated a boy named Devon for three years of high school and then had such separation issues once she went to Chicago for college and he went to Boston, she'd ended up dropping out of school and moving in with him. By the time her boxes were unpacked, Devon had broken up with her, saying she wasn't letting him live his life. After she came home to live with their parents, Julia told Maria, "Don't let any boys get in the way of what you want to do."

"Ultimate humiliation," says Maria. "Put that in the cons column."

"If you quit?"

"If I quit *or* if I stay in the chorus. If I quit, everyone will think I have a bad attitude and I'm jealous of people who got real parts. And if I stay, people will feel sorry for me. I mean, how many seniors are in the chorus? I wonder if I did something to piss off Mrs. Wilder."

Chloe draws a frowning face in the cons column, then takes a red pen out of her dachshund bag and colors it red. "Mrs. Wilder makes weird casting decisions every year. I wouldn't take it personally. I think it's menopause or something."

"What am I going to do?" says Maria. She looks at her uneaten turkey sandwich. She has no appetite today, but she steals a fry from Chloe's tray and chews on it. It's cold and mealy.

"About what?"

"My college applications. I planned on sending in a clip from the musical. Now what?"

"I have an idea!" Chloe says, standing up in excitement. The lunchroom table shakes from her sudden motion, and Maria grabs her swollen hand protectively. "Flash mob. At the mall! In the food court. Get people who work there to do it with you, and I'll film it."

"Aren't flash mobs like really 2014?"

"So what? Bring it back. You know what would be super awesome? If we could make our flash mob video go viral! It'd help us both get into college if everyone knows who we are."

Chloe wants to be a filmmaker, and she and Maria hope to go to college together in L.A. Years later, when Chloe is a famous filmmaker and Maria is a famous actress, and they collect their Oscars, they'll tell interviewers about how they've known each other almost all their lives, how they've always supported each other, how they've always believed in each other's dreams. They've fantasized about this since they were little girls.

"How am I going to get, like, a hundred people to be in the flash mob with me?" Maria says.

"Ask the people who work in the mall to help. They'd do it. I bet they're all so bored."

"But then everyone would have to leave their stores and they'd get in trouble."

"We'll figure it out," says Chloe, eyes wide with excitement. "This is *so* much better than a video of a musical. This will make you totally stand out from the other applicants."

When Chloe clears the remnants of her lunch from the table, she accidentally sweeps up the pros/cons list and deposits it into the garbage. She doesn't seem to notice, and Maria sees no reason why she should draw any attention to the list, now buried beneath the remnants of Chloe's uneaten fries.

AFTER SCHOOL, MARIA drives to the mall, where she has a four-hour shift. She enters the bathroom near the food court and wiggles into her yellow overalls. Then she yanks her chicken hat out of her backpack, places it on her head, and straightens the comb. She steps out of the stall and looks in the mirror and says, "Ultimate humiliation." There are many things in her life that are humiliating. Maybe this is what it means to be seventeen; maybe at this age life is just one long series of humiliations.

She leaves the bathroom and sees the back of a figure heading toward the men's room on the other side of the food court, and she swears it's the boy from school, the boy who might live in the underground tunnels, the one who told her to quit the musical. She hasn't quit, not yet at least. Rehearsals don't start for another week; she has time to contemplate. She wonders if it will look bad to colleges if she decides to not participate in the musical her senior year. Maybe it wouldn't be terrible to be in the chorus. There would be fewer lines to learn, less pressure. If she messes up, forgets a lyric or stumbles during a dance, no one would even notice.

"Hey!" she calls out as she shrugs her backpack onto her shoulders, but the boy has disappeared into the men's room.

"Hey, baby! You looking for me?" yells a man with a pile of tacos from Taco Bell spread before him at the table nearest the women's bathroom. Right now the food court is nearly empty—it's the time after lunch and before dinner.

"You have all these tables to choose from and you choose the one closest to the bathroom?" Maria says. Usually she ignores the men who shout rude comments at her, but today she's in a bad mood, can't keep quiet.

"Best view, mamacita," says the man through a mouthful of taco. He wiggles his eyebrows up and down.

Maria makes a disgusted, cat-hacking-up-a-hairball sound and storms off toward Chickety Chix. She hates men like this, men who think that just because you're stuck behind a counter, because you're young and working a job that requires you to wear a chicken outfit, that it's their right to say whatever they want, to stare at you lasciviously. One day things will be different. One day she'll be successful and famous, and this job in the food court will feel like a faint memory of a long-ago nightmare. And by that time, this man will be dead, his arteries clogged with cholesterol from taco meat. Behind the counter, Maria adjusts her chicken hat and stares at the men's room, but she doesn't see the boy exit.

"Maria!" calls out Jackson Huang.

"What's up?" says Maria. She likes when Jackson comes by. He helps the time pass more quickly, and he doesn't mind when it gets busy and she can't pay attention to him. He just goes to a table and reads one of his books with the animals dressed in Victorian clothing on the cover until she's free again. She fills a small cup with lemonade and hands it to him. He thanks her and takes it with one hand; the other hand is clutching a bag.

"I had an idea," says Jackson. He sets the lemonade on the counter and reaches into the bag. He pulls out a baseball cap, which is painted white. An orange construction-paper beak covers the bill and there are large googly eyes attached to each side of the hat. "It's a dove hat," says Jackson. "Did you know that doves and pigeons are pretty much the same bird?"

"I didn't know that."

"What happened to your hand?"

Her knuckles are now bruised, a dark purple. "Oh, nothing," says Maria, covering it with her other hand.

"Does it hurt?"

"Not too much," Maria lies.

"Really? It looks like it hurts."

"Tell me more about doves," Maria says, eager to change the subject.

"People think doves are beautiful and pigeons are gross, but they're the same species. Do you know some people call pigeons sky rats? I think that's mean to both rats and pigeons."

"I agree," says Maria, glad she's gotten Jackson back on the topic of animals. She hates rats and isn't too fond of pigeons, but she won't tell Jackson these things. She knows he loves all animals. "What are you planning on doing with the dove hat?"

"It's for you," says Jackson, holding it up to Maria. "For when you're my assistant."

When Jackson asked Maria to be his assistant in a magic act for his school's talent show, she assumed she'd wear a dress and heels, look like a bona fide magician's assistant, not a dove, which, in her mind, is only a miniscule step above dressing up as a chicken.

"I thought you could dress in all white and wear this hat and you wouldn't look like every other magician's assistant. Your chicken uniform gave me the idea. And if I can figure out how to make you pop out of a top hat, it would be even better."

"Can you do that?" Maria thinks a lot of magic tricks are done with mirrors, but she can't imagine how a mirror could help her appear to fit into a top hat.

"No," says Jackson. He pushes a straw through the cap on the cup of lemonade, takes a long sip, and says, "I know how to make a real dove appear out of a hat, but not a human dove. But I don't own a real dove, so I can't do that trick either." He drinks until his cup is empty and sets it back on the counter. "It's not fair. I'll find out how to do a trick online, but then I can't do it because I don't have a carpentry studio or money for supplies. But when I'm older, I'm going to be able to buy all sorts of stuff, and I'll be able to figure out how to make you pop out of a hat."

"By that time, I'll be too old to be a magician's assistant." After she says it, Maria thinks about being older, her hair gray, unable to fold her stiff limbs so she can fit into small spaces. She wonders what it will be like to be old, to not have men shout at her just because they think she's pretty. She wonders whether that will be better or worse than knowing people are only interested in you because they like the way you look.

"Do you think a corgi would be a good sidekick for a magician?" says Jackson.

"What? Are you thinking of replacing me with a corgi?" Maria is surprised by how insulted she feels.

"No," Jackson says, shaking his head. "An assistant and a sidekick are different things. You'd be my assistant and the corgi would be my sidekick. But I think only magicians who are funny can have animal sidekicks. Like Piff the Magic Dragon and his chihuahua. I don't think I'm funny enough to be a comedian and I don't own a corgi anyway, so I'll probably only practice serious magic."

"Right, serious magic," Maria echoes. She has no idea what Jackson is talking about—isn't the dragon named Puff?—but she's happy she's not being replaced as Jackson's assistant so she reaches for the dove hat and swaps her chicken hat with it.

Jackson stares at Maria and says, "I need to change the googly eyes. They're too silly. I'll paint eyes. Or maybe I can ask my mom to do it. She's good at art."

"I don't want to be a dove," Maria says, and Jackson's face falls. But right now she wants to stand up for herself. "I want to be an assistant in a fancy dress. And heels. Like how professional magicians' assistants dress."

Jackson looks like he's going to cry, and Maria feels a welling of regret because it's not Jackson she's mad at, it's Mrs. Wilder, and it's the crude man in the food court, and it's the lurking boy from school who thinks he has the right to tell her how she should live her life.

"I can't get you a real magician's assistant's outfit, but I can make you a dove outfit. My mom has this white sweat suit you could borrow, and I could get some feathers from the art classroom at school," Jackson says.

"If I get my own dress, can I wear it?" Maria is thinking about visiting the props closet at school, which is filled with racks of donated clothing. Surely, there has to be something there that is suitable for a magician's assistant.

"Okay," says Jackson, but Maria can tell it's not okay, that she's ruined his good idea, stomped on something he was excited about. Maria is still wearing the dove hat, and she's not sure what to do about it. Returning it to Jackson might upset him even more.

"Do you want more lemonade?" says Maria.

Jackson shakes his head, and Maria can see he's unhappy. Maybe she should invite him behind the counter to squeeze lemons in the juicer. That seems like something a nine-year-old would like doing, but she's already breaking a rule by wearing the dove hat, and the manager will be showing up soon, and he'd probably fire her for bringing a child behind the counter.

"Hey, you know what a flash mob is?" Maria asks.

Jackson nods.

"You want to help me put one together here? At the mall?"

The sadness in Jackson's eyes evaporates, and he nods.

"My friend Chloe can record it and we can put it online and maybe it'll go viral."

"What song will we sing?"

"I'm not sure yet."

"What about costumes?"

"I guess we'd just dress like regular people. So we'd all be walking around like we were just at the mall to shop, and then we'd start singing and dancing."

"Could we climb on top of the tables?"

"Definitely," says Maria, and a smile spreads on Jackson's face. She feels relieved.

"Okay, yeah, I can be part of it," says Jackson.

"Do you think you can do some magic? What would be cool to include as part of the flash mob?"

"It would be super cool if I could just appear out of nowhere standing on top of a table at the end. Or maybe float down from the ceiling like a bird. You know how sometimes you see sparrows inside the mall and then you wonder how they got in?"

"You could dress up like a sparrow," Maria says. She takes the dove hat off her head and holds it out to Jackson. This is her chance to return it to him without hurting his feelings. "Maybe if you painted this brown, it could be more sparrowish?"

"Yeah," says Jackson. "And you can wear a dress for the talent show. That would be okay."

"Yeah?" Maria says. "You sure?"

"Yeah," Jackson says. "This flash mob is going to be so cool." He places the dove hat on his own head, takes his empty cup to the trash, and heads back to the salon where his mother is styling an old woman's white hair.

MARIA'S SHIFT ENDS at six forty-five. After Jenna Dixon arrives at Chickety Chix for the night shift, Maria counts the till and writes down the amount of cash in her register. Then she rushes to the mall bathroom and stuffs her hat and overalls into her backpack and pulls on her jeans. Throughout her shift, Maria contemplated whether she should quit the musical, and right before she finished her final wipe-down, she made her decision. The musical would offer her nothing, and her time could be better spent doing other things. She'll somehow explain in her college applications why she isn't in the musical this year. She can say something about wanting to concentrate on academics or write an essay that spins untruths about having to make a difficult decision to step away from the musical for her mental health and describe how she, like so many kids of her generation, has found herself overextended.

Maria looks into all the brightly lit shops as she heads toward the exit. The mall is fairly quiet at this time of night, most of the customers home having dinner. As always, the bookstore is nearly empty.

Tonight, though, she wants to rummage through the props closet at the high school and find a dress that would work for the magic show. Tonight, before she quits, she still has the right to paw through the costumes meant for actors. She is certain no one will notice if one dress is missing. She's not stealing it—she plans to return it when she's done.

She glances back at the food court and thinks it will be a good setting for the finale of the flash mob. Jackson's excitement about the flash mob made her more enthusiastic about the idea. Instead of withering away in the chorus, she'll work with Chloe and Jackson on the flash mob; she will be in charge of how she moves and how she sings.

Maria pushes through the double doors of the mall and walks to Parking Area C and slides into her car. She can get to the high school in twenty minutes, maybe seventeen or eighteen minutes if she doesn't hit any lights. She knows the doors of the high school are open until at least eight on Tuesdays because the Robotics Club has their weekly meetings from six to eight. Before she got the job at Chickety Chix, she and Chloe would hang out and do homework until seven forty-five at Starbucks and then drive to the high school to pick up Chloe's younger brother, Christian, after his Robotics Club meetings.

Maria parks near the science wing—where she knows the door will be unlocked—and heads inside. The fluorescent ceiling lights still shine brightly, but everything is strange and empty. Without students crowding the hallway, Maria notices how many of the orange lockers are dented, how many scuffs there are on the floor tiles. The hallway smells like lemon disinfectant, and she sees a large gray garbage can on wheels and a mop in a rolling bucket. She hears one toilet after another flush in the boys' bathroom and thinks the janitor must be cleaning in there.

She walks upstairs and listens for any sounds in the auditorium, but it's silent. The silence is nice; once the rehearsals for *West Side Story* start, Maria knows the space will be filled with the sound of Madison Olafsson's reedy voice practicing "I Feel Pretty" onstage, every note a little flat. The auditorium is dark, and she's unsure where the light switches are, so she turns on the flashlight app on her phone. She proceeds down the long middle aisle, climbs the steps to the stage, pushes through the curtains, and opens the door to the props closet, the small room behind the stage. It is even darker back here, but her phone's flashlight does a decent job of lighting a few feet in front of her. She hears a rustling and freezes, holds her breath. A male voice calls out her name.

Maria can feel the thumping of her heart and is unsure whether she'd be safer keeping her flashlight app on or plunging herself into darkness. She slowly moves her phone around, illuminating the small room, until she sees Creepy Chester. She's not sure if she should be scared. He doesn't look threatening, but what is he doing hiding back here in the dark? He's sprawled out on the orange and brown plaid couch with scratchy upholstery that's always used whenever the school's plays or musicals have an indoor scene. It looks like he's relaxing in his own living room; his shoes are off and his socked feet are crossed at the ankle. He's also wearing a hat, which Maria knows was used as part of the Sky Masterson costume when the school put on *Guys and Dolls* her sophomore year. The boy is holding a small flashlight attached to a keychain and reading *The Turn of the Screw*, which means he's a junior and taking AP English.

"Hey, it's me," he says. He seems unsurprised to see her, almost as if he had been waiting for her.

"Chester?" Maria ventures.

The boy sits up and adjusts his hat so the brim is low on his forehead and she can't see his eyes. He puts his copy of *The Turn of the Screw* on the couch facedown, open to the page he was reading. "That's not my name," he says. He sounds irritated. He sighs, turns his flashlight toward Maria.

"What's your name, then?" Maria holds her hand up to shield her eyes from the flashlight and the boy moves it so it's aimed at the rack of clothing behind her.

"I know your name, Maria. It's disappointing that you don't know mine after all the time we spent working together on *Guys and Dolls* and *Alice in Wonderland*."

Maria waits a few seconds, but the boy doesn't say more, so she supposes his name will remain a secret for now. "What are you doing here?" She blinks at the light in her eyes.

"What are *you* doing here?" the boy asks. As if he owns the place, as if Maria has trespassed and entered his home without permission.

"And to answer your question, I just like hanging out here sometimes. It's quiet when there isn't a show going on; nobody bothers me here. Well, *usually* nobody bothers me."

Maria wonders whether she should run away. She should have texted Chloe, telling her where she'd be. Or she could have texted Seth. Her parents probably believe she's still at work; some nights she works until closing, and they won't be worried about her until after ten. She didn't tell anyone where she was going because she hadn't thought being at school at night would pose any danger.

"I know what you're doing here," says the boy when Maria doesn't answer his question. He stands up.

Maria takes a step backward. She reaches out and finds the light switch and flips it up. Suddenly, the small room is bathed in light, and everything seems much less threatening. They are just in the props closet, a small, airless room with its musty furniture and thrift store clothing. The boy is just a strange kid in an old-fashioned hat holding a tiny flashlight attached to a keychain. "Why do you think I'm here?" Maria says.

"You're pissed off."

"About the musical?"

"Well, yeah. I saw you punch the cast list."

She doesn't like that he was the only witness to her momentary loss of control. "Maybe, but I'm here for a reason unrelated to that."

"Yeah, right." The boy pulls the brim of his hat up and now Maria can see his light gray eyes again.

"I need a dress."

"You use this place as your closet?" The boy slides on a pair of too-big black dress shoes that were next to the couch. He leaves the laces untied. Maria is certain he found them here and they do not belong to him.

She's annoyed by this boy, annoyed by his presence in this place she was supposed to have to herself, annoyed by his questions. "It looks like you're using this place as your living room, and that's *way* weirder than using it as a closet."

"Hey, don't get mad at me. I'm sorry if I ruined your plans to destroy stuff."

"What are you talking about?" Maria says. She wonders if Robotics Club has let out yet. Will the janitor be locking up the school? She needs to get a dress and go before everyone else leaves. She needs to not waste any more time talking to this boy. She doesn't want to be in an empty school alone with him.

"Tell me you didn't come here to cause trouble."

"I did not."

"It never crossed your mind to mess up some stuff? Like maybe steal a few props?"

"I just came to borrow a dress," Maria says.

"What do you need a dress for?" he asks.

"I'm going to be a magician's assistant." Why has she told the boy the truth? Why didn't she just tell him it's none of his business? It's not as if he's been forthcoming about anything, including his name.

"Oh?" says the boy, and he says it in a harsh and sharp way, and Maria sees his body tense. He takes off the Sky Masterson hat and hangs it on a hook on the wall. Then he puts on a black top hat, which looks like it could be a magician's hat. "Who's the magician? Someone famous?"

Why would the boy think a famous magician would hire someone in high school to be his assistant? And are there even famous magicians in upstate New York? "He's nine years old. It's for his elementary school talent show."

"Oh, good, that's fine," says the boy, nodding.

That's fine? Maria thinks. How is it his place to tell her what she can and can't do?

"I'll just find a dress and leave. And you can continue reading and acting like you live here." She walks toward the rack of dresses and reaches for a sparkly black dress. She thinks it would look pretty with overhead stage lights reflecting off of it.

"Listen," says the boy, sitting back down on the couch, "you're better off not doing the musical. I saw the libretto. It's sanitized, scrubbed clean for delicate high school students. Adults think we're all special snowflakes. You wouldn't want to be part of it. You have too much integrity for that."

"What do you mean 'scrubbed clean'?" And what does he know about her integrity? Why does he keep acting like he knows her?

"Maria," says the boy, and she's taken aback by the way her name sounds coming out of his mouth, each syllable overarticulated. She hates the fact that he knows her name but she still does not know his. "Haven't you ever watched *West Side Story*? It's very racist. It contains words that no one got upset about hearing in 1961 but you can't say in 2018. It's also way too long for the attention span of an average high school musical attendee."

"How did you get to see the script?" Only a few pages were handed out to the students who'd auditioned. At this point, no one but Mrs. Wilder has access to the entire libretto.

"Nobody ever seems to notice me. I can do pretty much whatever I want."

Maria feels goose bumps on her arms, even though it's warm and stuffy back here, the heat banging and hissing through the old radiators. Is this boy dangerous? Is he just pretending to be dangerous? Does he know that the kids at school call him Creepy Chester? He must, judging by how irritated he got when she called him Chester. Is he mad at her for not ever noticing him, even though he's obviously been watching her?

"Let's burn the costumes," the boy says, and Maria is startled and lets go of the sparkly black dress and takes a few steps backward to distance herself from him. She wonders if she should punch in 911 on her phone, just in case.

"I'm not setting anything on fire. Why would you even think about doing that?"

"Let's bring them outside and burn them. How about the football field? It can be two birds with one stone. We burn the costumes and we ruin the field. A fuck-you to the drama kids *and* the athletes." He starts pulling blazers and coats off a rack and piling them on a small table next to the couch.

"Stop," Maria says, but the boy doesn't listen. He seems crazed, pulling more and more clothing off the racks. How had he gone from lounging around reading Henry James to this maniacal idea in a matter of minutes? Why is he talking to her like she's agreed to his plan? The room feels incredibly small now, crowded, clothing piling up on the floor and couch.

"We could burn stuff under the bleachers. There are no cameras there."

"I need to go," Maria says. There's something wrong with this boy, and she wants to get away from him quickly. Why hadn't she just left when she first saw him? Why had it been so important for her to take something from this closet?

"You don't have to be involved," says the boy. "But you'll know I did it for you?"

"God, no, don't do anything for me!" Maria doesn't want to spend one more second with him, so she quickly makes her way out of the props closet, across the stage, and through the curtains. She uses the flashlight on her phone to guide her out of the auditorium, then runs down the stairs, back into the science hallway. She sees a few students still lingering in the classroom where Robotics Club is held, their heads bent over a small robot that looks like a dog walking on its hind legs. She feels less panicked after seeing people around. If the boy follows her she can scream and they will help her. As she jogs toward the door, she keeps checking to see if the boy is behind her, but he is not. It isn't until she sprints through the cold night, gets to her car, and stops to catch her breath that she realizes she's left that sparkly black dress on the rack. She thinks how stupid it was to go to the auditorium and then into the props closet, to these parts of the school where she no longer belongs.

"Did you hear?" says Chloe the next day in second period study hall.

Maria shakes her head. She is exhausted, not in the mood to listen to Chloe's latest gossip. She just wants to slouch and put her head down on the desk, like many of the people around her are doing.

"Someone burned all the costumes from the props closet. Under the bleachers."

"What?" says Maria. Her heart starts pounding so furiously she wonders if other people can hear it.

"Yeah, first period gym class was out on the track, and it smelled all burnt and they found pieces of stuff that survived the fire."

"Weird," says Maria. "That someone would do that." She hopes she sounds normal, that her voice doesn't betray how stunned she is that the boy went through with his plan.

Chloe says, "We could make a film. Interview people, see if we can figure out who did it. I could film it and you could be the host and narrator, and we could use it for our college applications. This is probably the most exciting thing that's happened in our town all year."

"What are we now, investigative journalists? Are you applying to journalism school?" Maria snaps. "What about the flash mob?"

"Whoa," says Chloe, leaning back in her seat. "What crawled up your butt? This idea is so much better than the flash mob."

"Sorry," says Maria, rubbing her eyes. "I'm just tired."

"I don't get why you work so many hours at Chickety Chix. It's not like your family is poor."

"Let's go see the stuff," Maria says. "Let's both pretend to have to go to the bathroom and then go see what happened."

"Because you want to do some investigative work with me?" says Chloe. "Oh! We could call the film *Burned Dreams* and interview the theater kids too."

"Okay," Maria says because it's easier to agree with Chloe than argue with her. If Maria is lucky, Chloe will soon get bored with the idea and move on to something else, just like she moved on from the flash mob.

"You go first," says Chloe.

Maria asks the study hall monitor, Mr. Garland, if she can go to the bathroom, and he nods without looking up from the book he's reading. Maria walks into the hall, past the girls' restroom, and out the side door. No one stops her and Maria thinks about how easy it is to get away with things at this school. It's freezing outside, some snow from last week's storm still on the football field, and Maria wishes she'd grabbed her puffy jacket from her locker. There's an acrid scent in the air, and it gets stronger as she approaches the bleachers. It's not only clothing that has burned. Someone has dragged out suitcases and lamps and pillows, the props that fill the stage for the plays and musicals. Maria looks around to see if anyone is watching, but she's alone. She steps under the bleachers and then she sees it. The brick wall behind the bleachers is spray painted, in white paint, with "4MR." Each letter must be six inches tall. Maria knows what it means: for Maria Robles. Maria feels fury; he has pulled her unwillingly into his destruction.

"You didn't do it, did you?" says Chloe, who seems to magically appear under the bleachers. "I mean, it *would* explain why you're so tired." She laughs.

"Of course I didn't do it!" Maria says, and then she wonders if everyone else will think she's guilty.

"You'd have motivation," says Chloe, surveying the damaged props.

"I told you I didn't do it, so don't act like you're hosting *Dateline* and investigating me as the prime suspect."

"You know I was just giving you a hard time," says Chloe. "You're no fun today. Although it would be a pretty great twist ending if one of the filmmakers of *Burned Dreams* was actually the guilty party."

"I'm not guilty!"

Chloe raises her hands, says, "All right, all right. I never thought you were guilty. Can't you take a joke?"

"We should get back before Mr. Garland realizes we're gone."

"You think he cares at all about what we're doing? Did you take any pictures?" Chloe asks.

"Why would I take pictures? This is terrible. All this stuff is ruined."

"For our film! We could include still photos all Ken Burns style, with the camera panning in and out on the images." Chloe pulls her phone out of her pocket and spins in a slow circle, taking photographs of the debris. She stops when her phone is facing the wall that says "4MR" and says, "Maybe a clue?"

Maria shrugs. The wind is strong, and she wraps her arms around her chest and wishes again she had a jacket. She watches Chloe kneel on the ground, completely engrossed in taking pictures of the rubble. Maria has never kept a secret from Chloe, but if she keeps this one—as she knows she will, because she doesn't want to admit Creepy Chester burned all of this in some insane, misguided solidarity with her—they will no longer be constant coconspirators.

THAT AFTERNOON, AS Maria squeezes the juice from ten pounds of lemons at Chickety Chix, she thinks about the boy. She doesn't like the idea that he could be watching her, knowing what she's doing, even at the mall. She doesn't like that he probably thinks she owes him something. She wonders if he's watching her right now, hidden behind a pillar or at a table in the food court. She's sure he'll somehow know if she and Chloe make a film about the destroyed props and costumes and he'll watch the video again and again, his eyes following her on the screen, knowing that Maria is aware of exactly who the culprit is. And what can Maria do but watch the view count go up and up?

All of it now feels like a violation, the eyes of men on her, looking and seeing and judging, and she wants none of it. She slams the handle of the citrus juicer down hard and watches the juice spill out of half a lemon. She's glad she's made the decision to quit *West Side Story*. She can't imagine being onstage knowing the boy is watching her from the lighting booth. He'll probably think she quit because he told her to, but she will know she made this decision on her own.

She wants to quit Jackson's talent show, but she can't do that, especially since she will likely need to disappoint him by telling him the flash mob won't happen. If Chloe is no longer on board, then she's not going to be able to get others to join in. Chloe is convincing, can make people do things, can gather people together. Maria doesn't have the same power of persuasion.

But she has an idea, a way that will allow her to be Jackson's assistant. She slips her phone out of her pocket, looks up pictures of doves. She can be onstage as a strange and ugly dove; she can be onstage as long as no one can see who she really is.

During her break, she goes to Boscov's, where she never shops, because only frumpy old ladies buy clothes there. But this is exactly what she wants: old lady clothes. She finds a white sweat suit on the sale rack. It is a size XL, which is three sizes too big, but she doesn't want it to look good. She plans to use one of her father's belts to cinch a pillow around her torso, so she can have the fat, puffy chest of a dove. No one will even be able to tell if she's female or male once she's in her dove costume.

Maria removes a pair of orange knee-high socks from a hanging rack and wonders who in the world would buy these socks if they weren't intending them to look like orange bird legs. She will wear the sweat suit, which she'll glue feathers onto, and the orange socks and the dove hat, which she hopes Jackson hasn't transformed into a sparrow hat yet, and she'll be a magician's assistant who looks like a dove, not an assistant in a tight and sparkly dress. She places the sweat suit—on sale for eleven dollars—and the orange socks on the counter, and a saleswoman with glasses hanging from a chain on her neck looks up and says, "Well, hello, dear. Did you find everything you needed?"

Maria nods and says, "Yes, thank you, I did."

January

A Good Home

Kevin wants to be a different type of man. He wants to be someone who springs out of bed with the sunrise, fresh and eager to take on the day. He wants to be someone who can leave his house without first downing two mugs of strong coffee, doctored with too much half-and-half and sugar. He wants to be someone who jogs because he enjoys it. He wants to be someone who can afford a house, a real house with multiple rooms and more than one toilet. With a bathtub, in case the urge to take a long, lingering soak ever strikes anyone in his family. He wants to be someone with a job that's fulfilling and satisfying.

But Kevin is none of these things, and right now he's only one minute and forty-seven seconds into the second running segment of the No! More! Couch Potato! walk/run regimen he downloaded off the internet, and already he feels a stitch in his side and he swears there's a pebble transforming into a boulder inside his right sneaker. His wool hat is soggy with sweat. He bought extra-thin gloves made for runners—he knows he spent too much money on something for such a specific purpose—but those are doing little to keep his hands warm, and his fingers are ten stiff icicles.

All he has to do is run for forty-three more seconds and then he can walk for the next two and a half minutes. He made a New Year's resolution to be better, and he can't give up only two weeks into January. He can do it, he tells himself, as he sucks in a mouthful of freezing air. One step at a time and in a few weeks he'll be running for five minutes without stopping, and then six, and in a few months he'll have a pile of T-shirts from all the 5Ks he's completed. He'll look different, lean with muscular legs, and be more agile. His clothes will fit better and not strain at the seams. Right now he's not lean, but he's not fat; he's what his mother used to call husky. In the last few years he's developed a gut, and as he runs he can feel it jiggle. Once he goes down two sizes, he'll allow himself to buy some new clothes, maybe a few button-down oxfords, in light blue and pink, a few pairs of khakis. He'll tuck in his shirts and wear a belt. A real belt, made of leather, not something stretchy and elastic. He'll get rid of his old clothes, which Gwen calls *schlumpy*. He will cut up his cartoon-character T-shirts into rags for cleaning the house. He'll take Gwen out to dinner and she'll smile from across the table, happy to see him in a crisp shirt; she won't roll her eyes at his Darth Vader T-shirt, like she did the other day at Book Nook when she asked if he was supposed to dress "like an adult" while managing the store.

Maybe he'll shave off his beard, which he has let grow for the last two years, hiding how pudgy he's become, covering up most of his face and the upper half of his torso. If it were white instead of orange, he could take on a second job playing Santa at the mall. Children like him, he likes talking to people, likes making kids happy. If the mall doesn't close, maybe he'll look into working as a mall Santa next year to pick up some extra money. It wouldn't be too hard to get a fake white beard. And a fake belly because by next year his will be gone. How could it not be if he keeps up with this running?

Kevin checks his watch. He's run for two minutes and fifty-four seconds, twenty-four seconds over his required two minutes thirty seconds, and decides for his next segment he'll run only for two minutes and six seconds to account for the extra running. But, no, he tells himself: that's what the old Kevin would do. The new and improved

Kevin is not going to make a big deal over an extra twenty-four seconds of running.

Kevin puts his gloved hands on top of his head as he slows to a walk. He's not sure if this helps with breathing, but it's what his elementary school gym teacher made the class do after running around the gym, saying it opens up the lungs, and since Kevin hasn't been involved in anything athletic since then, he'll heed this old advice. Puffs of breath come out of his mouth as he walks toward the field where the cows that produce milk for the park's ice cream shop graze in the summer. Kevin is glad the shop is closed for the season because otherwise he might be tempted to get a cup—a small one, the child's serving—as a reward after finishing his run. He knows this line of thinking is a problem and has contributed to his belly. For the past few years he's been soothing himself with treats—rocky road ice cream, salt and vinegar chips, gummy bears—every time he feels down about himself.

He looks at the empty field, which is covered in a layer of snow. It is too cold for the cows to be outdoors, and Kevin wonders where they go for the winter. They are probably somewhere warm and comfortable, happily chewing on hay; only dumb humans force themselves to go outside and do absurd things like try to run on ice-slick ground in January.

Up ahead, he sees Dawn and Amy, his neighbors from down the street, and their three-legged pug, Wilford. The pug is out of the stroller and is bounding on its three legs, back and forth between the stakes of a wooden fence. Wilford is wearing a puffy blue vest, which is the exact same color as Kevin's puffy jacket.

Kevin stops the timer on his watch, telling himself it would be unneighborly to rush past them. Hasn't he earned this little break by running a bit extra? He knows he really hasn't, but he also knows he is the master at making excuses, at figuring out ways to wiggle out of the things he should be doing. His wife has been telling him more and more lately that he needs to stop making excuses, that he needs to be more productive. But this will just be a short break, and then he'll get back to running.

"I wish I had that much energy," he says, pointing to the dog, who is still springing back and forth, barking wildly at nothing.

"Enough, Wilford," says Amy. She bends down and snaps a leash onto Wilford's collar, but the dog continues to bark.

Kevin wants to make a comment about how the dog seems to be managing fine with just three legs, and how this is admirable, but he's not sure if it's rude to say it, so he stays quiet.

Suddenly, the dog seems to exhaust himself and plops on the ground, his three legs splayed. Kevin thinks how wonderful it would be if it were acceptable for adults to collapse whenever they're tired and rest for a bit. He imagines himself flat on the ground next to Wilford, their labored breathing making their matching blue outerwear move up and down over their chests. He looks at Dawn and Amy and reveals, "I'm supposed to be out for a run, but I haven't really gotten very far."

"It's good, though, that you got out the door, especially on such a cold day. That's the first step," says Amy. She manages to say it earnestly and not condescendingly, which Kevin both appreciates and is annoyed by. Amy is lean, athletic. Her cheekbones appear almost sharp. She looks like someone who would enjoy running, who might choose it as a leisure activity and not because her doctor told her that if she doesn't pull herself together she's going to have all sorts of health problems by forty, which is what Kevin's doctor told him two weeks ago. "You can't eat the same way at thirty-six that you did at eighteen. You have to learn to enjoy vegetables." He said this with a serious and concerned look as he handed Kevin a photocopied food pyramid. The doctor, like Amy, was thin and fit and tall and probably harbored a deep love for vegetables.

"If you ever want to run together, let me know," says Amy. "It would be fun."

"Oh, thanks," says Kevin. "Maybe one day." The idea of exercising with someone who can run for more than three minutes without stopping to gasp for air terrifies him.

"Just let me know," says Amy. "Happy to have company."

Kevin has lived in this neighborhood for a year and has never, not once, seen Amy running. He is certain she runs early, before he is even awake. Amy is a lawyer, at work, probably, before 9:00 a.m. By the time Kevin is ready to face the day, Amy has likely already run, showered, changed into a suit, driven to work, and started saving the world. Amy practices immigration law, which Kevin knows is a difficult profession, especially during this administration. Amy looks to be about Kevin's age, and he can't help comparing himself to those already far more successful than he'll ever be. He knows it's bad to be jealous of others' success, but he can't help how he feels.

"Have you ever run with Wilford?" says Kevin, looking down at the dog who is now snoring.

"That was actually the original purpose of going to the shelter," says Dawn. "Back when I was in grad school I was on an Ultimate Frisbee team and wanted a training partner on my runs."

"Oh," says Kevin. Maybe once Wilford had four legs and was a good runner, despite his small size. "And back then he ran with you?"

Dawn laughs. "No, never. I went in wanting a big dog, and I came out with Wilford. He came with that name, by the way. The ladies at the shelter thought he looked like Wilford Brimley."

"He's a pug, right?" says Kevin. He looks at the dog's smushed-in face and flat nose, from which mucus is slowly dripping.

"Half pug," says Amy. "We're not sure what the other half is."

"The lady at the shelter said he's 'half pug, half perfection.' She was very convincing. Convincing enough for me to bring home a three-legged dog when I'd wanted a running companion," says Dawn. "But it all worked out. I busted my knee a few weeks after getting Wilford and haven't run much since."

He thinks perhaps this small, sleepy three-legged dog might actually be the right running partner for him, might not be impatient when they have to slow down, might peter out as quickly as Kevin does.

"I had this idea," says Kevin. "For a business that involves dogs." He explains about the border collies and hopes Dawn and Amy will tell him it's a good plan, a perfectly legitimate way to make a living. He hopes they don't exchange knowing looks about how foolish he is, how dumb to think this won't be akin to lighting all the money in his checking account—which isn't very much money at all—on fire.

"It's a great idea," says Amy. "No chemicals, the dogs don't hurt the geese, and no one has to clean up goose shit."

Excellent, Kevin thinks. Amy, who is a gainfully employed dog owner, believes this is a *great idea*. Maybe his wife will think the same when he tells her about it. Maybe she won't sigh and tell him it's too impractical. She didn't give the honey business enough of a chance, insisting he get rid of the hives once Sammy got stung. Who knows how successful that business could have been if she'd let him try for a little longer. "It's just the matter, of course, of finding the dogs. And training the dogs. And housing the dogs," says Kevin. "Housing them might be an issue."

"You're still in the tiny house, right?" says Dawn.

Kevin nods. His three-hundred-square-foot house is too small for one person, let alone a family of four. Sometimes, looking around his house, he wants to cry. If regret could be symbolized by an object, that object would be a tiny house.

"I admire the paring down it must involve," says Amy. "I wish I could simplify like that. I think just the paperwork in my home office would fill your entire house."

Kevin imagines piles of paper, imagines clutter, imagines not being able to find something because it's been lost among the things crammed into a house, and he feels envy ripple through his chest. "It's been nice living simply," Kevin says, although of course that's not true. He hates it, feels like he's made an awful decision. Their tiny house is parked in his mother-in-law's backyard. She has encouraged them to move into her house, tells them it's been lonely since Kevin's father-in-law passed away two years ago, but there's some stupid pride that won't allow Kevin to move his family, even though they hauled dozens of boxes of their possessions—including costumes from all the Halloween parties he and Gwen threw over the years—into his mother-in-law's attic and basement because they won't fit in the tiny house. He loves his mother-in-law's house, with its plush carpets, and an oak dining room table that can expand to seat twelve, and the small wicker basket housing seashell-shaped soaps in the downstairs bathroom. He loves that basket of soaps—it's so completely unnecessary—and he now covets unnecessary things, since he's had to pare down his life. The tiny house—which he spent his family's entire $10,000 savings on—makes him feel like he's in some absurd experiment, like he's trying to prove how little they can survive on. But experiments have ending points, and it seems like there's no way out of the tiny house short of winning the lottery.

Suddenly, an enormous sneeze emerges from Wilford, and when Kevin looks down, he sees a trail of dog mucus on the cuff of his sweatpants.

Amy reaches into a sack slung over her shoulder and takes out a wad of tissues. She hands half the tissues to Kevin and then uses the other half to wipe Wilford's face. "Sorry, he's a mess," she says.

"It's okay," Kevin says. He kneels to wipe his pants and is suddenly reminded of when his children were younger and they would spit up or sneeze on his shoulder as he held them, and how he'd clean them up and change his shirt and how easy it felt to solve these small, everyday problems. He remembers how happy Gwen seemed back then, how she talked about her friends' husbands being unwilling to tackle the messier parts of parenthood, how she liked that he never complained about diapers or vomit or staying up all night with a feverish baby. He wipes at his cuff until he can barely see any trace of Wilford's sneeze and feels a deep longing to care for something in that uncomplicated, easy way, of doing something so simple that could make everyone around him happy and content.

"Look who's here," says Dawn out of the side of her mouth, and Kevin stands up and sees Ro Goodson. She's wearing a long black wool coat and a bulky white knit hat. She walks slowly around the pond, stopping every once in a while to throw ripped-up pieces of white bread plucked from a plastic bag to the few stubborn ducks who have not flown south.

"She's something," says Kevin. He tucks the dirty tissues into his jacket pocket. He knows Ro has issues with most everyone who lives on the street. She doesn't like Kevin because he doesn't have a great job, doesn't like that he's married to a Black woman, doesn't like that he lives in a tiny house. She hasn't said any of these things outright, but there's always a subtext to her comments, and he can tell she's always judging him, judging his family. Kevin is sure Ro doesn't approve of Dawn and Amy. Even though they have a beautiful, large house and good jobs—lawyer and biotech engineer—their marriage likely doesn't pass muster with Ro. Joan, who has lived next door to Ro for over forty years, has been tight-lipped about her neighbor, and refuses to join in when Kevin and Gwen complain about her. "She's nearly ninety," Joan always reminds them. She tells them that Ro is old and lonely, and it reflects poorly on them if they can't find it in themselves to treat her with basic courtesy. Kevin felt furious when Joan defended Ro after Sammy got stung, saying, "She helped him, Kevin. Can we ask any more of neighbors than for help when we're in trouble?" But Kevin thinks everyone should ask—no, *demand*—much more than help in dire circumstances. He thinks neighbors should work to form a community, work to understand each other, to accept each other. He knows he might be too idealistic sometimes, but if he ran the world, things would be different. But of course he doesn't run the world, he runs a small bookstore in a mall. That is it. Nothing more. And the only reason he is the manager of the bookstore is because he's been around the longest. Other people went off to better jobs or school or pursued their dreams. He's the one now considered a lifer, and that's not the way he ever envisioned things turning out.

"Every time we're pushing Wilford in the stroller, she looks at us as if we're ridiculous, but it's not an affectation," says Dawn. "He's twelve and has arthritis! Fresh air is good for everyone, and just because he's not as limber as he once was, it doesn't mean he shouldn't get outdoors."

"It's okay," says Amy, rubbing Dawn's back. "She's not worth getting worked up over." She bends, lifts Wilford, and settles him in the stroller. Kevin is reminded of his twins, and thinks longingly of four and five years ago when he buckled each of them into the double stroller, how every day, unless it was raining or snowing, he would take them out for a walk. There was a nice rhythm to his days when his children were young and he was in graduate school. He was still hopeful he'd be hired for a position in the English department at a good school and would write a well-received book that would earn him tenure. Back then, he still thought the world was full of opportunities.

"She's waving," says Dawn. "Is she waving at *us*?" They all look at Ro, who is slowly making her way toward them.

Amy sighs, grips the handles of the stroller, and the three of them wait silently. Kevin listens to Wilford's wheezy breathing as he sleeps in the stroller.

"Mrs. Goodson," says Kevin when she appears close to them.

"Hello, you three," says Ro when she arrives. "Or, I suppose I should say 'you four.'" She points at Wilford. "He looks content."

Kevin sees Dawn clench her jaw, sees a vein emerge in her forehead.

Ro stares at Wilford's small stump where his right front leg is missing. "Did he come that way?"

"Come?" says Dawn.

"I mean, was the leg missing when you acquired him? Or did it happen under your watch?"

Kevin's eyes flit between the three women. He wonders if something might blow up right here, right now. And if it did, what should he do? Should he jump in as a referee, do something to smooth everything over? His mother-in-law's reminders that Ro is old and lonely echo in his head, but do these factors excuse her habit of running her mouth whenever she wants?

"Do you mean did we chop off his leg?" says Dawn.

"Well, no, of course I know you didn't chop off his leg. What use is a dog leg to human beings? It's not like a rabbit's foot."

"Chopping off rabbits' feet is barbaric," says Amy. "How could anyone feel lucky with one in their pocket?"

"My husband used to carry one, and I'd like to believe it brought us some luck," says Ro. "And I assume the rabbits' feet come from rabbits that have already been slaughtered for food."

"I can tell you the real story," Dawn says, and Kevin sees Amy shaking her head and mouthing the word *stop*. "An old lady used to own Wilford. But she was a busybody and paid more attention to her neighbors than to her dog. And one day she was so busy being nosy about the couple that lived a few houses down the street that she forgot to check her rearview mirror and ran right over her dog and severed his leg! Can you believe it? Animal protective services came and took Wilford and we adopted him the next day. And we gave him a good home."

Ro's face crumples as if she has just been speared through the heart. She says, "I never said you didn't give him a good home."

"All right," says Amy. "We should go."

"But I came over for a reason," says Ro.

"Do you need a ride home?" says Kevin. As soon as he says it, he remembers he did not drive to the park. His wife dropped him off on her way to the library.

Ro shakes her head. "I drove." She pauses then adds, "And I looked carefully in the rearview mirror when pulling out of my driveway. I've never run over anything, man or beast, in all my years of driving. Not even a squirrel."

"How can we help you?" says Kevin. The rock in his shoe is irritating him again, and he kicks his shoe off and turns it upside down. A pebble—barely the size of a grain of rice—drops onto the pavement. Would it be pathetic to ask Ro for a ride home? Yes, Kevin decides, it would. He will walk home, as planned. He will not allow her to do anything for him or his family ever again.

"I was just wondering if you have seen any suspicious characters on our block lately."

"Besides us?" says Dawn, and Amy gives her a harsh look.

"It's just that someone keeps stealing my deliveries, and I was wondering if anyone knew anything about it."

"I haven't seen anybody suspicious," says Amy.

"I haven't seen anybody suspicious either," says Kevin. He wants to ask Ro whether by suspicious she means "not white." He wonders if Ro is only asking the three of them this question because they are all white and thus she can assume their innocence in criminal matters, despite all the flaws she believes they possess.

"You should get a dog," says Dawn, pointing at Wilford. "A vicious guard dog, like this one. It'll keep suspicious characters away."

Ro looks at Wilford, then up at Dawn, then she shakes her head, crumples the bread bag hard in her hand, balling up the few slices that remain in it. "I'm sorry," she says. "I'm sorry I always say the wrong thing."

A FEW HOURS later at the bookstore, Kevin regrets not wearing his running sneakers. Instead he's wearing clogs his doctor recommended, but they feel hard, and his heels hurt. When he told his doctor about the pain in his lower back and knees, his doctor suggested the clogs chefs wear for hours and hours in busy kitchens, and Kevin bought a dark green pair online. After they were delivered—to Joan's doorstep, of course, not his, because his tiny house doesn't have an address— and he took them out of the box and slipped them on, his daughter asked why he was wearing gnome shoes. And thus the gnome costume was born. He found a pointy red hat for seven dollars, and paired it with striped shirts and striped socks and rolled up the cuffs of his pants and now, every few weeks, he reads a book about gnomes during story hour. It's amazing how many books feature gnomes.

He stares out into the mall and sees teenagers gathered near the food court. A group of five boys is sharing a paper cup of french fries. One of the boys shoves a fry up each nostril. Teenagers rarely buy anything at the mall besides snacks in the food court, but Kevin supposes the mall is a good enough place as any for them to go after school. It's safe, it's indoors, and as long as they don't cause trouble, they can stay for as long as they want. Sometimes they come into the bookstore and thumb through magazines. Sometimes they leave sticky, sugary fingerprints on *Skateboarders Monthly* or *Cosmo Girl*, but Kevin doesn't care. He likes it when kids read, even if it's not literature. Hell, he's had enough literature for a lifetime.

He emerges from behind the register, walks to the shelf holding books about animals, and takes down *The Perfect Dog for You*. He flips to the page on border collies and admires a glossy photograph of two dogs running through a field. They're beautiful dogs, aerodynamic looking, their black-and-white coats gleaming in the sunlight. He reads: "Border collies are energetic dogs that need a great deal of space. They are not recommended for apartment dwellers." He slams the book shut and shoves it back onto the shelf. He has known this information since he started researching border collies, but he gets a flare-up of irritation every time he sees it in print. It doesn't matter, though, that he lives in a tiny house. He could find places for the dogs to run, parks or hiking trails or soccer fields. He'd figure out a comfortable home for them. What if he built a second tiny house, one just for the dogs? It doesn't matter if he becomes the laughingstock of the neighborhood. It doesn't matter if Ro peers out of her upstairs window, shaking her head at the foolishness of a tiny house for humans and another tiny house for dogs.

"Hey."

Kevin turns and sees one of the girls who works at Chickety Chix. The smell of fries and grilled chicken wafts off her uniform. He's purchased plenty of chicken kabobs from her, but he doesn't remember her name. His eyes dart to her nametag.

"Hey, Maria," he says. "On break?"

"Yeah," she says.

Kevin stares at her hat for a moment and wonders if she'd ever be willing to read *Chicken Little* for story hour. She told him once that she was in the school musicals, so she must like acting, and reading to kids is a little like acting, especially if you do voices for all the characters, which Kevin always does.

"I'm looking for a book," Maria says.

She's come in before looking for books on acting, and he's about to point to a new memoir by a young actress he thinks she might find interesting, but she says, "I don't really know which section to look in, but I was wondering if there were maybe some books about dealing with stalkers."

"Like a psychology book?"

Maria shrugs. "Yeah, maybe."

Kevin leads her to their small psychology section. "Maybe you can find something here?"

"Okay, thanks," says Maria.

"Are you writing a paper for school?"

She stares at the shelves for a few seconds, then shakes her head. "It's personal research, I guess. I'm not saying I have a stalker, but there's a guy that's kind of following me around and watching me. I've seen him at the mall."

"Oh," says Kevin, alarmed. "Do you know who he is?"

"He's from school. I thought maybe a psychology book could help me figure him out."

Why is she telling him this? Does she need help or is she just desperate for someone to talk to? Or is there something about him that she trusts? Maybe he's an adult who doesn't quite seem like an adult, someone who can be confided in the way *real adults*—people who don't wear Darth Vader T-shirts or dress as gnomes—cannot? When he was a graduate student, his students often came to his office hours under the guise of talking about their essays, but then they'd tell him things about their lives and ask for advice and sometimes he was even able to help them. It's silly, Kevin knows, but on Rate My Professors, one of his students wrote: "Good dude. Genuinely cares about his students. Wish more professors were like him." He returned to that comment often; reading it made him happier than it should. The next semester, another comment appeared: "My favorite professor in the whole English department because he actually cares about us and listens to us." Never mind that he was just a graduate student, not a real professor; the students never seemed to know the difference, didn't know he was being paid $13,000 a year for his work. But who is he to Maria? Not her teacher, not really anything. Just the guy who works in the bookstore whose only responsibility is to lead her to this shelf of books and then step away. But maybe he can help. "Do you think you should report him to mall security?"

Maria laughs. "They don't ever do anything. The building could explode and they'd just keep drinking Orange Juliuses and playing games on their phones."

She is right, mall security is a joke. But then who? "Maybe you can talk to someone at school. A guidance counselor or a teacher?" Should he offer to call someone? In graduate school, they were told to call Public Safety or walk students over to Health Services if there was an emotional or mental health issue, but he's not sure how much he should get involved. Would it stress Maria out more if he inserted himself into the situation? Maybe this is a case of her just needing to tell someone; maybe she intentionally didn't go to anyone who she thought might insist on calling the police or taking some other proactive action.

Maria doesn't respond to Kevin, doesn't look at him, her eyes scanning the books on the shelf. "Sometimes I see him in the food court, but by the time I'm on break, he's always gone."

"What does he look like?"

"He's really pale and thin, and his eyes are gray, and he usually wears clothes that are gray too, like he doesn't want anyone to notice him. He's got dark hair that flops into his eyes."

Kevin thinks he knows the boy. He's come into the bookstore quite a few times. He's different from other boys his age, quiet and always alone. He likes to look at books about American history, and one day he creased the spine on a book about Revolutionary War artillery. Kevin thought about reprimanding him, but the boy looked so miserable slinking out of the store that Kevin said nothing. At least this kid cared about something, was interested enough in history to want to spend some time reading in a bookstore. That's more than Kevin can say for a lot of teenagers. But should he be concerned that the boy is interested in guns? Aren't a lot of history buffs drawn to them?

Kevin says, "I think I remember a boy who looks like that, but I'm not sure if it's the same one you're talking about."

"Has he ever bought a book? Maybe with a credit card?"

"I don't think so."

"I don't even know his name," Maria says. "I'm probably making a big deal out of nothing."

"Maybe you're not," Kevin says.

"He's just got me creeped out. Some people at school call him Creepy Chester."

"I think if you feel creeped out, you should tell someone." Maybe this is serious; but then Kevin thinks of the boy, and he seems more sad than threatening. Maybe the nickname is more about teenage cruelty than about anything else.

"I don't think there's anything anyone can do."

Kevin contemplates what he hopes someone would do if his daughter ever went to them with a concern like this. "Listen, if you want, I could call your school and maybe talk to a guidance counselor and explain the situation? I know I'm not your dad or teacher or anything, but if you need me to talk to an adult in your life, I could do it."

Maria pauses for a beat, and Kevin thinks she'll take him up on his offer, but then she sighs. "There's nothing to say except 'Maria feels weirded out,' and there's nothing anyone can do about that, can they?"

Kevin feels powerless; this is not a problem he knows how to solve. This might not even *be* a problem. But it might be. He has no idea. He considers jotting his cell number on a slip of paper and telling Maria she can call him if she's ever in a situation where she feels threated, but he's a thirty-six-year-old man and she's a teenage girl and he doesn't want anyone to get the wrong idea. "Well," says Kevin, "you know where I am." He pats the counter by the register, as if this will somehow help Maria remember where he spends his days. "Come find me if I can help, okay?"

"Sure, thanks," says Maria, but she looks embarrassed, as if she regrets telling him anything. She waves and walks out of the store. Now Kevin thinks that maybe he too has weirded her out and is grateful he had the good sense not to offer his phone number. And although he doesn't think he's done anything wrong, he feels he hasn't done anything right either. He feels he has failed Maria in a significant way.

AT HOME, IT'S Gwen's night to put the twins to bed, so she's up in the loft while Kevin is working on his laptop, using Wi-Fi from his mother-in-law's house. As always, the twins dawdle, demand multiple books be read, cite thirst and lack of tiredness as reasons they should be allowed to stay up. Since they've moved into the tiny house, their bedtime has drifted later and later because there's only one overhead light, and Kevin and Gwen need it on while they clean up after dinner. After that light goes out, and after the children are in bed, Kevin and Gwen putter silently on their laptops so they don't wake the children.

Sammy and Simone sleep in the loft. Most nights Gwen sleeps up there too, her body perpendicular to the top of the ladder, a barrier so the children don't roll off. Kevin knows that moving their family into this house was a concession—it was his dream to build this house, to live simply, to give up anything unnecessary for survival. He didn't think it through, though. It was a temporary dream, a fun idea, but now it's stifling. He wonders how much Gwen wishes for a different life. She has not complained about the house; maybe she's just picking her battles, intent on pushing him to finish his dissertation before demanding they live somewhere less confining. He wonders if she longs to sleep in the queen bed in the guest bedroom of her mother's house under a thick down comforter.

Kevin sleeps on a foldout downstairs, the bed a couch during the day. As a couch, it is adequate, but as a bed it's uncomfortable, metal bars pushing into his back. Physically, Kevin has never been in closer proximity to his family, but he's also never felt so far away. He's not sure when he and his wife last slept in the same bed, when they had the space for intimacy and privacy.

Kevin stares at a color printout of *Landscape with the Fall of Icarus*, which Gwen taped on the wall above the desk two weeks ago. She told him it was inspiration for her new poems. He wonders whether it's good for his children to absorb this grotesquerie, looking at Icarus's legs sticking out of the water after his plunge from the sky, dislocated feathers in the ripples surrounding him. It's one of two things on the wall. The other is a photograph of Simone, taken at the mall during her audition a few months ago to be a model. The name of the modeling company is stamped across the photograph, right across Simone's face, in gold ink. The auditions turned out to be a scam, meant to convince parents to spend hundreds on headshots. Of course Kevin and Gwen hadn't purchased the headshots, but Simone liked the photograph so they taped it to the wall.

Since they moved into the tiny house, Gwen has been writing poems about falling. She told Kevin that Auden and William Carlos Williams wrote poems based on *Landscape with the Fall of Icarus* and she's working with old ideas mixed with contemporary concerns. Editors like these poems, and Gwen has been on a publishing streak, which makes Kevin simultaneously proud and jealous, and he detests the jealousy that seeps into nearly every facet of his life. Gwen has written so many poems about falling she has enough for a book. He hates that Gwen is so obsessed with falling, even though this preoccupation is apparently good for her writing.

He blames himself for moving the family out of their cheap three-bedroom Victorian rental downtown to this tiny house where Gwen worries about their children tumbling out of the loft. He suggested moving their beds downstairs, but there isn't room for anything besides the small kitchen table, the couch that folds out into a bed, and the miniscule fold-down desk where Kevin pretends to work. He volunteered to sleep with the children, to be the human barrier, to buy a gate to put at the entrance to the loft, but Gwen insists on sleeping there every night. "I'd be too worried if I wasn't with them," she says, and Kevin feels guilty for adding this extra worry to Gwen's life.

Now, Gwen is reading the children a book about a possum that steals pies cooling on windowsills. It's one of Sammy's favorite books, the one he's asked for every night for the last three years. Kevin wonders if Sammy is too old for this book, whether he should urge his son to move on from picture books. "Blueberry is always lovely!" says Gwen, using a British accent for the possum's dialogue. Are there even possums in Britain? Kevin doesn't know. Kevin always voices the possum with a Southern accent. It seems more appropriate.

Kevin is supposed to be finishing his dissertation in the evenings so he can finally complete his PhD, but he doesn't care about the dissertation anymore. He cared a lot more when Gwen's father was his adviser in graduate school. He wanted to prove himself to Earl, to show he was smart and scholarly and worthy of his daughter. His own father died of a heart attack when Kevin was twelve, and Kevin always longed for a role model, but no one before Earl ever paid him much attention.

When Kevin got to graduate school, he took Earl's Modernism class his first semester. Then, on a whim, he took a poetry writing workshop and there was Gwen Walker, clearly the best poet in the creative writing program, so obviously skilled beyond the rest of the class. Why was she at a school not known for its creative writing offerings? She should have been somewhere much better, much more prestigious. Kevin wondered if Gwen was only at the school because her tuition was free as the daughter of a faculty member. They began to date a year later and Earl told Kevin he could no longer be his adviser because of the conflict of interest.

By the time Earl died suddenly two years ago, Kevin felt far removed from the subject of his dissertation. Horchester Glinton was a minor British poet who died in 1942. Kevin only focused on Glinton because Earl once called him overlooked and underappreciated, and Kevin thought there might be more opportunities if he studied someone unknown, instead of Eliot or Yeats or other popular poets.

What Kevin didn't realize was that studying the unknown would involve more digging, more travel, more initiative. He realized halfway through graduate school that there was a difference between being an enthusiastic reader and a scholar of literature. A teaching job, especially a tenure-track job, would mean he would have to produce scholarly work for the rest of his career. The thought made him claustrophobic and dizzy.

Now, Kevin's biggest regret is not telling Gwen years ago he wasn't cut out to be a scholar. She always had a fantasy of the two of them being an academic couple, teaching at the same school. She knew how hard it was to find an academic job—but she always held out hope that one day, if she could publish a book, she would find a tenure-track position. This is why she's willing to drive all over town adjuncting for $3,000 a class, which probably boils down to about twenty cents an hour when Kevin adds up Gwen's time prepping and grading. She thinks more experience will lead to a better job. Sometimes Kevin thinks Gwen's hopefulness about getting a tenure-track position in this job market is even more outlandish than his ideas about making a living selling honey or chasing geese off lawns. Maybe if one of his ideas takes off, if he's able to make a lot of money, then Gwen will give up her dream of them teaching together. Maybe it will be enough for her to teach and for him to do something else.

"How's it going?" says Gwen, who appears behind him, staring at his computer screen, open to his halfway-written dissertation. Instinctively, Kevin looks up to the loft to make sure no one is in danger of falling. He is surprised to find a baby gate.

"When did we get that?" Kevin says.

"My mother gave it to me this afternoon. She had it in her attic. It's vintage, from my childhood," she says. "I'm just borrowing it."

"It still works? The rubber on it hasn't dried out?"

"I'm not that old," Gwen says, smiling. "Not as old as you are."

"You're only three years younger."

"Which means that for as long as we live, I'll always be younger than you."

"Haven't you heard that one can reverse aging with good nutrition and exercise? I'm a runner now, you know."

"I'm glad you're getting out of the house more," Gwen says. "I think exercise might help your brain get going too, you know, help clear your mind so you can be more productive."

Kevin nods, tries to ignore the comment about his lack of productivity. He suspects Gwen knows he's hardly done any work on his dissertation in years and has been trying to figure out the best way to push him to finish.

"Let's step outside," says Gwen. Kevin is glad to leave the laptop behind. He and Gwen never leave the tiny house when the children are sleeping, but maybe the gate will change things. Maybe they can sit outside and drink a beer on warm nights, maybe they can watch the sun set and the stars emerge in the summer.

Gwen and Kevin slip on their down jackets and move outside. Kevin's breath fogs the air in front of him. He sees stars dotting the dark and clear sky. "You know Dawn and Amy's dog, Wilford? He was wearing a dog version of my jacket today."

Usually, Gwen would laugh at this kind of thing, but tonight she looks serious and unhappy. "We have a problem," she whispers. "Follow me." She leads him across the yard to her mother's garage and punches in a code on a keypad outside the garage—Kevin knows the code is Earl's birthday—and the garage door rises. Once they're inside, she presses a button so the door closes.

"Is everything okay with your mother?"

"She's fine. But look." Gwen points to a pile of boxes in the corner.

Kevin bends to examine the packages. They're all addressed to Rosalie Goodson. Who would steal Ro's boxes and hide them in Joan's garage? "There's no way your mother would do this, would she?"

"No, of course not!" says Gwen. "Our children!"

"Oh my God," says Kevin. His children are the suspicious characters Ro mentioned at the park. He leans back against Joan's car and pulls at his beard, which feels frizzy and dry.

"I think they were inspired by the possum story. Like if something is outside someone's house, you can just take it. Maybe they don't comprehend the difference between a cooling blueberry pie and a package addressed to someone else. Not that they should be stealing pies either."

"Why'd you read them the book again tonight if you already knew they were thieves?" Kevin asks.

"Because I thought there would be too many questions if I refused to read a book we've read every night for the last three years."

"What were they planning to do with all this stuff?"

"I don't know. Nothing. They just wanted to take it. They'd actually been piling it up behind my mom's garage. She found the boxes this afternoon when she went to check the levels on the propane tanks. She had a conversation with them about how stealing is bad, and then Sammy told her you said Ro is bad."

"Oh, right," says Kevin, remembering how he'd flipped out after he'd discovered a weepy, bee-stung Sammy. "I might have said some stuff about her. Do they think it's okay to steal from a bad person?"

"I have no idea what was going through their minds. If it were anyone else, we would have to make the kids apologize to the person they stole from, but, my God, Kevin, we cannot have our kids confess to Ro. If she learns they took her stuff, all her suspicions about us will be confirmed. You have to sneak it all back."

"Just pile it up on her porch? Isn't that suspicious?"

"What other option do we have?" says Gwen.

"Aren't you going to help me? There're a lot of packages here."

Gwen stares hard at Kevin. "I need to say this to you? I can't be seen in the middle of the night with stolen packages."

"But if we wait until Ro is asleep—"

"*Kevin,*" says Gwen. "How do you not understand after all these years we've been together? The rules aren't the same for me as they are for you. A white man moves packages in the dark of night and people come up with reasons why he's probably doing something helpful."

"Right," Kevin says, and he tugs hard again on his beard until his face hurts. Why is he so stupid sometimes? Why does he forget that his family moves through the world in a different way than he can? How can he simultaneously feel so protective, yet say the wrong things so often?

"Just leave the boxes on her front steps. When she finds them in the morning, she can draw whatever conclusion she wants. And if she asks us, we know nothing."

"What if I say I took the stuff?" Kevin thinks about movies where fathers lie and say they've committed their children's crimes. Those fathers are willing to take the fall, willing to go to prison. He could be that kind of father.

"No," says Gwen. "Ro is always asking my mother when you're going to get a real job. She doesn't need to think you're into petty theft to make a few bucks."

Kevin had no idea Joan and Ro spoke about him, and he feels a pain blooming in his chest as he imagines the two women, leaning across the rosebushes, talking about his lackluster employment history. But his job is a real job, and he spends forty hours a week there and is a store manager and the health insurance for his entire family comes from his job, even though it eats up a large chunk of each paycheck. He knows Gwen works harder than he does, teaching as many classes as she can, but it's his job that provides the bulk of the money they survive on.

"I don't know why you needed to tell me that," Kevin says. "About what Ro said about me. It's hurtful."

"This isn't the time for you to get your feelings hurt, Kevin."

"Well, I can't help how I feel."

"Actually, you can. Controlling emotions is a large part of being an adult."

"I'm an adult," Kevin says, and as soon as the words come out of his mouth, he realizes how childish he sounds.

"Adults control their emotions and get things done."

Is she talking about returning Ro's boxes or about his dissertation? There's so much subtext to everything Gwen says lately; or maybe that's his own guilt about dragging his feet, about not completing what he set out to do so many years before.

"Please," Gwen says. "Just take care of things, okay?"

"Okay," Kevin says, although he's not one hundred percent certain what he's agreed to.

Gwen presses the button that raises the garage door, and when they walk out into the cold and dark night Kevin sees a light next door, Ro in the window, squinting down at them.

Ro's light doesn't go out until after midnight. Kevin waits another hour for good measure, hoping this will give Ro time to fall into a deep sleep. Then Kevin carries all the stolen boxes around the side of Ro's house and stacks them outside her door, fourteen in total. Seven trips between Joan's garage and Ro's front door.

In the morning, the children board the school bus at seven forty-five, Gwen leaves at eight thirty to teach her Forms of Poetry class, and Kevin allows himself to remain in the uncomfortable fold-out sofa bed until ten, although he can't fall back to sleep after the children wake him. He is completely worn out. His arms feel heavy and sore. How had his very small children managed to haul the boxes behind Joan's house? What will he say to the twins about returning the stolen packages? How will he explain needing to do it in the dark of night? Sometimes he is utterly exhausted by being an adult, by being someone expected to explain the world to younger people, as if he's in possession of the right answers.

In the shower, he grows angrier about sneaking around in the middle of the night. He wishes he could have just apologized and returned the boxes and then Ro would have been gracious enough to say, "It's okay, they're just kids." He hates that Ro is always there, always watching over them, always judging them.

Kevin steps out of the shower and wipes the fog off the mirror above the sink. He looks old and tired. He wishes, as he does most mornings, that he could be someone else. He wishes there were some escape hatch from the life he's constructed. He wishes he could pull a lever to make everything different. He'd even settle for who he used to be. When he was younger, Gwen was drawn to him because he was fun. He threw good parties, made friends easily; he was someone people liked being around. He had big ideas, like the summer they spent backpacking around Asia two years before the twins were born. But his ideas lately have been failures and he fears Gwen is running out of patience with him.

Kevin stares at his face in the mirror and is flooded with a desire to change, and there's only one thing he can think of doing that will create immediate results. He pulls on a sweatshirt and slips on his clogs. In the kitchen, he takes a pair of scissors out of a repurposed coffee can, which also holds a wooden spoon and a spatula.

In the backyard, he grabs his beard with his left hand and cuts with his right. He releases a handful of hair into the wind and imagines birds finding these hairs and using them in their nests. He cuts again and again, trims as much as he can without having a mirror to guide him. He turns to look at Ro's house and sees the packages are gone.

Back inside the tiny house, he looks at his face in the small, round mirror and laughs because the face staring back at him is so unfamiliar. He looks doughy and unformed. What's left of his beard is patchy, messy. After work he'll go to CVS and buy a razor and shaving cream and shave it all off, but he feels a desperate need to do one more thing before his shift starts at two. He has one more big idea, and this time he thinks he can make it work.

At the Humane Society, Kevin asks to see the dogs. There is quite the assortment. Two dozen have just been rescued from a hoarding situation but are not yet ready for adoption. When one dog barks, it sets off the others in a series of howls. "Do you have any border collies?" he asks, and a woman named Wendy, leading him through the shelter, laughs. "That's not how things work here," she says.

"I just thought maybe you had some housed in the back."

Wendy laughs again. "This *is* the back. We could probably find a dog that's about the size of a border collie, but it's not too often we get purebreds."

"Right, of course," says Kevin. "You know, I was talking to my neighbors. They have a dog that's half pug. And they said the woman at the shelter told them the dog was 'half pug, half perfection.'"

Wendy nods. "Well, every dog is perfect, don't you think? Have you ever had a dog before?"

Kevin shakes his head.

"And you want an active dog?"

"I'm looking for one that's good at chasing geese," says Kevin.

"That's awfully specific," says Wendy. "Do you have a goose problem at your house?"

"Not exactly," says Kevin, and Wendy blinks at him, looking confused.

"Do you have a big yard?"

"Average-size yard," says Kevin. He says nothing about the much-smaller-than-average-size house. He also says nothing about the yard belonging to his mother-in-law.

"Here are a few dogs you might like," Wendy says, gesturing

toward three muscled, sturdy-looking dogs with blocky heads. They all look like they could run quickly, sink their pointy teeth into thick, heavy fallen branches, and carry the branches in their mouths for miles. They look like dogs who, despite being at the Humane Society, will have good lives once they're adopted. They look like winners who are only being briefly waylaid. Perhaps he can adopt all three, and they can be his crew, can be trained to chase geese. Maybe a good dog can be trained to do anything.

He turns and sees another dog, one who is small yet plump—about the size of Dawn and Amy's half pug—with light orange fur growing in patches. The dog holds Kevin's gaze for a long moment, then looks down to the floor of its cage and whimpers.

"That's Frito," says Wendy. "She's a senior dog. She's been here for almost a year."

"Why hasn't anyone adopted her?" Kevin imagines a camera focusing in tight on Frito's face in a commercial for the ASPCA. *Don't,* he tells himself. *Don't fall for a sad face.*

"Senior dogs are hard to adopt out. People want puppies."

Kevin sticks a finger into Frito's cage, and the dog raises her head, gives Kevin's finger a lick.

"Why is she named Frito?"

Wendy shrugs. "She came with that name. Based on her physique, I'd say she probably enjoyed eating Fritos with her previous owner."

"Can she run?" he asks.

"She'd prefer a slow walk. Walks are good for her in light of her weight issues. She needs exercise. She's a calm dog. She'd be excellent with children, as long as they're not too rough. Do you have children?"

Kevin nods.

"Frito's owner died and no one from the owner's family wanted to take her. She's unfortunately had some issues with mange. The owner was elderly and couldn't properly care for her. But her fur has been coming in better since we've been treating her. It's a slow process."

Kevin's hand rises to touch his own patchy beard.

Wendy says, "I would be happy to waive the adoption fee. I can tell she likes you."

Kevin tries to harden his resolve. *No, no, no.* This is absolutely not the kind of dog he wants. This is a sad and pathetic dog, a loser of a dog. An unlucky dog. A literal underdog. He is almost certain this dog would be scared of geese, would not be able to drive them away or herd them. "I don't know," he says.

"Let me take her out of the cage," says Wendy, reaching in front of Kevin to unlatch the door. "You can play with her and then make your decision."

"Oh, no, that's okay," says Kevin. He thinks about Dawn going to the shelter to get a dog to run with and leaving with three-legged Wilford. He needs to be stronger than Dawn was. He is here for a reason.

"You two might be a perfect match," says the woman. "I have a sixth sense about these things."

"I'm not sure," says Kevin, and he wonders if he should be insulted by Wendy saying he and the pitiful-looking dog are a perfect match.

"Here you go," says Wendy, as she places Frito in his arms. "Can you just imagine what it must be like to live with someone all your life and then lose that person and get taken to a shelter where you live most of the day in a cage? Can you imagine?"

Wendy looks at Kevin with her head slightly tilted, and now she too looks like one of the goddamned sad animals in the ASPCA commercials. He thinks about the speech class he took in college and the rhetorical strategies he learned and wonders if the people who volunteer in shelters are given a list of them to employ. What is this one? Appeal to pathos?

"She likes you," Wendy says. Frito is resting her head on Kevin's chest, and he feels the warmth of the dog's body through his sweatshirt, feels her chest rise and fall.

"I can't believe she's been here for almost a year," says Kevin.

"A lot of people can't look past appearances," says Wendy, and she seems to be staring at Kevin's beard as she says it.

There is something solid and good about having this dog in his arms. There is so much that's not good in his life: he knows he'll never finish his dissertation, he knows his wife will be haunted by images of falling from a great height, he's uncertain if he can ever afford a real home for his family, he's upset about his children emulating the actions of a cartoon possum, he worries about not helping Maria from Chickety Chix do something about the boy who might be stalking her, he worries that he can't find it in himself to have empathy for a very old and lonely woman, he is angry with himself for repeatedly forgetting he moves through the world in a different and more privileged way than the rest of his family. Maybe he can, for once, do something right. He can take this dog home and give her a good life. He could build her a house, not as big as his own, but elaborate for a doghouse. He could walk her every day, and the two of them could lose weight together and next year, when he goes for his annual physical, the doctor will exclaim that Kevin now has an appropriate BMI and Kevin will say he owes it all to his new dog Frito, who, by that point, might be renamed after something healthy, like Brussels Sprout or Cauliflower.

Wendy smiles at him. "We'll give you a bag of weight-loss dog food to start you out. And come over here and stand in front of the I'm Adopted! wall so I can take a picture to post on our Facebook and Instagram pages. You don't know what a hero you're going to be to all the volunteers here. We love Frito and we've just prayed and prayed that she'd find a good home. And, well, you're the answer to our prayers!"

But Kevin hasn't said he'll take Frito, and he wonders if this is another rhetorical strategy being used against him. After you tell someone they're a hero who has answered prayers, can the supposed hero actually hand the dog back and say, "No thank you"?

Kevin walks toward the I'm Adopted! wall and looks at the lettering painted on it. On one side, in purple paint, it says, I'VE FOUND MY FUREVER HOME and on the other, in blue paint, it says, WHO SAVED WHO?

"Whom," says Kevin.

"What?" says Wendy, and Kevin shakes his head. "Smile!" she orders. "I'll get your full name in a minute so I can tag you in the Facebook post."

Kevin holds Frito and looks into the camera and thinks that if anyone googles him—say, an old classmate who wonders how his life turned out—they will find just this photograph of him and this forlorn dog. They won't find books or articles he's written because there are none. They won't find a photo of him smiling, posing in front of a full bookshelf, on the faculty page of any English department. All they will find is this image of him and his patchy beard standing against a wall holding this patchy dog.

PART II

February

Consider the Possibilities

The mall is closing.

Last week, Jackson's mother received what she called "a notice," which said the mall would shut down in four months, in June. Everything, all the stores, the food court, the salon. "What will you do?" Jackson asked his mother after she set the notice down on the reception desk.

"Four months is a long time," she said. "I've got time to figure it out."

But Jackson knows four months isn't that long. It's approximately 120 days. It is only one-third of a year. It's not enough time for an artichoke to grow from a seed and be ready to harvest. It's not enough time to gestate a baby hippopotamus, giraffe, or walrus. It's not enough time to figure out a new life.

The day after Jackson learned the mall was closing, the architects arrived. Jackson's mom said the group with rolled-up papers under their arms and clipboards and tape measures were figuring out what was going to happen to the mall once the stores were vacated. From one of the stylists' chairs, Jackson watched the architects move around the mall. When his mother was busy with a client, he left the salon and followed them around like a wildlife photographer shadowing a cheetah, ducking into stores before they could notice he was tracking them.

Jackson is interested in one architect in particular. He is Asian, maybe Chinese, like Jackson. And, like Jackson, he has a cowlick at the back of his head, even though the architect has put gel in his hair, keeping it in a mostly neat pushed-back style. Last week, Jackson got his first pair of glasses, and the architect wears glasses too, round-framed Harry Potter–looking glasses, just like Jackson's. But what's most interesting is the way the architect trails behind the others, as if he doesn't quite belong. When the architect lags behind, he becomes distracted, picking things up in stores, examining them, maybe thinking about buying them, and when he looks up, the others have moved on, far down the hallways, measuring or tapping or examining something new. He never really seems part of the group.

Jackson understands what that's like. He wishes he had a group to hang out with at school. On rainy days, when they can't go outside for recess, Jackson wants to play Clue with Seth Stark and Matty Doyle, but he's too afraid to ask. He doesn't want them to say no, even though Clue can be played with three people. When the weather is nice and Jackson's class goes outside for recess, he watches the group of girls jumping rope, watches the way they hop on one foot and spin their entire bodies quickly before they need to jump again. He wants to join in, but again, he's too afraid to ask. What if he messes up? What if he trips on the rope and they have to start over again? It's better to just sit with his back against the old oak tree in the playground and read a book. When he's reading, he's not bothering anybody.

There is a good reason Jackson is so interested in the Asian architect. Since his mother doesn't talk about Jackson's father, he needs to figure out who his father is himself. And so every Asian man who might be around Jackson's mother's age is a potential father. He knows it's silly, knows that the chance of just stumbling into his father is tiny, even infinitesimal, which was one of his vocabulary words last week. But not knowing his father has always bothered him, has always felt like a mystery he is supposed to solve. Jackson only knows a few facts about his father: he's someone his mother used to know, he's Chinese, and he's the same age as his mother. He lived in Albany ten years ago, but maybe he doesn't live here anymore. Or maybe he does. So perhaps there's a chance the architect is Jackson's father, but if he is, wouldn't his mother recognize him? Would she hide because she doesn't want him in her life? Or in Jackson's life? But what if, after the mall closes, their new life can include Jackson's father? Would it be so bad for their new life to be very different from their old one? It would not be a terrible thing to have both a mom and a dad. He knows he can never say this to his mom because she would feel that she is not enough, and she is enough, has been enough all of Jackson's life. But having more than enough is a good thing too.

Now, the architects are in the bookstore talking to Kevin, who is dressed up like Max from *Where the Wild Things Are*. Jackson wonders what they think about Kevin's costume, if they think he's a silly and strange adult. In the salon, Jackson's mother is flipping through a magazine.

"Mom," Jackson says, "what if you tell the people who own the mall that you won't leave? What if you handcuff yourself to your chair?" On TV, he saw a woman do this with the door of an old hospital set to be demolished. The demolition was delayed for four days, but finally the police sawed off the handcuffs and the building was knocked down. Maybe it could work if the other people in the mall handcuffed themselves to heavy objects in their stores too.

His mother looks up from her magazine. "Oh, honey," she says, "people only handcuff themselves to places they care about."

"You don't care about the salon?" says Jackson. How can she not care about the place where she spends so many hours? How can she not care about the place where she earns the money they need to live?

"There are other salons. I don't want you to worry, okay? It's my job to worry, not yours."

"Why is it your job to worry?"

"Because I'm the adult." She looks down at the magazine again, flips a page. She pulls open a flap, rubs her wrist on the perfumed page, then lifts her wrist to her nose. Jackson is annoyed. She doesn't seem worried. She seems totally fine, not concerned about what they'll do once the mall closes and she no longer has a job.

Jackson sees the architects approach the salon, but the Asian man is missing. A woman with a shiny brown bob—his mother taught him the name of this hairstyle—knocks on the wall, pokes her head in, and shouts, "Knock knock!"

Immediately, Jackson dislikes her. Why *both* knock and say "knock knock"? There's no door to the salon. They don't have to be invited in. They can just walk in like everyone else.

Jackson's mother stands up, puts her magazine on the chair, and a man holding a clipboard says, "Oh, please carry on with what you were doing. We just need to look around and take some measurements. We'll be out of your hair in a few minutes."

"Actually, I'll get out of the way," says Jackson's mom. "I don't have any appointments for the next hour. I'll grab a drink at the food court. You want to come, Jackson?"

Jackson wants to stay and talk to the architects. They know how to build things, and Jackson needs someone who knows how to build things to help him with his act. The talent show is coming up in three weeks, and he wants to do something spectacular. If he can impress everyone at school, then maybe they'll want to be his friend. And what if his father is the Asian architect and is on his way to the salon right now? Maybe he can help Jackson build props for his act. "I'll stay here," he says.

"All right," says his mom. "But keep out of everyone's way. They're here to work."

He nods and hopes his mom will be gone for a while. He hopes she might go to the bookstore and flip through magazines for ten or fifteen minutes before picking out a new one to buy.

Jackson tries to concentrate on his book about cameras, but he's distracted by the movement of the architects and has trouble remembering what he's read about apertures and f-stops and his eyes travel over the same sentences again and again. A few minutes later, the Asian architect appears in the salon.

"Hi," Jackson says, as he turns his chair to face the man who probably isn't but could be his father.

"Hello." The architect reaches up, pulls a pencil from behind his ear, and it almost looks like a magic trick, the pencil Jackson hadn't noticed before appearing in the architect's hand. The architect looks down at the pencil then shoves it back behind his ear. Maybe he forgot he has no paper to write on. The others are huddled around one of the hair-washing sinks, playing with the knobs, as if they're unsure if the sink can produce water.

"What are they doing?" Jackson says.

"Getting a sense of the space."

"Why?" says Jackson. "Are you going to build another mall here? Are you going to turn Sunshine Clips into a different salon?"

"We don't know yet," says the architect. "We need to first assess the overall structure and the existing electrical and plumbing systems."

"Would you build another mall? A fancier one?"

"Maybe, but my guess would be apartments. My firm was hired to draw up plans for the space."

"How will you decide what to build?"

"*I* won't decide anything," the architect says. "I'm the new guy, so I have no say. We'll research what would be most profitable, consider the possibilities. But our firm might not even get the job. It all depends on what other firms propose."

Jackson looks toward the food court and sees his mother sipping a cup of lemonade at Chickety Chix, talking to Maria behind the counter. Maria has agreed to be his assistant for his magic act, but she's been sworn to secrecy. Jackson doesn't want his mom to know about his magic yet. If he can get the architect to help build something for his act, if he's certain the act will be spectacular, then he'll tell his mom about it.

"What's your name?" says the architect, walking to stand next to Jackson's chair. "Mine's Edison, but you can call me Eddie."

"Jackson."

"Like Michael Jackson? Or Jackson Pollock? Or neither? I guess they're both problematic, huh?"

"Michael, but I know who Jackson Pollock is. I don't really like his paintings, but my mom says his paint spatters are energetic."

"I don't like his stuff either, but what do I know? My paintings aren't on display at the MoMA." Eddie shrugs.

"Were you named after Thomas Edison?"

"Yeah. I guess my parents were hoping for a scientist or an inventor."

Jackson likes that they are both named after famous people. He likes that they have something in common besides the cowlick and the Harry Potter glasses. "You're a painter and an architect?" Maybe Eddie has two jobs, two ways to earn money. Having two jobs seems like a good plan, especially if something happens, like the closing of the mall, that prevents you from doing one of them.

"I guess I'm not much of an artist anymore. I haven't painted since college, and that was a while ago."

Jackson examines Eddie's face. How old is he? Ages are confusing for Jackson. Everyone can be sorted into one of four categories: babies, kids, adults, and old people. Jackson's mother and Eddie both fall into the adults category, but this doesn't mean they're the same age.

"Do you like being an architect more than being an artist?" Jackson asks.

Eddie shrugs. "It's more stable. But this is my first job out of grad school, so I don't really know yet if I really like it." Eddie looks over at the other architects, but their heads are bent together as they discuss something, and they don't seem to have noticed Eddie's arrival in the salon. "I got hired last month. This would be my first major project."

"What kind of buildings do you like to make?" Jackson asks.

"You want to see one of my projects?" Eddie says, taking his phone out of his pocket.

Eddie crouches so he can show Jackson his phone. "Our assignment was to build something that solved a problem. So I built inexpensive, portable modules for the unhoused." He shows Jackson a photo of a box on wheels with an awning that pulls down in a curve like the back of an igloo. When the awning is open, sunlight can filter into the box, and when the awning is down, the box is long enough for someone to sleep in.

The pictures remind Jackson of Kevin's tiny house. Kevin showed him photographs on his phone one day when Jackson went to take photos of Frito at the bookstore. Jackson thought it was neat that Kevin built the house by himself, that it could be hitched to a truck and transported other places, but now he feels sad because the tiny house is something someone might give to a homeless person. "The wooden parts are made from reclaimed shipping pallets in order to keep costs low. And everything can fold down and be attached to the back of a bike."

"Cool," says Jackson. He feels a swell of pride, an expanding in his chest. Eddie is using his skills to do something good. This is the kind of man Jackson would like to have as a dad. "Did you give it to someone?"

"Yeah," says Eddie. "This guy in L.A., where I went to school. This kind of thing wouldn't work with the weather in New York, especially not upstate."

"Is he still living in it?"

Eddie pauses a moment, looks like he doesn't want to answer the question. Then he says, "I don't know. I hope so, but we didn't stay in touch."

Jackson is disappointed. People can be found, if you want to find them, if you have enough information about them. "Maybe they can make apartments for homeless people in all the stores in the mall," Jackson says.

Eddie laughs. "It's a nice idea," he says, "but the people who own this property want to make money, not start a charity." Eddie looks at the other architects, who are now measuring a back wall. "I should go," he says. "But good talking to you, Jackson Not Pollock."

"Wait," says Jackson. He scans the food court and is glad to see his mother still talking to Maria. "You're good at building things, right?"

"I'm okay."

"Can you help me figure out how to make something?" Jackson asks. His heart thumps in his chest because he knows this is a lot to ask, but he needs to ask now before his mother comes back.

"Maybe," Eddie says, and Jackson sees his eyes flit to the group of architects at the back of the salon.

"I'm doing a magic show, and I need to build something for my assistant to hide in."

"Like a wooden box?"

Jackson nods. "My idea is that my assistant dresses up like a dove. And then I put her in a box and use a saw to cut her. But you know how magicians usually saw their assistants in half? I want to saw her in four."

"I thought assistants got sawed in half because they can fold their bodies up and hide in half a box and then you can stick fake legs out the other half," Eddie says.

"Sometimes," says Jackson. "But there's another way to do it where there's a secret compartment for the assistant's legs in the table below the box. There's a body double in the other half, dressed the same, with their head and upper body bent down into the bottom of the table and with their legs out, so they can wiggle their feet."

Eddie laughs. "That sounds elaborate. Are you performing in Vegas?"

It sounds like Eddie is making fun of him. Jackson thinks of Larry Bornstein, the magician from Las Vegas he'd met in the food court, who makes videos explaining how to do tricks. Now Jackson has just done the same thing, revealing secrets to Eddie. Jackson wishes he could talk to Larry Bornstein again, ask him if there's a way to do the sawing-in-four trick.

"The magic act is for my school talent show," Jackson says.

"Can't you do a card trick or something?" says Eddie.

"I want to do a trick everyone in the auditorium can see. Only the first few rows would be able to see a card trick."

"It'd be easier to get a deck of cards than to build a fancy box," says Eddie. "Plus you'd have to get the box to school. And you'd have to get a saw there too. Do you even have a saw?"

"I could probably find one. Do you have a saw? And I don't only want to cut her in four. I want to open up the four boxes and have a real dove in each box. And then as the audience is looking at the four doves, the spotlight goes up to the beams above the stage and the human assistant is sitting up there, like she's flown up like a real bird."

Eddie rubs his chin, pushes his glasses up the bridge of his nose. "You want me to tell you the truth?" he says. And before Jackson can answer, he says, "This trick sounds impossible."

"Edison!" calls out one of the other architects, waving him over. Jackson is surprised they've finally noticed him.

"I admire your imagination," Eddie says. "Good luck with it." He pats Jackson on the back and jogs over to the rest of the architects.

Good luck with it is a way to wiggle out of something without seeming rude. It's an adult's way of saying they're not helping, and they don't believe it can be done and good luck, kid, with your wild and impossible plan. Good luck, *dumb* kid.

Jackson's mom returns and hands Jackson a cup of lemonade. She watches the architects move around the salon, but no look of recognition crosses her face, and Jackson is certain she doesn't know Eddie. All along, Jackson knew there was little chance Eddie could be his father, but for a few minutes—right after he saw the portable housing Eddie built—he desperately wanted to be his son. But now Jackson feels relieved. He doesn't want his father to be someone who doesn't believe in his ideas, who doesn't want to figure out how an impossible trick might become possible.

"Did I miss anything?" says Jackson's mom, picking up her magazine from the chair next to Jackson.

"No," says Jackson. He takes a long sip of the lemonade and lets the cool, sweet liquid sit in his mouth for a moment before he swallows. "You didn't miss anything."

So it will have to be close-up magic using small, everyday objects. There is one spectacular trick that doesn't require big and heavy things, but that trick is even more impossible than cutting Maria into four. That trick is the bullet catch: an assistant shoots a bullet across the stage, and the magician catches it in his teeth. Or in a metal cup in his mouth, so the bullet hitting metal makes a loud sound that every person in the room can hear. The bullet catch has been called the most dangerous trick in the world because sometimes it goes wrong. Magicians have died doing it.

The trick can be performed with a real gun or a trick gun that fires blanks or wax bullets. It always involves sleight of hand, so the magician is only pretending to catch a bullet. The most famous magician to have died doing this trick is Chung Ling Soo, who was shot in the chest in 1918 when a real bullet was fired, instead of a blank that was supposed to come out of a tube below the barrel of the gun. Soo was really a white man named William Ellsworth Robinson, who pretended to be Chinese. He was an unsuccessful magician who was not good at stage banter, like magicians are supposed to be, so he stole an act from a Chinese magician named Ching Ling Foo and he claimed he couldn't speak English, so he no longer had to say much onstage during his performances in America, just mumbled some words audiences thought to be Chinese. William Ellsworth Robinson shaved his head except for a long, black braid, dressed in Chinese silk jackets, and no one in the audience figured out he was a white man. Jackson is not sure how people could have been so dumb, but back then people didn't have cell phone cameras and the internet in order record things and scrutinize them.

William Ellsworth Robinson died the day after he was shot onstage performing the bullet catch. The gun used in the act malfunctioned because Robinson hadn't cleaned it well enough, causing a real bullet—which had been loaded for show—to fire instead of the blank. Maybe that's the problem with stealing an act; maybe you're not really as good as the magician whose tricks you're stealing. Maybe Ching Ling Foo would never have left his gun improperly cleaned. There's something wrong, Jackson thinks, in stealing someone's name and act and even his race, but there's also something very appealing about pretending to be someone completely unlike yourself and getting popular doing so. It's interesting to think you can erase who you are and where you've come from and no one would know. But who would Jackson be if he wasn't himself?

If Jackson wanted to do the bullet catch, who would sell a gun, even a trick one, to a nine-year-old? And who knows what would happen if he brought it to school. So far his school hasn't installed metal detectors or forced students to use clear plastic backpacks, but he knows a lot of schools do these things. Every year, all the kids in his school have to watch a video about gun violence, and the only good thing about that terrible and sad video is that they get to skip gym to watch it. Jackson knows if he brought a gun to school, he'd probably be tackled, dragged to the principal's office, and told to never come back again.

ONE WEEK BEFORE the talent show, Jackson asks for a bathroom pass during lunch. Instead of going to the bathroom, he walks to the computer room. No classes are there, since it's lunch period, but one of the computer teachers, Ms. Hines, sits at the front of the classroom eating a Thin Mint and staring at something on a screen. There are barking noises coming from the computer, and Jackson wonders if she's watching dog videos. He steps into the room, and Ms. Hines doesn't look up. He waits for a few seconds and she still doesn't notice him. He thinks of shouting, "Knock knock!" the way the architect with the bob did at the salon, but instead he clears his throat and says, "Excuse me, Ms. Hines?"

Ms. Hines looks up and sticks the rest of the Thin Mint into her mouth. Then she holds up her pointer finger while Jackson waits for her to chew her cookie and stop what's playing on the screen. "Sorry about that. Did you leave something in the classroom? Is this your glove?" she says, holding up a tiny pink glove with a magenta heart on it. It looks like it would fit a kindergartener.

"That's not my glove."

"No, it doesn't look like it would be, Jack," she says, looking at the glove for a moment and then placing it into a lost-and-found box on her desk.

She always calls him Jack, even though he's told her many times that his name is Jackson. He doesn't understand why she's so forgetful. She's not old enough to forget such a simple thing as a name; she told his class in the fall that she was twenty-two and graduated from college in May.

"I was wondering if you could help me with something for the talent show?"

"I'll be there," she says. "I'm in charge of the mic and the speakers."

"I'm doing magic," Jackson says.

"Oooh! Abracadabra!" she shouts, grinning and splaying all ten fingers. Jackson can see some Thin Mint stuck between two of her teeth.

"I'm going to do close-up magic, and I was wondering if you could film it and at the same time project it on the screen at the back of the stage."

The tricks Jackson will be doing will be hard for people beyond the first few rows of the auditorium to see if they aren't projected onto a screen. The first trick Jackson wants to do is called Bottle Tops. He'll call a member of the audience up to the stage and pull a coin out of his pocket and place it on a table. Then he'll tell the audience member to put the coin under one of four bottle caps lined up on the table while his back is turned. Then he'll turn around and lift up the bottle cap on top of the coin. The secret is to tape a small piece of hair to the bottom of the coin, and the hair will stick out of the bottle cap, and he'll know which cap to choose. He plans to use one of Mrs. Goodson's white hairs. A white hair will be hard for anyone in the audience to see.

"Oh," says Ms. Hines. "I'm not sure. I mean, I was told I have to do the sound, and that might be a lot of work. And I'm not really supposed to do anything without getting permission from the administration, and there's a lot of paperwork to be filled out for, like, anything anyone wants to do around here."

"What if I ask the principal?"

"I don't want to bother the principal. Just make your movements big and people will be able to see them."

"I don't think they will. The auditorium has fifty-two rows." Jackson knows this because each row is labeled with a letter, and the rows are marked A through ZZ, running through the alphabet twice.

"I don't know if it's worth it for one act, you know? If I do it for you, then I'd have to accommodate everyone else's requests and things can get complicated." Her phone buzzes, and she picks it up and starts texting.

"You can use the camera that's used to record school plays and concerts. And there's a screen that comes down at the back of the stage. You don't have to set it up." Ms. Hines is still texting, so Jackson isn't even sure she's listening.

Ms. Hines puts down her phone, then looks at the box of Thin Mints, and Jackson can tell she wants him to leave so she can eat another. "Aren't you supposed to be somewhere?"

"Lunch," says Jackson.

"You should get back. Jack, look, I'm sorry. I would help, but it's just not fair if I can't help everyone. Here," she says, holding out the box of Thin Mints.

Jackson shakes his head. "No thank you," he says, although what he wants to say is, *Thanks for nothing.*

When he returns to the lunch table, Kenny Parker says, "Did you poop? You were gone for a million years." The other boys at the table laugh, as if what Kenny said is the funniest thing ever. Jackson does not particularly like these boys, but they are his assigned lunchmates for this month. He is glad for the assigned seating because without it, he worries that no one would sit with him.

"I didn't," says Jackson. "I've never pooped at school in my life."

"I didn't know if you were coming back, so I ate your Cheez-Its," says Reggie Joyce.

"He's probably extra hungry now because he pooped everything out," says Kenny. Everyone laughs again.

"I didn't poop!" says Jackson, but everyone is laughing so hard he doubts they hear him. He picks up his apple—all that's left of his lunch; his ham and cheese sandwich is also missing—takes a bite, and thinks how everyone he knows is so completely disappointing.

THAT AFTERNOON, AFTER the bus drops him off at the mall, Jackson goes to the food court before going to the salon. Maria is working, so he can talk to her about the talent show. He tells Maria each act is given five minutes, so he should be able to do three tricks. He pulls the Bite Coin out of his pocket, shows her how it can look like he's taking a bite out of a quarter, but tells her he thinks this trick works better one-on-one, not on a stage. He's not sure anyone in the audience would be able to see the fake coin. He wishes he'd bought something better suited for his act. Because his only store-bought trick won't work, he'll do Bottle Tops first and then a mind-reading trick and then, for the grand finale, he'll do Miraculous Money, where he'll use three small envelopes, two filled with folded paper and one with a twenty-dollar bill loaned by an audience member, and he'll rip up the two envelopes of paper and then open the envelope with the money inside and return it.

"What if you accidentally rip up the money?" Maria asks.

"I won't," says Jackson.

"It would be a pretty expensive mess-up if you do."

"Do you really think I'll mess up?"

"No," Maria says. "If you could read my mind, you'd know that I have the utmost confidence in your magical abilities."

"I can't really read minds. The mind reading trick is called Black Magic, but it's not anything bad. Black magic usually means when you summon up evil spirits, but that's not what we're doing." Jackson explains the trick. He'll leave the room with someone important, like the principal, to watch over him and make sure he can't hear what's going on in the auditorium. Then, with the help of the audience, Maria will pick an object in the room. When Jackson comes back, Maria will point to a bunch of objects, and Jackson will select the object she chose.

"It's called Black Magic because you'll point to a black object right before you point to whatever you picked. So you could point to a speaker or the microphone and then the next object you point to will be the one you chose. The audience won't know the trick's name, though. That's just for us to know."

"Your secret's safe with me," Maria says, pretending to zip her lips shut.

She picks up a few paper straw wrappers from the counter, balls them up, and throws them into the trash can. "Hey, did you invite your mom to the show?"

Jackson shakes his head. "She's not into magic. Plus, she'd have to leave work, and there's no one to cover for her."

"I don't think it would matter. Hardly anyone is coming to the mall anymore."

"I'm not going to be doing anything spectacular," says Jackson.

"Is anyone else doing magic? Let me guess, everyone else is singing or dancing."

"Mostly. Some girls are doing a cheerleading routine."

"Boring," says Maria. "Not spectacular."

"They're popular, so no one at my school would ever call them boring."

"Well, just think about inviting your mom," says Maria. "Your magic is pretty cool."

"Maybe," says Jackson, but he wants to change the subject because he is definitely not going to invite his mother to the talent show. "Can we try Black Magic?"

"Yeah, sure, one time quickly and then I have to get back to work," says Maria. "Okay, I've picked my object." She points to the Hot Dog Charlie's sign with blue and red lettering, and Jackson shakes his head. She points to an orange plastic tray someone has returned to the shelf above the garbage cans. Jackson shakes his head. She picks up a white packet of sugar, and Jackson shakes his head. She points to a black sweater on a mannequin in the window of Old Navy, and Jackson shakes his head. And then she picks up a lemon from a bucket of lemons waiting to be squeezed, holds it up in front of Jackson's face, and he nods. Maria grins and says, "Magic!"

AT THE TALENT show, Jackson waits backstage for his turn. The music teacher is there keeping everyone in order, shushing them. Jackson watches two girls and two boys—all popular kids—doing a dance called flossing to a song he does not know. The audience loves it. At the end of the song, one of the boys, Bobby Callahan, does a backflip as he runs across the stage, and the cheering in the auditorium is so loud that Jackson can feel the stage vibrate under his dress shoes. So far, the only act that Jackson thinks showed talent was Isabelle Kaplan, who'd played a few minutes of a Mozart flute concerto, but the applause for her was quiet and polite, since she is not one of the cool kids.

Jackson looks at Maria. She had to get special permission to be here from her parents and the principal of the high school, even though she said she was only missing lunch, study hall, and gym. Jackson feels guilty that she had to leave school, thinks that if his act is bad she will have wasted her time. Maria is the tallest person backstage, besides the music teacher, and now he feels weird about having a high schooler as his assistant because no one else brought someone from outside to join their act.

Maria is dressed as a dove, which seems stupid now. She looks weird and funny, and Jackson worries that people will think they're doing a comedy act. He's not doing the trick with real doves and a human dove who appears high up in the auditorium, so it doesn't even make sense for Maria to be dressed this way.

After the flossers, two fifth grade girls, Cassie and Gemma, go onstage. The audience is applauding loudly again, and Jackson isn't sure if it's because they're impressed or because the girls are popular and blond and pretty. In unison, Cassie and Gemma shout, "Go, team! Win win! We're the best! Winners year after year! Other teams better fear!" It seems silly to be cheering onstage without a team to cheer for.

"We're next," Jackson says. "Are you ready?"

Maria nods. She stands like the cheerleaders on the stage, right hip jutted up and hands in front of her bulging dove belly, as if she's holding pom-poms, then says, "Other acts better fear!" and Jackson can't help but laugh, even though he's so nervous his hands are sweating and his stomach is clenched up.

When the cheerleaders are done, the applause is loud, but not as loud as for the flossers. Jackson takes a deep breath, then nods at the janitor, who brings a table onto the stage and unfolds the legs. The auditorium is silent, and Jackson can hear the jangling of the janitor's keys as he walks off the stage. Jackson looks down at his own outfit, a white button-down shirt, too-short dress pants he wore to a wedding last year, and an old vest his mother found in her closet. It's black and shiny in front with embroidered flowers on the back in a material that reminds him of an old lady's couch. It's a few sizes too big. He takes a deep breath and emerges from backstage with his assistant dressed like a fat dove.

He stares out at the audience, and most of the kids look bored. He sees people fidget and slump. If he walked out on the stage with a huge buzz saw, they would sit up and pay attention. But he has to get them to pay attention to bottle caps. He lines up the caps on the table, then takes out a nickel with a piece of Mrs. Goodson's white hair taped to one side. He makes sure the taped side is flat to the table. "I need a volunteer," he says and looks to the audience. No one raises their hand. A few seconds later, Mrs. Cole, his first grade teacher, stands up. She jogs to the stage, her gray curls bouncing as she climbs the stairs, and Jackson hears kids giggle. Mrs. Cole is old, and it is unusual to see her jogging, but right now Jackson is happy to have anyone onstage with him. He tells her he'll turn around while she slides the coin under one of the bottle caps behind his back.

"All done," says Mrs. Cole, and Jackson turns around. His hands hover over the bottle caps, as if a feeling will tell him where the coin is, but he knows its location because he can see Mrs. Goodson's hair sticking out. Second bottle cap from the right. Jackson allows himself a quick glance at the audience, and they still seem bored, and he wonders how many of them can even see what's happening onstage. He looks at Ms. Hines sitting near a speaker next to the stage, not doing anything, not paying attention to his act, and thinks she could have easily projected his act, so even people sitting in row ZZ could see.

With a flourish, Jackson lifts up the correct bottle cap. He picks up the coin, making sure the side with the tape and the hair isn't visible to the audience. The audience is silent.

"Why, that's wonderful!" says Mrs. Cole, clasping her hands. "Truly magical," she says, and Jackson smiles, even though he wants to cry. She is speaking to him as if he's still in first grade, as if reading a picture book or tying his own shoes or pouring apple juice into a cup without spilling are magical acts. He says into the microphone, "Everyone, please give Mrs. Cole a hand!" He tries to sound enthusiastic, even though he feels like his heart is being squeezed. The audience claps unenthusiastically as Mrs. Cole leaves the stage.

"And now for some mind reading!" Jackson says. He looks down at the principal, Mr. Hendrix, sitting in the front row. He tells the audience he will go into the hall, accompanied by Mr. Hendrix. While he's outside, the audience will help Maria pick an object in the auditorium. He hands the microphone to Maria, descends the wooden staircase, and walks toward Mr. Hendrix. It feels like it takes forever for them to walk the length of the auditorium, as if he is making his way through a pool of sticky caramel to the heavy door into the hallway. Jackson can feel the weight of everyone's boredom and impatience in the overheated auditorium. In the past, Jackson has always just been someone to be ignored. Now, he's worried this magic act will make him into someone to be made fun of.

Once the door to the auditorium swings shut, Mr. Hendrix says, "Good job with your first trick. I can't wait to see what you do with this one."

Jackson nods, but he knows Mr. Hendrix is just being polite, just being a good adult. Jackson wonders what Maria is doing onstage. He knows she wants to be an actress, and maybe she's doing something—singing or dancing or pretending to be an actual dove—that's more entertaining to the audience than his magic. He looks at his watch—a gift from Mrs. Goodson; it used to belong to her husband—and sees four minutes have passed since his act started. He won't have enough time to do his third trick, his best trick.

"How did you learn magic?" says Mr. Hendrix.

"From books. And YouTube," says Jackson.

"Just between you and me, I think it's far better to learn magic from YouTube than to learn how to floss from it. Who even knew flossing was a dance? I thought it was something you did to your teeth."

Jackson nods again. He thinks Mr. Hendrix might be making a joke, but he might not be, so Jackson doesn't laugh. One of the back doors to the auditorium pops open and a boy sticks his head out. "You can come back," he says. Jackson and Mr. Hendrix walk back up to the stage, and Jackson feels like he's moving in slow motion again. Onstage, Maria holds out the microphone to Mr. Hendrix and says, "You, sir, are the principal of this school, are you not?"

Mr. Hendrix nods.

"And we all know that principals are truthful and honest, right?" Maria looks out at the audience, and no one says anything. "I can't hear you!" Maria shouts and then the audience shouts back, "Right!" and Jackson is glad Maria is his assistant because even though she doesn't know very much about magic, she knows how to get an audience to participate.

"I need to ask you a question, and I need you to answer truthfully," Maria says.

"Of course," says Mr. Hendrix.

"When you and Jackson were out in the hall, could you hear what was happening in here?"

"Not at all," says Mr. Hendrix.

"Excellent," says Maria. "You can return to your seat." She holds her hand out toward Mr. Hendrix's empty seat next to the vice principal, Mr. Salisbury.

"Now, Jackson," says Maria, "everyone in here knows what object I'm thinking of. Do you know?"

"Not yet," says Jackson. "Have a seat," he says, pointing to a spot next to the table where there is supposed to be a metal folding chair. But the chair is leaning on the wall at the back of the stage. The janitor was supposed to set up the chair when he set up the table. Jackson jogs to get the chair, and he hears giggles again in the audience and he feels a pain in his chest. He's sure his five minutes are already up. He's been onstage for too long, and there's been too little payoff. Maria sits, and Jackson stands behind her and puts two fingers from each hand on

Maria's temples. Jackson closes his eyes, says, "It's coming to me, I'm reading your mind." He opens his eyes, takes his hands off Maria's face, and sees his fingertips are covered in white face paint.

"Okay," says Maria, standing up. "I'll point to items in this room and you tell me if they're what I'm thinking of." She points first to a large pink bow in the hair of a girl in the front row. Jackson shakes his head. Then she points to the frosted-glass light fixture on the ceiling. Jackson shakes his head again. Then she points to Ms. Hines, who looks bored sitting next to the speakers. "What about the green sweater of that woman who is clearly fascinated by magic?" The audience laughs, perks up a bit, and Ms. Hines's face turns pink. "*No way*," says Jackson, and the audience laughs again. Then Maria points to Mr. Salisbury's shiny black shoes, and Jackson shakes his head, but now he knows that whatever Maria points to next will be the object. She points to the windows on the right side of the auditorium and says, "What about these red curtains?" and Jackson nods, says, "Yes, you're thinking of the curtains!" Maria says, "You are correct!" and Jackson looks away from her to the audience. No one seems impressed.

"Let's give our magician a hand for his amazing mind reading abilities," says Maria, and then there's some quiet clapping, and Jackson hates that Maria had to ask for it.

Maria steps next to Jackson, and he sees her slide her thumb to turn off the microphone. "Take a bow," she whispers. She holds her hands out, palms up, toward him, encouraging the audience to keep clapping. Jackson doesn't want to bow because it's all been a failure, everything so small, so unremarkable. But he takes a bow because Maria's set him up to do so. He bends deeply at the waist, making sure he doesn't touch his black pants with his fingers that are covered in white face paint, and when he rises, he hears one person clapping louder than the rest. He scans the crowd and he sees his mother, far back, in maybe row LL or MM and he wonders how he hadn't noticed her before. Even though people are staring at her, his mother continues to clap, and her smile is so wide, and she's looking at Jackson as if he's done something spectacular.

March

Patron of the Arts

The mall is closing.

Ro assumed the mall would at least outlast her, but it is not to be. It will only be open for three more months, and every day there's more evidence that this place is on its last legs. Yellow poster board signs in the windows proclaim HUGE SALE!, the broken faucets in the ladies' room have not been repaired, and the lights in the food court continue to flicker until they fade away. Although she would never admit it to anyone, Ro has an immense fondness for the mall. It is where she goes when she wants to spend time outside of her house, to talk to people who are the closest thing she has to friends.

After the announcement of the mall's closing, Ro took up mall walking as an excuse to visit every day. Today she is wearing her new sneakers, an awful pair of bright white Nikes sold to her by a young man at the Foot Locker down the corridor from Sunshine Clips. He insisted they would cradle her heels and make even the longest walks comfortable. She must concede they are, indeed, comfortable, but all the cushioning makes it look like she's wearing marshmallows on her feet. She sees the other mall walkers, observes their ridiculous outfits, the warm-up pants, the sweatshirts, even the terry cloth headbands, as if they are breaking a sweat looping around the mall. Ro will not dress as if she's trying out for the Olympics; she will not strap one of those godforsaken fanny packs to her waist or put a headband on her head. Her regular clothing—sweaters, slacks or skirts, turtlenecks, purse—paired with the marshmallow shoes will do. And she will not pump her arms back and forth just so everyone can see she's exercising. If anyone asks, she'll say her doctor insisted she take up exercise, but that's not true. At her physicals, her doctor revels at her health, impressed by the numbers that come back on her blood work. "What's your secret, Ro?" Dr. Patel says every year. "Clean living," Ro always says. "And a positive attitude." But, really, she knows it has more to do with genetics and luck than anything else.

And perhaps it is lucky she's been healthy for so long. She can care for herself and her house and her garden, and even at ninety she doesn't have to pay someone to help. She watched her husband die slowly and painfully, and she is grateful her only ailments are sore joints when it rains or snows and a back that is curved more than she'd like. Sometimes, though, she wonders if she'll live for ten or fifteen more years and if, by that point, she'll need assistance with the matter of daily living. At what point have you lived too long? At a certain point, you start outliving most of the people you know, and if you spend your time grieving the dead, you'd spend all your waking hours mourning.

But this ending—the closing of the mall—there's something different about it than death, and the news has sent Ro into a profound state of sadness. Where will she go? She can go to a coffee shop, but she doesn't like coffee or sitting in one place all day. At the mall she can poke around many stores, she can move about. She can walk briskly and buy a cup of weakly brewed tea at Panda Wok and sit for a while watching the people in the food court. She can watch young mothers with their toddlers in strollers, urging them to take a bite of a chicken nugget. She can watch teenagers goofing around, spilling soda and running to grab large piles of napkins to clean it up. She can watch bored-looking mall employees eating pizza and playing on their phones during their breaks. And she can do this every day. It doesn't matter if it's snowing or if the wind is blowing fiercely or if the sun is beating down hot on the sidewalks. In the mall, there are no slippery patches of ice. The mall is temperature controlled and bright and safe. It is where she spent her ninetieth birthday last week, even though she told no one it was her birthday. She bought herself a cupcake at Dotty's in the food court, but the thing was overly sweet and tasted of artificial vanilla and she'd dumped most of it into the trash.

Ro walks by the bookstore and sees Kevin inside with his dirty-looking dog resting in a dirty-looking round dog bed near the magazine racks. She doesn't think Kevin is allowed to have a pet in the bookstore, but no one seems to care now that the mall is closing. Today the dog is wearing a pink vest, and Ro wonders if Kevin pretends the dog is an emotional support animal in order to keep her in the shop.

"Hello," says Ro, entering the bookstore.

"Hi," says Kevin.

Ro swears she can see him sigh, sees his chest rise and sink, even though no sigh comes out of his mouth. The sad-looking dog does not look up.

"Hello, Frida," says Ro to the dog.

"Fri-*to*," says Kevin.

"Freedo?"

"Frito. Like the chip." Kevin pantomimes putting a chip in his mouth and chewing it.

"Why have I been thinking all this time that the dog is named Frida?" Ro says.

Kevin shrugs. "Maybe you just haven't listened."

Ro bristles. She knows Kevin doesn't like her. She has tried to be kind to Kevin and his family, even though she figured out his children stole the packages delivered to her house, knows Kevin returned them to her doorstep in the dark of night. She saw him out there. She thought the girl twin would be smarter than to steal things she had no use for. But maybe her brother got some idea into her head; maybe he passed along the bad things Kevin told him about Ro. Maybe the children wanted to hurt her and this was the only way they could figure out how to do so.

"Is Freedo your emotional support dog?" Ro says. She knows she's mispronouncing the dog's name, but she wants to irritate Kevin, who always seems so angry with her. She knows nothing will change his mind about her; he will never be able to see beyond what he believes her to be.

"*Frito* is just a regular dog."

"Then why is she outfitted in a vest?"

"She's wearing the vest because she has a skin condition and she bites at it. So the vest keeps her from aggravating her skin," says Kevin.

Ro wants to know why Kevin chose to adopt this ugly little dog with a skin condition. There had to have been cuter dogs with fewer medical conditions at the shelter.

"She seems like a calm dog," Ro says. She considers telling Kevin it was a good thing he did, adopting this unsightly little creature, but she can't bring herself to say it, so instead she adds, "Very calm."

"She is," says Kevin, and his demeanor softens. "She's great with the kids."

Ro nods, unsure of what else to say. The dog's calmness seems to be its only redeeming feature.

"You can pet her if you'd like," Kevin says, and Ro recoils. She stares at the dog's patchy fur, its wet nose, its fluttering eyelids, the creature deep in dreamland.

"I'll let her sleep in peace," Ro says. She looks up at Kevin and notices he's lost some weight. He's still pudgy, but less pudgy than before. She has seen him walking the dog around the neighborhood, and maybe this has done him some good. And he's managed to keep his face shaved for the past few months. Perhaps, most surprisingly, he is wearing a shirt with buttons and a collar. He's not even wearing a costume, as he often does at the bookstore. Maybe once this mall closes, he can get a better job now that he no longer looks like a vagabond. Maybe there's some hope for him after all.

Behind Kevin, Ro sees a large poster taped to the wall with Gwen's face on it. The top of the poster states BOOK PARTY!, and the smaller print says there will be a reading and party for Gwen's forthcoming book of poetry, *Plunging from a Great Height*, next Friday at the bookstore.

Ro points to the poster. "I didn't know Gwen wrote a book," she says. Ro knows Gwen writes poetry but she didn't know about a book. Once, Ro wished to write her own books of poetry, but that was a long time ago, before she decided she was a better reader than writer.

"It's not out yet," says Kevin. "She won a contest and the prize includes publication of her book, and I figured, why not, let's celebrate her at the bookstore. The contest was a big deal."

"Well, that's impressive," says Ro.

"Thanks," says Kevin. "I'm not sure if anyone will come, but I just wanted to do something nice for her. She works really hard, you know, with writing and teaching, and the kids, and who knows what I'll be doing when her book is published. So why not throw an event at the store."

"Will you get in trouble if someone in charge finds out?"

Kevin shrugs. "I think I'd get in trouble if I was trying to sell her book. I'm going to pay for some snacks with my own money, and set up a microphone, and Gwen will read a few poems. There's nothing wrong with that, is there?"

"I suppose not," says Ro. She reaches into her purse and pulls out a receipt from the hair salon. She turns it over and takes a pen out of her bag. She looks up at the poster and then writes down the date and time for Gwen's book party.

"What are you doing?" says Kevin.

The dog wakes up, yawns, and shakes one leg out hard, as if it's gone numb.

"I'm writing down the information for Gwen's party."

"Why?" says Kevin.

"Because I don't want to miss it," says Ro. She is unsure if she wants to attend out of curiosity or if she wants to support Gwen, but her motivation doesn't matter. All that should matter to Kevin is that Ro plans to come. He should be glad to have an audience for his against-the-rules book party. "I'd like to hear Gwen read her poems."

"Really?" says Kevin, looking surprised. "You don't have to. Please don't feel obligated."

It is clear that Kevin doesn't want her to come, but she wants to show up. Ro shakes her head. "I never feel obligated. To anybody. I should go. I'm mall walking. I don't want to let my heart rate slow down too much." And she hefts her purse straps, which have slipped down her arm, back onto her shoulder, pivots in her marshmallow shoes, and speed-walks out of the bookstore.

AT HOME, RO hauls the step stool from the kitchen to her bedroom closet. It is absurd, she knows, hiding things in her house when she's the only person living here, has been the house's only inhabitant for over twenty years. Hiding things made sense when Lawrence was alive, but now, who cares about what she's got shoved away behind boxes of old photographs and tax documents on a high shelf in the closet. It's silly, she knows, but some things feel private. She quickly finds what she's looking for, something she hasn't seen in a decade.

She holds Earl Walker's first book of poetry. On the back, there is a small, black-and-white photograph of Earl, a portrait of how he looked when he and Joan first moved in next door. Ro sits on the step stool and stares at the back cover of the book. Earl looks so young in the photograph, without the deep lines that developed between his nose and mouth, and with a full head of dark hair, before it grayed and receded to just two small strips above his ears. He is wearing glasses with thick frames that look too big for his face. He looks incredibly young. How had this man—and this book—caused such disagreements between Ro and Lawrence?

Ro settles into the armchair near the window. She opens the book and smells the aged pages. She remembers when she first read this book over forty years ago, and she remembers how she felt strange sensations of respect and admiration. She remembers disbelief that her ordinary neighbor, who opened the front door each morning in slippers, pajamas, and a blue robe to retrieve the newspaper, and who mowed his lawn every Sunday morning wearing drab brown sweatpants, could write such beautiful words. Many of the poems were about nature and gardens and there were fourteen poems—Ro had counted—about different types of flowers, and Ro was astounded by Earl's knowledge of the natural world.

Lawrence brought the book home after attending a reading given by Earl and a Black woman poet at a bar in downtown Albany. Lawrence told her he had to stay late at work because someone was coming to service the lights in his illuminated Snellen chart. She discovered his lie the next day when Joan leaned over the rosebushes separating their properties and said she and Earl were so grateful to Lawrence for coming to the reading and buying a copy of Earl's book. Ro nodded politely but felt a hot fury coursing through her body. Why was Lawrence so insistent on befriending the Walkers? What was Lawrence trying to prove? What would the other neighbors think if they knew Lawrence was going out of his way to spend time with them? It was one thing to be neighbors—that was circumstance, which could not be avoided—but all they had to do was coexist, not become the welcoming committee.

"I didn't think you'd want to go," said Lawrence, after Ro confronted him about it. He spread peanut butter on a piece of toast, carefully covering every inch of the bread, and his slow fastidiousness only made Ro's irritation swell. Ro had cooked Chicken à la King for dinner, one of Lawrence's favorites, but the pot was hidden in the oven because she was furious at his betrayal.

"Well, I *wouldn't* want to go. And are you now some beatnik who goes to poetry readings?"

"I'd like to think I'm a good neighbor," Lawrence said, taking a large, noisy bite of his toast. "And I figured you'd try to stop me, so it seemed easier to say nothing."

"You didn't *say nothing*," said Ro. "You lied. If you can lie about this, what else might you lie about?" It was an unfair thing to say because Ro knew Lawrence was trustworthy, and if he were to have any fault it was that he was overly kind, but she was angry and wanted to hurt him. "Who knows, maybe you have a woman on the side, and those other nights you say you're at work late, you're really with her."

Lawrence laughed, took another bite of his toast. "If that's what you want to believe, then go ahead."

"And what's this about buying a book?"

"I bought his book of poems."

"And when was the last time you read a book of poetry?" said Ro. "Why do you insist on wasting money?" If anyone was a reader in their house, it was Ro. She'd been an English major at Vassar, had once been serious about writing poetry, but she had difficulty with meter and rhyme, struggled to come up with the right words to describe the images she could see in her mind. She could identify greatness in the work of others, but she could not achieve it herself, so she stopped writing her senior year of college. Lawrence had been a biology major at Cornell, and Ro had never known him to read anything that wasn't a textbook, instruction manual, or newspaper.

Lawrence shrugged, crumpled the napkin his toast had rested on, and dropped his knife into the sink, where it clanged. "He's a great poet. You should have heard him read, Ro. It's something to see someone so passionate about what they do."

"You're passionate about ophthalmology."

Lawrence shrugged. "It's a good profession but hardly a passion."

Ro knew Lawrence's true passions were his model trains and the town he built surrounding them. The trains and the ever-growing landscape around the tracks were taking over the basement. In the early years of their marriage, when Ro complained about the money he spent on them, Lawrence said one day they'd have a child—maybe a son—and he would feel awful if he got rid of the trains before their child could play with them.

"Well," said Ro, "you might as well show me the book."

Lawrence smiled. "I didn't know you liked poetry."

"You don't know a lot of things about me." Lawrence and Ro met after she'd graduated from college, after Ro was done with poetry. She thought it unimportant to mention it to Lawrence. What would she even say? That this was something she'd once done, but then she'd given up because she was not good enough?

Lawrence smiled again, and said, "You're a woman of great mystery. For instance, the mystery of where you've socked away the dinner you've cooked. It smells good in here."

Ro ignored him and waited quietly while Lawrence fetched the slim volume of poetry. There was a photograph of a large, manicured garden outside a stone manor on the cover, and Lawrence explained Earl had taken the photograph when he'd gone to England to research his dissertation. "Maybe we should go to England one day," he said. "Earl says the gardens are magnificent."

"One day," said Ro, taking the book of poetry into her hands. "One day we'll do everything we've always talked about doing. One day a million years away."

THAT NIGHT, AFTER Lawrence fell asleep, Ro went downstairs, sat in the olive-green armchair, turned on a lamp, and opened Earl's book. On the title page, Earl had written, "For Lawrence, neighbor and friend. With gratitude for your support and encouragement, Earl Walker." Irritated by Earl's use of the word "friend," Ro forced herself to turn the page and read the first poem. And then, after that first poem, she kept reading until the end. The book was breathtaking, and for a moment Ro deeply regretted not hearing Earl read his poetry aloud. He was able to find such precise words to describe flowers and birds and the sky and ponds and streams, and Ro could see the imagery of each poem vividly in her mind. Years later, she found Earl's other books of poems at the library and hid in the stacks reading them, not wanting to check them out and have them on her library record, not wanting her name written in pencil on the borrowing cards, but she'd never liked any of the subsequent books as much as she'd loved the first. The later poems were more political, dealing with race relations in America, and Ro found these lacking the beauty of Earl's earlier work.

As the sun began to rise and the birds in the backyard commenced their wild early-morning chirping, Ro closed the book and placed it on the table next to her chair. She took a deep breath because she felt dizzy, overcome. What was she to do with this admiration? With this respect? With this jealousy about Earl managing to capture the world in a way that felt beautiful and true, in a way she never could. She couldn't tell Lawrence how much she'd loved the poems, and she certainly couldn't tell Earl or Joan. It was a secret—one that felt weighty—she had to bear herself.

It became difficult, after that night with Earl's book, to look at him when they passed on the sidewalk during their evening walks. She felt her heart pound in her chest, the way it might if she were to encounter a movie star. How had this thin man with the oversize glasses and battered leather briefcase written such a thing of beauty? Did he write in the house right next to hers? Had he ever looked out his window, onto her garden, and found inspiration? If Earl had been someone else—someone different—she could have asked him questions, could have invited him and his wife over for dinner and a few bottles of wine, could have asked about being a writer and what it felt like to write something so sublime. But of course she could do none of these things. When she passed him on the sidewalk, she merely said "Good evening," or "Nice weather tonight," and moved along.

Many years later, when Lawrence was sick in the hospital, Earl came to visit, bringing Lawrence books of crossword puzzles, sneaking in chocolate-glazed doughnuts and bottles of Dr Pepper, both Lawrence's favorites. Earl visited every Monday and Wednesday after his afternoon class, and each time he brought something Lawrence loved, and Ro wondered how Earl had come to know her husband so well. A week before Lawrence died, Ro asked if Earl had just been lucky with the gifts he'd brought—the doughnuts and soda and caramels and slices of cheesecake from the Sparrow Street Bakery and crossword books and magazines about model trains and golf and sailing (an interest of Lawrence's, although he'd never owned a boat)—and Lawrence said, "We're friends."

"No, neighbors," Ro said, bending a plastic straw so Lawrence could take a sip from a large plastic mug of ice water. Ro thought then of the inscription Earl wrote all those years ago, calling Lawrence a neighbor and friend. Ro always thought Earl was only being polite, so he wrote something kind and untrue.

"Friends," said Lawrence, taking a slow, pained sip. "We had lunch together every Wednesday for twenty-five years. At the diner near work." He lowered his head back onto the pillow, coughed a phlegmy cough, and closed his eyes.

Ro sat quietly, stunned. How had she not known?

But of course it was possible to keep secrets from the person you lived with, the person with whom you shared a bed every night. Ro kept a secret from Lawrence for much of their marriage. It is a secret, she is certain, she'll take to the grave.

It was Lawrence who wanted children, who felt a child would complete their family. Ro was less certain. It was, of course, what everyone expected, and all the married couples on their street back then had children. If you didn't, people thought something was wrong, and Ro certainly didn't want people talking about them behind their backs. But Ro didn't have the same fantasies many other women did about raising little girls, tying ribbons in their hair, teaching them to bake cookies, and planning birthday parties. She didn't look at things—like Lawrence's train set—and think about how a child might play with it. She wasn't in a constant state of preparation for a baby to enter their lives, but she always assumed she would have to, within a few years, bear a child. After college, she found a job in Albany as a copy editor for a company producing travel guides, and she loved that work, loved the precision of it, loved spending her days with words, even though by then she was no longer writing anything herself. She liked flipping through the travel guides and imagining herself flying all over the globe, meeting new people, seeing new places, even though she'd never left the country. Her job felt neat and useful and productive, and she didn't want to give up working to care for a child, who would likely be messy and unruly, who wouldn't come with the tidy rules of grammar and punctuation.

After two years of marriage, Lawrence said it might be time to add a child to their family. They made love often, but one year and then two and three passed and by that point having a child seemed less a project of passion than a failed biological experiment. Maybe it was God's will. Maybe God knew she'd be a lackluster mother and prevented sperm from fertilizing egg. Maybe it was for the best.

Six years into their marriage, Lawrence's career was thriving, and he said in a few years Dr. Klein planned to retire and Lawrence could take over the entire practice. Lawrence told her she no longer had to work, but it would be fine if she wanted to, until their first child was born. Ro knew Lawrence thought he was being kind and generous, but she also knew she would rather work than change diapers or breastfeed a baby or boil and puree vegetables to make baby food. But these weren't feelings she could share. People—Lawrence especially—would have found these statements monstrous and wonder how her wiring had gone so wrong as to not have the maternal urges expected of women.

When Lawrence was thirty-four and Ro thirty-three, he insisted on going to doctors. "We don't have all the time in the world," Lawrence said. Ro felt a sense of relief when it turned out they both had fertility issues. This way no one was at fault, and they could settle into a life of just the two of them, and if people wanted to talk about them behind their backs, then so be it.

But Lawrence decided the next step was adoption. "It's perfect," said Lawrence. "This way we can adopt a boy. I'd have someone to share my train set with. You would be okay with a little boy, wouldn't you?"

Ro shrugged, remained noncommittal. Lawrence was patient, brought up the idea every few months, then dropped the subject when Ro refused to engage. She hoped she wouldn't have to tell Lawrence to give up, to look for other ways to find fulfillment. She wanted him to be able to read her mind.

But then, behind her back, Lawrence made an appointment at a local adoption agency. He came home with his eyes bright, a photograph in his briefcase. "Look," Lawrence said, holding out a photo of dozens of baby girls in cribs in a Chinese orphanage.

"Why?" said Ro, feeling a tightness in her chest. "Why do I need to see this photo?"

"We could adopt one of these girls," Lawrence said. "Diane, the social worker at the agency, said there's a need for homes for these girls, and she said that just this year Congress passed legislation allowing for intercountry adoption."

"Intercountry adoption," Ro said. "That sounds awfully complicated."

Lawrence was silent, and when Ro looked at his face, she understood. "You already have your heart set on one of these girls, don't you?"

Lawrence nodded. "She's not in this picture, but there's a file on her. If you come with me to the agency, we can begin the screening process. Please, would you come? Diane told me that at thirty-four I'm already considered old for being a first-time parent, and I don't want to wait any longer."

It was, in this moment, impossible to say no. Ro would go with Lawrence to the adoption agency, and maybe the social worker would deem them unacceptable. She would be firm in saying she was not planning to give up working. She would bring up their ages, say that by the time the child was ready to leave home for college, they would be halfway through their fifties. She would figure out some way to stop the adoption from happening.

A FEW DAYS later she found herself at the adoption agency with Lawrence, sitting across a desk from the social worker, Diane.

"I wish we could take them all," said Lawrence, sliding the photograph of the babies in cribs across the desk.

"And run an orphanage out of our own home?" Ro snapped. Diane looked startled, and Ro felt her face warm. She wanted to come across as an unsuitable parent, not as a cruel person.

"Let me get you the file on Mei Li," said Diane. "I'll show you her photo, Mrs. Goodson. We have some notes from the orphanage. They say that Mei Li translates to 'beautiful.' Isn't that lovely?"

"Wouldn't it be nice to have a little girl?" said Lawrence, and Ro heard a dreamy quality to his voice, and she knew he was imagining carrying Mei Li to the basement, placing a miniature blue-and-white-striped conductor's hat over her straight black hair, and showing her how to turn on the train set, teaching her how to pour mineral oil into the smokestack of the engine, showing her how to turn on the switch that lit up the entire village. It was clear that it wasn't necessary anymore for Lawrence to have a boy to play trains with.

"We'll need to think about it, of course," said Ro as Diane ran her fingers over file folders in an open cabinet drawer.

"Yes, of course," said Diane. "There are many steps—interviews, paperwork, home visits. I can go through the entire process if you'd like."

"We'll be back," said Ro, standing. "Lawrence and I will talk more about this at home first."

"But the photo," said Diane. "Don't you want to see Mei Li?" She held up a photograph, but Ro refused to look.

"Next time," said Ro.

And because Ro was already up, had already shrugged her jacket on and lifted her purse onto her shoulder, Lawrence stood up, shook Diane's hand, and followed his wife out the door.

LAWRENCE TOLD Ro she'd embarrassed him, had maybe ruined their chances of adopting Mei Li. "Why do you even like the girl so much?" Ro asked, and Lawrence said there was something intelligent and gentle about her eyes. He said he was good at reading people by looking into their eyes, and he could tell Mei Li was smart and creative and kind. He said they could give the girl a good life. "Sometimes you just get a feeling about things." He was always going on about feelings, intuitions, dreams, and Ro found this strange coming from a man trained in science.

"Fine," Ro said because she knew arguing about this, about the one thing Lawrence had ever pushed for, might ruin their marriage, and if there was one thing in the world Ro could not be without, it was Lawrence. "But I still don't understand how you can tell so much from just one photograph."

So they marched through the adoption process because it was what Lawrence wanted, was all he could talk about. Ro subjected herself to interviews where she pretended to be happy and enthusiastic about the idea of bringing a child from across the world to New York. She showed her home to social workers to prove they would have the space for a child to live comfortably. Ro pretended and pretended and pretended. Inside, she thought of all that would be lost once this child entered their home. Already, Lawrence was too devoted to his work, and with the combination of taking over the practice and raising a child, there would be so little time left over. Ro's life would change completely, dedicated to this little girl from morning to night.

One Saturday, Lawrence painted the walls of the home office pink. He bought a stuffed elephant wearing a gingham dress from a toy store downtown. He bought a cookbook with Chinese recipes. Ro found the cookbook on the shelf next to her *New York Times Cook Book*, and she left it there, untouched, thinking Lawrence could cook the dishes himself. Lawrence bought a set of records to teach him to speak Mandarin, and each night he spent twenty minutes repeating after the people on them, filling the living room with odd, unfamiliar sounds. Through all of this, Ro felt herself disappear. Lawrence talked only of the future, of their life with their little girl. It was as if the life they built together wasn't enough. But it was enough for Ro. It was all she wanted.

One day, Ro called the adoption agency, pretended to be someone named Lillian, and asked about white children. Maybe it would be better to adopt a white child, then Lawrence wouldn't have to learn a new language or learn to cook different food. Surely, there were unwanted babies in America. The woman who answered the phone—who, thankfully, was not Diane, who might have recognized Ro's voice—seemed irritated by the question and explained that while there certainly were white children up for adoption, the wait was longer. Currently, there were more Chinese babies than there were good homes for them. However, if she was interested in a disabled white baby or child, the list to adopt was much shorter. "I am not interested in a disabled child," said Ro, before hanging up the phone.

After the phone call, Ro stormed outside and grabbed a pair of pruning shears from the garage. The garden always calmed her, and when she was angry, the steady work of pruning helped slow her heartbeat. She pruned her rosebushes and stewed. Having no child at all was preferable to adopting a child from China, one who Ro did not think she could ever come to fully understand. And it wouldn't be good for the child either to be ripped away from her homeland, to have to deal with people who didn't understand where she came from, to have to listen to people who spoke a strange and foreign language.

But the ball had been set rolling, and Lawrence was eagerly awaiting the arrival of Mei Li in three months, and it seemed there was nothing Ro could do stop it.

As she pruned and cut away more than she knew was healthy for the plants, Ro came up with a plan. It made her uneasy and it felt immoral, but it was the only thing she could think to do.

SIX WEEKS BEFORE Mei Li would be flown to America with a caretaker and several other soon-to-be-adopted girls from the same orphanage, Lawrence went to Cleveland for a conference. One afternoon while Lawrence was out of town, Ro left work early and drove herself across town to the adoption agency. She asked to see Diane. She had to sit in the waiting area for nearly two hours because Diane was with other prospective parents, and Ro felt sweat drench her dress from the anxiety of what she was about to do. She planned to tell

Diane Lawrence was ill—terminally ill—and the adoption could not go forward. She would deal with all the paperwork, and she would tell Diane not to call their house to speak to Lawrence.

Diane came into the waiting room and invited Ro into her office.

Ro slumped into a seat. She felt tired and hot and angry, and she did not need to act to make her face look believably distressed as she prepared to lie about Lawrence's health.

"Did you hear already?" asked Diane. Her eyes were red and puffy, as if she'd been crying.

"Hear what?"

"About Mei Li. I was going to call you this afternoon but it's been so busy and, well, it's not easy to say this. Did someone from the agency already call you?"

"I've heard nothing."

"But then why are you here?"

Ro would not answer until Diane revealed what she had to say. "What do you need to tell me?"

"Oh, Mrs. Goodson, I'm so sorry."

"Sorry about what?" said Ro. She watched tears fall from Diane's eyes. Ro looked hard at her, really looked at her for the first time, and saw how young she was. She saw the heavy application of mascara on her eyelashes, the cheap blue polyester dress, the flipped bob, an obvious imitation of Jackie Kennedy's hair. All of this now seemed like a costume to make her look older, more respectable. How old was she? Twenty-three or twenty-four? She was nearly a child herself.

"Mei Li died yesterday, Mrs. Goodson."

Ro felt a tug in her heart, an unexpected and profound sadness. But wasn't this the solution to her problem? She wouldn't even have to tell a lie. And yet something had suddenly been lost in Ro's and Lawrence's lives. The adoption of Mei Li would have sent them down a particular path, and that path was one they could no longer travel. "What happened?" Ro said.

"They said it was an infection. It spread quickly and was too much for her small body to handle. Oh, Mrs. Goodson, I'm so sorry." Diane put her head in her hands and wept, her body heaving.

"Lawrence can never know," Ro said.

Diane looked up with wet eyes, and Ro saw her tears darken the blotter on the desk. "What do you mean?"

"I'll tell him she was adopted by a distant relative. I think it would be too much for Lawrence to bear if he knew she died."

Diane nodded. "I won't tell him."

"I'm sorry about Mei Li," Ro said. "It's a terrible thing."

"It is."

"I should go," Ro said, and Diane got up from behind the desk.

"But why did you come?"

What could she say? She could not tell Diane the truth. "I wanted to see the photo. Of Mei Li."

"You waited all those hours just to see the photo?"

Ro nodded. "I never saw it the first time. I'm sorry. I realized that I should see Mei Li before she arrived in our house." She didn't want to see the photo now; seeing it would just make everything feel more awful, but what else could she do? What other reason would she have for being here? Diane stood up, opened the filing cabinet, and took out the photo of the tiny girl.

"I don't think anyone would mind if you kept it," Diane said, holding it out to Ro.

Ro took the photo and stared at it for a moment and felt her eyes grow hot. She willed herself not to cry; she was not someone who cried in public. But looking at the photo, she could see what Lawrence talked about, the intelligence and warmth in the baby's eyes. "You can put it back in the file," she said. "It would be difficult for Lawrence to look at it now."

Diane nodded, but kept the photo on her desk. "I'll walk you out," Diane said. She could hardly get the words out.

Tears had darkened the front of Diane's dress. "Come here," Ro said, and Diane seemed to fall into her arms, and Ro hugged her tightly and it felt odd to be offering a near stranger comfort. She felt Diane's tears, hot and wet on her shoulder, but she did not let go until Diane did.

"I know you and Mr. Goodson would have been great parents." Diane sniffled as she walked to the door.

Would they have been? Ro knew Lawrence would have been a wonderful father, but did she have the capacity to be a good mother? Well, perhaps if she could hug a young woman she barely knew, offer her some comfort Ro was not aware she was capable of offering, maybe she could comfort her own child, even if that child was not her biological daughter, even if that child looked nothing like her.

"I suspect we'll be back," Ro said, walking toward the door. She surprised herself by wanting to come back, wanting to find another child that would delight Lawrence as much as Mei Li had, and she realized that this was what she wanted too. "Once this all settles down, we'll try again."

AFTER SHE LEFT the adoption agency, Ro walked to the travel agency down the street and booked a trip to England. They would depart in two weeks. A trip would cheer Lawrence up, and away from their everyday concerns they could regather and figure out their next step. "My husband and I would like to see gardens," said Ro to the travel agent, who was as young and wide-eyed as Diane, and the girl clapped her hands in delight and suggested the gardens at Sissinghurst Castle and Hidcote Manor.

When Lawrence returned from his conference, Ro told him she'd spoken to Diane and that a distant relative of Mei Li's had come to adopt her. It was the gentlest lie she could come up with.

"I'm so sorry, Lawrence," Ro said.

"Why didn't you call me in Cleveland?" Lawrence asked.

"What could you have done?" said Ro. "Family takes precedence over strangers from America."

Lawrence conceded that there was nothing he could have done.

"But there are other girls," Ro said. "We could think about another girl. Or what about a boy? There are children out there who need homes."

"This feeling," Lawrence said, holding a hand up to his chest. "I think I need some time."

"You know, Diane said we'd make good parents," Ro said.

Lawrence looked thoughtful for a moment, then said, "Maybe it's a sign. Maybe it's just not to be."

"I don't believe in signs," Ro said. But maybe this *was* a sign, a big statement from the universe. She wondered if she'd somehow wished this into being by not wanting to be a mother, not wanting to adopt a Chinese baby, not wanting to share Lawrence with a child. Maybe, somehow, all of her awful thoughts had caused Mei Li's death, and she was to blame for this terrible thing.

A FEW WEEKS later, they flew to London and walked the city streets, explored museums, strolled through majestic gardens, discussing whether it would be possible to create topiary birds on their property back home. Ro felt happy to be spending so much time with Lawrence while simultaneously she was filled with a heavy sadness about keeping Mei Li's death a secret. But if thinking she'd been adopted by a relative caused Lawrence such grief, what would happen if he knew the truth? Ro felt certain she made the right decision. Throughout the trip, Ro tried to bring up the possibility of adoption, and Lawrence quickly ended each conversation, saying he wasn't ready to talk about it.

A month after their trip, Lawrence spent an afternoon painting over the pink walls of the nursery, hauling his desk and typewriter back into the room after the eggshell-white paint dried. Ro knew they would not pursue adoption again. This was what she wanted all along, so then why did everything feel so dreadful?

RO HAS SPENT the years since Lawrence's death secretly compensating for her behavior around the adoption. Or at least trying to compensate. The lingering, simmering guilt is why she tries to be nice to Jackson Huang, the son of her hair stylist. The *Chinese* son of her hair stylist. Jackson is a good boy, quiet and bookish, always reading, the type of boy Lawrence would have loved to have as a son. Ro has taken to bringing him presents—all things that used to belong to Lawrence—when she gets her hair styled. She's given him Lawrence's Pentax camera, a model ship, the cookbook of Chinese recipes Lawrence bought in preparation for Mei Li's arrival, Lawrence's Waterman fountain pen, an Omega watch, and a box of silk pocket squares, which, it turned out, delighted the boy, who said he could use them in some sort of magic act. Tina keeps insisting Ro should not give so many gifts to Jackson, but Ro tells her she would donate them to Goodwill if Jackson didn't take them.

Ro likes Jackson a great deal; he is one of the few children in the world who does not irritate her. She makes her appointments for the afternoons since he's only there after school. But now the mall is closing, and when Ro asks Tina if she'll move to another salon, Tina is noncommittal, says maybe this is an opportunity for her to pursue something else. What Ro wants to say: she wishes she could see Tina and Jackson outside of the salon. She can't say this sort of thing, though, to someone who might only be kind to her because she pays for her services. But the idea of never seeing Jackson or Tina again causes Ro a great deal of distress.

Ro wishes she was the type of person people wanted to be around, someone others will seek out even after the mall is closed. She has a plan now, something she's certain will at least make Kevin's feelings soften toward her. Kevin is her neighbor; he does not have to go out of his way to see her, and wouldn't it be nice if her neighbor did not actively despise her? She will be a patron of the arts. She has withdrawn ten crisp one-hundred-dollar bills from the bank. Tonight, she is going to Gwen's party at the bookstore, and she's going to give Kevin that $1,000 and tell him it's an investment in Gwen's career as a writer. She'll tell him part of the money is for a copy of Gwen's book, which she hopes he'll deliver to her house as soon as it's published, but to consider the rest a gift, a way for Gwen to work less and spend more time writing.

Ro will tell no one about this act of generosity—who is there to tell anyway?—but she wishes Lawrence were here to see she's someone different now. And she will do one other thing at the reading: she will tell Gwen how much she loved her father's first book of poetry. She will say it out loud, and after all these years she'll at last be unburdened of one secret. She has already placed Earl's book on top of the short bookshelf in her living room. She plans to begin a new ritual and read a poem from it each morning as a way to start her day.

Ro surveys her closet. What does one wear to a book party? She knows one thing for certain: she will not wear her marshmallow shoes. It is a party, so she'll wear a dress. Even though there's still a chill in the air, she won't bring a jacket. She doesn't want to lug it around all night, and, besides, she'll only be outdoors for the walk to the car from her house and then from her car to the mall. She takes a dark green dress patterned with magenta and yellow flowers off a hanger. She bought the dress forty years ago, but the fabric is good, the construction sound, and it has not fallen apart. She smiles, remembering how she thought she was too old to wear such a bold pattern when she bought it, and thinks of Lawrence telling her not to talk that way about herself. She remembers Lawrence saying she looked beautiful in the dress, even as she insisted she looked silly, that the dress was too bright.

Ro emerges from her closet with the dress, a pair of black stockings, black shoes with one-inch heels. She slips the dress on and examines herself in the mirror. She is angry about the small hump in her back, but there's nothing she can do about it. She tries to convince herself she doesn't look ludicrous in the flowered dress. She tells herself that once you reach a certain age, things reset, and you can get away with wearing anything, just like a child.

She walks downstairs, bringing the envelope of bills from the bank. She is not used to going out in the evenings; it feels strange and delightful. And a book party! She has never been to such a thing. Ro picks up her purse and is ready to go, even though there are still two hours before the party starts. Well, she can go to the mall early and get some walking in, even if she's not wearing her marshmallow shoes.

AFTER THREE LAPS around the mall, Ro is thirsty and needs to sit down. She'll buy something in the food court, not hot tea this time, something cold. She'll sip it slowly and watch the people come and go—the teenagers, the parents and children, the shoppers loaded with bags—until it is time for the party.

As she approaches the food court, Ro feels something she hasn't felt in a long time: anticipation. She reaches into her purse, runs her hand over the envelope of hundred-dollar bills. She imagines Kevin's face after she hands it to him, tells him what it's for. She wonders if this gesture will be enough for him to forgive all the ways he believes she's wronged him. She is eager to hear Gwen's poems and feels certain they will be as beautiful as her father's. Ro doesn't know how she knows this, but she does. She's known Gwen her entire life, and she was a quiet, smart, perceptive little girl. Besides Jackson, Gwen is one of the only children that didn't bother her a bit. Imagine that. The two children she likes best in the whole world are a Black child and a Chinese one. What would Lawrence think about that?

Ro sees a bubbling tank of lemonade with a few halved lemons floating on top and decides a cold cup will be the perfect thing to quench her thirst. A beautiful girl wearing a chicken outfit waits as Ro makes her way to the counter. She wonders how much the girl detests wearing the chicken costume, but then she thinks maybe she doesn't. Maybe she knows she's pretty enough that even the costume won't detract from her good looks.

"I *love* your dress," says the girl as Ro nears the counter.

Ro is taken aback; she had not expected any compliments tonight. "Can you believe I bought it forty years ago?"

"It's super retro in a good way," says the girl. "You're rocking it."

Ro doesn't know exactly what this all means, but she can tell from the tone of the girl's voice that it's something positive, so she thanks her, then orders a lemonade. She wants to ask the girl what ethnicity she is—her hair is dark and wavy and her skin is tan—but Ro has learned that one is not to ask that question, and so she doesn't. She's just curious, and she finds people who aren't clearly one thing or another to be interesting, like a puzzle to solve.

"I'm going to a book party," Ro says, and she's not sure why she tells the girl this. "I know the poet who wrote the book."

"That's very cool," says the girl, as she hands Ro her lemonade and her change. Ro tilts her hand to let the change—two dollars and forty-seven cents—fall into a tip container. She has never placed money in a tip jar before and pauses to listen to the sound of coins falling into the plastic container.

"Thanks!" says the girl, and Ro nods. As Ro walks away, she hears the girl say, "Enjoy your book party!"

Ro will sit at the small round table near Panda Wok, where she usually drinks the dull-tasting tea she buys for eighty cents. It is a good spot because you can see almost all of the food court and also out into the mall, and you can watch so many people going about their lives. As Ro turns her back to Chickety Chix to head toward her table, something catches her eye. There is a boy, and he is so pale it seems as if sunlight has never touched his skin. His chin-length hair is greasy and lank and every piece of his clothing, from his denim jacket down to his sneakers, is gray. He is charging into the food court from the direction of Sunshine Clips and at first Ro thinks he is running toward her, but she follows his gaze and thinks he is heading toward the girl who sold her lemonade. Then she sees him raise an arm and in his hand Ro sees a gun, black and solid, and she knows what is about to happen and she thinks she must stop it but how can one stop something as fast as a bullet? And then, before Ro can figure out what to do, what she *should* do, she steps to her right—her body reacting before her mind can sort anything out—and there is a blast, a sharp bang, and the cup of lemonade drops from her hand, the plastic lid coming off, the ice cubes clattering to the floor, the liquid drenching her dress, the smell of freshly squeezed lemons filling the air.

Soon after Ro and Lawrence were married, they moved to California, where they lived for a year while Lawrence completed an internship. Ro would take this one year off from working and spend time caring for their home. They rented a small, run-down house, and the landlord told them if they were at all handy, they should feel free to make any modifications they wanted. "Paint the walls whatever color pleases you. Plant a garden," the landlord said, and Ro planted lilacs and poppies and morning glories and yarrow outside that house, her first garden.

That year was glorious, how happy Lawrence and Ro were, how adult they felt with a whole house to themselves. It was the first time Lawrence lived without roommates, the first place—besides college—Ro lived without her parents. She bought a sewing machine and learned to make curtains and tablecloths and napkins and even dresses for herself and shirts for Lawrence. She sewed colorful curtains for every room in the house. Her favorite time of day was late morning on breezy, sunny days, when she could open all the windows and watch the curtains she'd made billow.

A month before they were set to return to New York, Ro saw a small lemon tree for sale at a nursery where she purchased fertilizer for her garden. She bought the tree and, while Lawrence was at work, she planted it near the house so that one day, when it grew big and produced lemons, anyone lying in bed upstairs could look out their window and see bright bulbs of yellow dotting their view. The woman at the nursery said it would take five years for the tree to bear fruit. By that point Lawrence and Ro would be long gone.

In bed that night, Ro talked to Lawrence about the tree. She said one day there'd be a tall lemon tree with more fruit than a family would know what to do with. On windy nights, she hoped, the scent of lemons might drift into the house through an open window. "Whoever lives here could reach right out their window and pluck a lemon off the tree," said Ro. "Can you imagine that? Wouldn't that be nice?"

"*You're* nice," said Lawrence, kissing Ro on the temple. "What a nice thing to do, to plant a tree for the people who come after."

"Maybe I can plant one in New York," said Ro.

Lawrence laughed. "I'm not sure if lemon trees do so well in upstate New York, but you can try."

"I want to plant a garden in New York. When we buy our house. I want to plant all sorts of flowers," Ro said.

Lawrence nodded. "*Our* house," he repeated. "That sounds nice too, doesn't it?"

"It all sounds nice," said Ro.

It was a warm night, and they left the bedroom window open halfway. The orange curtains with the daisy print blew in the light breeze. Ro saw the moon—bright and nearly full—high in the dark sky. She nestled her body against her husband, closed her eyes, and felt such certainty that good things lay ahead.

April

How to Go On

Two weeks have passed, yet Tina keeps looking into the mall, expecting to see Ro. Out of the corner of her eye, Tina has seen other women with white hair walking by, but when she turns to look, it's never Ro. Of course it can never be Ro again.

There were only two clients in the morning and no one scheduled for the afternoon, but Tina wants to keep busy, keep moving, so she cleans and organizes the salon. She gathers small accumulations of dust and stray hairs from behind objects at each station on the blue puff of a Swiffer duster. She looks to the floor and sees a strand of white hair stuck beneath her chair and thinks of all the haircuts she's given Ro over the years. Did this hair belong to her? And if it did, what should she do about it? Pluck it out from the spot it's wedged itself into? Save it in a plastic bag? Tina is usually not subject to sentimentality, but Ro's death has left her at a loss about how to behave, how to keep going on.

Ro's absence fills the salon, expands into an always-present cloud. Maybe Tina has been so deeply affected because of how Ro died, the violence of it, the fact that it happened inside the mall. Maybe if she'd just slipped away in bed one night, Tina would feel differently. Were they friends? Can you be friends with someone who pays you to perform a service? Should she have asked Ro more about her life? Maybe their relationship was what Ro needed; Tina was someone Ro could see each week, a part of her routine. If Tina asked questions, if she tried to pry and learn more about Ro's life, Ro likely would have shut down, perhaps even stopped coming. Tina sprays Windex on the mirror, polishes it until there are no fingerprints, scrubs the paper towel hard against the glass so loud squeaks fill the empty space.

Now there's talk of fast-tracking the closure of the mall. There was already the sense of decay, and now the mall is the site of a murder. Who would want to come here and do those ordinary things—eat a soft pretzel, shop for khakis, buy new running shoes—one does in a mall? Forget about the movie theater, the only place that was still doing reasonable business; now movie theaters are for sitting ducks. No one wants to stew in dark uncertainty, unsure of what danger lurks nearby. Tina doesn't even want to come back to the mall, even though she has to. Or does she? What would happen if she just stopped coming? Who would care? The salon's manager, Belinda, has already retired to Florida. Ro might have been the only person to care if Tina stopped coming to work. And now she's gone, her sheet-covered body wheeled away as Tina—and everyone else at the mall—watched in disbelief.

"Hi, Tina."

Tina sees Maria and ArtyAnnieAmazing, YouTube artist extraordinaire, standing at the entrance of the salon. Maybe a few weeks ago she would have been stunned about the coincidence of Annie appearing here, but now strange, incomprehensible events seem part of everyday life at the mall.

Today, Maria is wearing regular clothing—faded jeans and a blue UCLA sweatshirt—not her chicken costume. Tina opens her arms and envelops Maria in a tight hug. They aren't close—they haven't spent much time together—but they've been through something together now. According to the news, the shooter was a boy from Maria's high school, and there is speculation he was angry with someone from his school who worked at the mall. His bullet might have been intended for Maria. No one has said her name on the news, maybe it's been kept silent for legal reasons, but Tina knows there were suspicions of unrequited love, and the bullet was aimed toward Chickety Chix, where Maria was working that night. There were some comments online, and Tina is certain Maria knows that people are whispering about the shooter's obsession with her.

Maria leans into Tina hard, and Tina thinks if she lets go, Maria will fall to the floor. "I'm so sorry about everything," Tina says. She has not seen Maria at the mall since the shooting.

Tina lets go gently, and Maria takes a step backward. "I quit my job," she says. "I didn't want to come back here."

"I completely understand," says Tina. But why is Maria back now? And why has she brought Annie with her?

"This is Annie," says Maria. "We go to school together." Annie extends a hand, and Tina shakes it. She can't help but think about all the artwork this hand has created and hopes for some transfer of talent and skill, like osmosis, through their handshake. It's strange that Tina knows so much about this girl but must pretend this is the first time she's encountered her. "We came to talk to you," says Maria.

"Me?" says Tina. What could she possibly offer these two?

"We're working on our senior projects," says Annie. "And I thought I'd do mine about Rosalie Goodson."

"What kind of project?" says Tina. She bristles because she is certain Annie did not know Ro. Annie seems like an opportunist, a vulture swooping down to pick at someone else's tragedy and misfortune for her own gain.

Annie says, "A tribute. I was thinking of working on something mural-sized and then, who knows, maybe we can get the city to approve painting the mural about Rosalie Goodson's life somewhere."

Tina is annoyed by the way Annie keeps saying Ro's full name, as if she's someone famous, someone like Walt Disney, George Washington, or Helen Keller, someone always referred to by both first and last name.

Maria says, "Annie didn't know her, but she asked me since, well, you know, I was around when stuff happened. And I didn't really talk to Mrs. Goodson except the night it happened. But I know she was always in your salon, so I figured you would be a good person to start with."

Tina wants to say she barely knew Ro either, even after all these years. She looked for an obituary in the paper and online, but couldn't find one. She has no idea what became of Ro's body, whether she's buried somewhere. She hopes there was a relative—no matter how distant—who ensured Ro was treated with respect at the end.

"Are you part of this tribute?" Tina asks Maria.

Maria shakes her head. "I haven't figured out what I'm doing for my senior project yet. And anyway, I didn't really know Mrs. Goodson."

"Neither did she," Tina can't help but say, while pointing to Annie.

"I don't think an artist necessarily has to be well acquainted with her subject. If you can find out enough about the subject, you can capture her essence," Annie says. "I mean, do you think Kehinde Wiley and Amy Sherald knew Barack and Michelle before painting their official portraits?"

Tina has nothing to say to that ridiculousness, irritated that Annie insists on calling Ro by her full name while acting as if the Obamas are her close personal friends she can refer to by their first names only, so she turns to Maria and says, "Are you thinking of doing something with acting for your project?"

"No, I don't think so," says Maria, shaking her head. "I don't feel like performing right now."

Tina can understand why Maria wouldn't want to be onstage in front of people thinking about how the boy who shot Ro was maybe in love with her, how she might have, just by existing, been part of this murder.

"Can I interview you now?" says Annie. "I brought a notebook. And I have a sketchbook too, in case there's anything related to Rosalie Goodson I can draw." She sits down in a stylist's chair and opens her notebook, holds her pen above a blank page, making herself at home.

Tina thinks of telling Annie to talk to Kevin at the bookstore since he was Ro's neighbor. But, for now, she'll spare Kevin the interrogation. "I've got a few minutes," says Tina.

"The more specific you can get, the better. And if you know anything unusual or interesting about her life, that would be awesome."

Tina glares at Annie. She's acting as if she's on a scavenger hunt, collecting clues that will lead to a prize at the end. Well, there probably is a prize, or at least some certificate for best senior project, and of course Annie would be gunning for it.

"I'll go read a magazine at Book Nook," Maria says. "I'll be back in a little bit."

Tina sees her walk toward Chickety Chix, sees her pace slow as she nears the spot where it all happened. Tina turns her back. She doesn't want to watch her. She will give Maria her space.

"So what can you tell me about Rosalie Goodson?" says Annie.

"I can tell you I miss her," says Tina. "More than I thought I would. I mean, she was just a customer but in retrospect it all feels like something more."

Annie nods, but she doesn't write anything down. She looks a little bored.

"She came in every week. She was loyal, even after most of my other clients went to other salons."

"Okay, but do you know any facts about her life? Like, what was her job? Who was in her family? If you were going to paint her, what would you imagine she'd be surrounded by?"

Tina thinks about Ro's garden, which she talked about often. She might have loved that garden more than anything else. Once, Ro mentioned a lemon tree she planted outside a house she and her husband had rented in California, and Ro wondered if the tree was still there and, if so, how big it had become and how many lemons it produced each summer. But Tina feels stingy with the few details she knows about Ro's life, unsure how Annie will manipulate them for her own purposes. She will reveal something small, something that would be difficult to render in a painting. "She told me that, long ago, she wanted to be a poet. But I guess life got in the way."

"Well, then, if she didn't become one, there isn't much to say, is there?" says Annie. "I mean, *wanting* to be something is nothing."

Tina stares down at the perfect part in Annie's hair. She wants to do something to shake Annie out of her perfection. She makes Tina's skin feel itchy with her certainty about everything, her superiority, and, maybe most of all, her talent and skill. What would Annie say if Tina told her she wants to be an artist? Would Annie demand to see a portfolio? Would she ask about credentials and degrees? Would she laugh and tell Tina she's too old to be anything besides what she already is? The word *nothing* echoes in Tina's mind, and she decides she will not reveal any more about Ro. She won't tell Annie about Ro's garden, or about the old camera and pocket squares she gave Jackson, or even about Ro's fondness for her son. None of these things are any of Annie's business.

"She was in the circus when she was young," Tina says, the lie bursting from her mouth. After all, Annie asked for "unusual" and "interesting," so Tina is complying. Annie looks up with wide eyes, says, "Oh my God, really?" This is what Annie wants—not the truth, but something colorful and false—and Tina will provide it.

"She performed the high-wire act in a traveling circus. I can't remember the name of the circus, but she was the star. She said she was on all the posters, but of course she didn't use her real name. Her name was something with the word Amazing in it. Maybe Rosalie Amazing?" Tina fights the urge to grin. Maybe Rosalie Amazing doesn't have the alliterative charm of Annie Amazing, but Tina wants Annie to at least consider there are other people in the world who might be amazing too. Maybe she's gone too far—maybe it's too obvious now that she's lying, maybe she's shown her hand and Annie will know Tina watched all her YouTube videos and knows Annie's screen name. But until Annie says something, Tina needs to keep going, needs to bring this lie to some sort of conclusion, plausible or not. "Then, one night, she fell and broke her neck and never returned to circus work again."

"No way!" says Annie, and from her tone Tina is certain Annie hasn't caught on to the fact that she's being mocked. She scribbles in her notebook, then she flips open her sketchbook and draws a woman on a tightrope, and Tina is stunned at how quickly Annie draws, how well she captures a scene of a full audience enraptured by an agile woman balanced precariously on a thin rope high above their heads. How is Annie able to conjure that scene in her mind without photographic references?

"She recovered enough to walk again, but not enough to perform."

"And what happened after that?" says Annie.

Tina thinks about cartoon villains who rub their hands together when doing something devious and wishes she could do this right now, rub her palms together until they feel hot from the friction. But she must maintain her serious façade, must keep charging along with more ludicrous lies. "After that, she joined the CIA. Obviously she couldn't tell me much about her work there, but she spoke six languages. She told me she'd met seven U.S. presidents in her lifetime and worked closely with two. But she wouldn't tell me which two."

"She was *so* interesting!" says Annie, not looking up from her notebook, which she's filling with small, neat notes. "I could probably figure out which presidents she worked with if I do a little research."

"Yes, do that," Tina says. She wonders if Annie would ever consider anyone who'd lived an ordinary life—someone who got up in the mornings and went to work, someone who tried their best to be a good parent, someone who didn't get everything they wanted in life—to be interesting. The answer is clearly no. Someone would have to be extraordinary, *amazing*, in order to be interesting. "But she did say she had a code name in the CIA. Something with the word *Bumblebee* in it, I think." Ro told Tina about her annoyance with the beehives Kevin placed in his yard, and she thinks Ro would have found this lie funny. Tina knows she is more than twice Annie's age, and she should start acting like an adult, but Annie just sets her off, makes her feel immature and petty. In a small way, Tina is glad Annie is here; she gives Tina someone to direct her anger toward, gives her a way to distract herself from how unwieldy her sadness about Ro's death feels.

"This is going to be so, so good," Annie says.

Tina turns to look at the food court, and she sees Maria sitting at a table, alone, her head bowed, hair hanging over her face. Tina doesn't know if Maria is crying, but it's obvious she needs some time alone. She is still unsure whether Annie and Maria are friends; they seem so different that Tina finds it hard to imagine them hanging out, trading gossip, bent over a textbook studying for a quiz.

"You want a haircut?" Tina says. She doesn't want Annie storming into the food court and interrupting whatever is going on with Maria. "I've got nothing to do right now, and I think we should give Maria a few minutes." For Maria's sake, she'll do a good job and will fight every urge she has to butcher Annie's perfectly neat hair.

Annie's eyes flit to the food court, and when they land on Maria a look of understanding crosses her face. "My mom cuts my hair at home," says Annie.

Tina examines Annie's hair, and it looks good—*really* good—if it is the work of an amateur.

"Is your mom a hair stylist?" says Tina.

Annie shakes her head. "She's a pediatric nurse. She just knows how to do all sorts of random stuff."

"You should tell her she does nice work," Tina says. No wonder Annie is so good with her hands; there must be something in her genes.

"There is something I've been wanting to do with my hair, though," says Annie, sounding shy, breaking eye contact with Tina, and Tina is surprised at the sudden lack of confidence and certainty. "I was thinking of dyeing the ends bright pink. What do you think?"

"That would be a change," says Tina. She is good at making statements that don't contain value judgements. This skill is useful when clients ask for awful things she knows will be unflattering—bangs or a perm or, God forbid, a mullet—but she doesn't know the clients well enough to try to change their minds. She wonders if Annie's parents would approve of pink hair. Are they strict Asian parents, like Tina's were, or are they of a new generation of lenient Asian parents, rebelling against their own rigid upbringings?

"I'm just tired of being so ordinary, you know? Ordinary, boring Annie." She sighs. "I've had the same haircut since I was three. And before that, I had almost no hair."

Tina is taken aback. Annie is many things—annoying, insufferable, superior—but the last thing Tina would think her to be is ordinary. Even if everything else about you is ordinary, being extremely good at something makes you extraordinary. "I think a lot of people your age feel that way, that they need to do something to stand out."

"It would be nice if I stood out a little. I'm not like Maria," Annie says, waving a hand toward the food court.

"Like her how?"

"Beautiful. Everyone knows the guy who shot Rosalie Goodson was stalking Maria and was mad she didn't want to date him. They found all these pictures of her on his phone. He was obsessed."

"Oh," says Tina. "I hadn't heard that." This sounds absolutely horrific and she can't imagine how frightened Maria must feel.

"People are talking about it at school," Annie says. "It's not being reported on the news."

"It's probably best not to spread this stuff around." Annie should keep her mouth shut and try not to make things worse for Maria. Doesn't Annie understand Maria will be haunted by this forever? And it's not over; right after he shot the gun, the boy was tackled by a few college football players who were eating pizza in the food court, then the police arrested him, and now he is awaiting trial and Maria likely will have to testify, and that will make the trauma feel fresh again. "It's a very hard time for Maria. You know that, right?"

"Yeah, I get it. She hasn't talked about any of it with me. We're not really friends. I mean, we're not *not* friends, but we were in our capstone class and I mentioned doing a tribute to Rosalie Goodson and she said she would introduce me to you, and I said okay because it sounded like she wanted to bring me here or something."

"Maybe she wanted to come back here but didn't want to come alone?"

"She could have brought her boyfriend."

Tina didn't know Maria has a boyfriend. Maybe the relationship is new or something Maria is uncertain about. Maybe something changed between them after the shooting. "It's probably simpler going with you."

"Yeah, simple, ordinary me," says Annie, sighing melodramatically and looking down into her notebook and doodling swirls and circles in the margins. Tina's first reaction is to roll her eyes at Annie, who has no reason to feel sorry for herself, who has such a bright future ahead, who has a world of possibilities in front of her. But maybe life is harder and more complicated at seventeen than Tina remembers, and there's something valid about Annie's feelings. Tina has spent a lot of time longing to be young again, wishing she made different decisions, but Annie makes her remember how uncertain everything feels at that age.

"How about we clip in some extensions?" Tina says, turning the chair so Annie is facing the mirror. "Some bright pink ones. So you can have pink hair temporarily but you don't have to commit to it. I can teach you how to put them in and take them out, so you can wear them whenever you want." There are some clip-in extensions in the back closet that one of the stylists forgot to take when she left.

"Really?" says Annie. "You can do that?"

"I'm actually pretty good with extensions," Tina says, trying to mimic the confidence she hears in Annie's voice in her YouTube videos.

"I don't have any money, though. I mean, I have nine dollars, but that's to get fries and my mom wants me to pick up a copy of *Real Simple* at Book Nook."

"It's on the house," Tina says.

"I feel weird about it," says Annie. "I should pay you."

"Don't feel weird," says Tina, as she takes Annie's two notebooks and sets them on the small table at her station. She picks up a brush and runs it through Annie's hair.

"Thank you," says Annie. "This is so strange. I came to the mall to interview you and now I'm going to leave with pink extensions. I've been wanting pink hair forever."

"Funny how life works out," says Tina. Two weeks ago, Tina would not have believed all that has happened: Ro is gone, murdered, and because of this Annie Amazing has popped out of the computer and into the salon. And now Tina is standing behind her, and she has come to understand that Annie is young and insecure and misguided and maybe not actually the absolute worst person in the world.

TINA AND JACKSON have driven to three parks with two loaves of soft white bread. The bread is for ducks, but at each park there has been a DO NOT FEED THE DUCKS sign next to a pond, so Tina keeps searching, keeps driving to find if there are any parks where one can feed the ducks all the carbohydrates they desire. She would have dumped the bread near the first pond at the park a mile from their house, but Jackson is a stickler for rules, and Tina doesn't want to encourage him to start breaking them.

Tina has taken the day off from work. She asked Kevin to put a sign outside the salon saying it was closed for a family emergency. This isn't true, but it gives her a reason to be gone. She has no appointments for the day, even though it's a Saturday, generally the busiest day for salons. It feels like it's time for her and Jackson to talk about what happened to Ro. They haven't had that conversation yet, and she knows how deeply he's been affected by Ro's death, even if he hasn't been willing to talk about it. He's been different, quiet and sullen, not interested in watching animal shows on TV, only picking at his dinner, unable to eat a full meal.

Tina pulls into a gravel parking lot, and Jackson takes the bread out of the car. There is a small pond with four mallards floating calmly in it. Jackson insists on walking around the circumference of the pond to make sure there are no signs prohibiting them from feeding the ducks. Once they've made a complete circle, Jackson decides they can toss out bread. A few moments after he opens the twist tie on one bag, the ducks speed over and Jackson and Tina throw pieces of bread into the water. And then, a few moments later, two geese dash from somewhere in the park, running in their flappy-footed, wobbly way. Jackson stands close to Tina, who pretends not to be scared for Jackson's sake, but she too is frightened of those beaks.

"Just keep feeding the geese," says Tina. "As long as they're eating, they shouldn't hurt us." She tries to hurl a piece of bread, but it's so light that it lands only a few inches from her feet. One of the geese waddles over and snatches up the bread then takes a few steps away to eat it. She thinks about that business Kevin mentioned to her months ago about dogs chasing geese away and wonders whether he's still thinking of it as a good business or whether he's moved on to something else.

"Why do you think parks have rules against people feeding ducks and geese?" says Jackson.

"I guess it's not healthy for them to eat too much bread. And maybe they stop wanting to try to find food for themselves."

"Yeah," says Jackson. His bag of bread is still nearly full, although Tina's is almost empty. She wonders how long it will take to empty his bag. He is pinching tiny pieces to throw into the water, and at this rate it will take all day to get through his loaf. "I read online that people get mad about foie gras."

Tina laughs. Jackson has pronounced the words correctly, with a bit of a French flair; she wonders if he listened to the pronunciation online. "Well, people think it's cruel to fatten up geese just to eat their livers."

"Do you think the people who are in charge of parks are worried that if the ducks and geese get too fat they'll be killed for their livers so people can make foie gras?" Jackson says.

"People don't want to eat geese from parks. The geese people eat are usually raised on farms."

"But someone *could* kill a goose at a park and then take it home and eat its liver."

"I guess someone could, but that doesn't mean they will," Tina says, and then she realizes where this line of questioning is coming from. Jackson now lives in a world where there's potential for violence at every turn. If a boy can march into the mall with a loaded gun, what would stop someone from coming to the park and shooting some plump waterfowl in order to harvest their livers? This is her chance, her entryway into the conversation, but Tina's still figuring out what to say. Maybe the right words will come if they start walking, if she keeps her legs moving. She takes the last four pieces of bread in her bag, squeezes them into a dense golf-ball-size mass, and throws it far into the grass. The geese take off after it. She drops her empty bag into a green trash can.

"How about we dump the rest of the bread with the ducks and take a walk?" Tina says. "Or if you're worried about the geese eating too much bread, we can take your loaf home."

Jackson pulls the twist tie out of his pocket, closes the bag, and says, "We can bring it home." Tina takes the bag from him.

So now they will have some time without distractions. How will Tina talk to Jackson about Ro's death? What's the right way to speak to a kid about something so incomprehensible? If there had been a funeral—some official event—they could have gone and it might have opened the doors to conversation. But there was no funeral, no obituary, no closure. A terrible thing happened, and it is up to everyone to figure out how to deal with it on their own.

Jackson was at the mall that night. After Tina heard the shot, before she even knew what was going on, she grabbed the old iPod she kept at her station, swiftly unraveled the headphones, turned on her eighties playlist, and shoved it into his hands. She told him to hide inside the supply closet at the back of the salon and pushed the earbuds into his ears. Telling him to hide in a closet wouldn't protect him if the gunman decided to come for them, but what else could she do? Tina heard screams and saw people scrambling toward the escalators and stairs. It was impossible in that moment to understand what was happening. She stood motionless for a few seconds in the middle of the salon and then ran into the closet with Jackson, who was hunched over, and she squatted and enveloped him in her arms, her heart beating so hard she was certain Jackson could feel it, and they hid together until she thought it safe to open the door.

Now, Tina and Jackson follow a trail with green blazes on trees. A sign at the beginning of the trail says the loop is 1.7 miles. A chipmunk skitters across their path and disappears into the underbrush. They walk silently for a minute, the only sounds birds chirping above them and the rustling of leaves.

"Mom!" Jackson says. He points, and Tina looks into a thicket of trees and sees a hawk sitting on a high branch. Tina pulls out her phone and takes a photo, but when she looks at the screen, the hawk is just a brown speck. She zooms in and tries again, but the photo is blurry.

"I wish I had a better camera with me." Tina looks at Jackson and says, "Like the one Mrs. Goodson gave you."

Jackson nods, says nothing. They continue on the path.

"We haven't talked about Mrs. Goodson," Tina says. "I know you must be very sad."

Jackson keeps walking with his head down, stepping over a few tree roots that have pushed up to the surface.

"I miss her," Tina says. She stops, picks up an acorn, rolls it around in her fingers, tosses it into a patch of ferns. "It was nice to see her every week, wasn't it?" She doesn't know how to get Jackson to talk about his feelings, but she thinks it's not good for him to keep everything packed tightly away inside.

Jackson nods again. Then he mumbles, "I turned the music off."

"What music?"

"After you gave me the iPod, I turned off the music. I heard screaming."

Tina feels a hot fury about the boy with the gun. How many lives has he affected with one stupid, violent action? She wants to kick a boulder, pound on the rough bark of a tall tree with her fists, scream into the forest, but she knows she needs to appear calm for Jackson's sake.

"I thought it was a trick at first. A magic trick. There are trick guns that don't shoot real bullets," Jackson says.

"Did you see it happen?" Tina holds her breath, desperate for Jackson to say no. It would be better if he wasn't a witness, if he didn't see Ro collapse. Tina only heard it happen, and that's been enough to keep her up at night, to make the sounds of the gunshot and the chaos and terror cycle through her mind night after night.

"I saw it," Jackson says, and Tina releases a quick stream of breath. Jackson stops, bends, and ties his shoelace.

"You saw him shooting the gun?"

Jackson stands up, pushes his hair out of his face, says, "Yeah, I saw him shoot it. I saw him run into the food court and shoot it and I thought it was a trick gun, but when Mrs. Goodson fell down, I knew it wasn't. She never played along with magic tricks. I was so stupid to think it was a trick gun."

"Baby, no, you weren't stupid." Tina pulls Jackson to her, but his body is stiff, not accepting comfort. She lets go.

"I saw him take out the gun," Jackson says. He steps away from Tina. "He stopped outside the salon and took the gun out of his jacket pocket. He stood there looking at it and nobody saw him except me. I could have called the police or said something or tried to stop him."

There are footsteps in the distance, and Tina and Jackson move to the side of the trail as a man in a Yankees cap walking a small black-and-white dog comes around the bend. "Hey there!" he says cheerily, and Tina forces a smile onto her face. The dog sniffs in Jackson's direction, but Jackson doesn't lift a hand to pet it. Suddenly,

Tina has a thought that makes her feel breathless: What if Jackson *had* brought attention to the boy? What if Jackson had said something to the boy, asked about his gun? What if the boy turned the gun toward her son?

After the man and dog disappear down the path, Tina says, "I'm sorry, baby. I'm sorry about everything and I'm sorry you had to see that."

"It's weird that people say they're sorry when bad things happen," Jackson says. "I think maybe everyone says they're sorry because there's nothing good to say. But you're only supposed to say sorry when you make a mistake."

Tina wants to weep but she tries to never cry in front of Jackson. She agrees there's nothing good to say, but isn't it her job to say something? To somehow make this better for her son? Who can she ask for help? Maybe she will call Jackson's school and ask about a therapist who works with children, someone trained in the right things to say to help children who've experienced something traumatic.

"It's not your fault," says Tina. "You did nothing wrong. It wasn't your job to stop things."

"I feel guilty," Jackson says. He lets his body drop onto a large rock, sits with his head in his hands. Tina can tell he's trying to keep tears from falling, but he can't, and he sucks air into his lungs and his chest heaves. He takes his glasses off and holds them in one hand while he rubs his eyes with the other. Tina wants to pick him up and hold him tight to her chest and rub his back, just like she used to do when he was a baby.

"You should only feel guilty if *you* did something wrong, and you didn't," Tina says. "That boy did."

"I never gave Mrs. Goodson her film. I don't know why I kept it."

"What film?"

"In Mrs. Goodson's camera case. There was a roll of film and I never gave it back. On purpose. I wanted to get it developed and see what was on it, but I thought it was wrong to do that, so I didn't, but I also didn't give it back and now I can never give it back." He's having a hard time speaking through his tears, his voice juddering. Tina understands what's going on—the film is something Jackson can control. He can choose to develop it or not. Everything else is out of his control.

"Do you have a tissue?" Jackson says, and Tina shakes her head. How can she help Jackson when she can't even remember to carry tissues?

She sits next to Jackson and puts the loaf of bread on her lap. "I have an idea," she says. She unties the bread bag, takes two pieces out, and uses one to dab each of Jackson's cheeks. She is surprised by how well the bread works to absorb his tears.

"More absorbent than the leading two-ply," Jackson says, imitating a paper towel commercial they see when they watch *Talent Abounds!*, Jackson's favorite TV show. Tina breaks down laughing and Jackson joins in. She realizes this is the first time since Ro's death she has heard her son laugh.

"You think the birds and chipmunks would eat soggy bread?" Tina asks, once she catches her breath.

Jackson nods. "The ducks are fine with wet bread."

Tina dabs again at his cheeks and drops the slices on the ground. "I guess it'll be a little salty too. The animals might like that."

"You need one," Jackson says, pointing to Tina's face, and she realizes she's been crying too. Tina pulls more bread out of the bag, pats her wet face, and deposits it on the ground with the other two slices. She feels better now, like something has cracked and released everything that was trapped inside for the last three weeks, and they can begin to move forward in some way.

Jackson stands up from the rock and brushes off the back of his pants. He takes another deep breath, wipes both eyes with the cuffs of his sweatshirt, and puts his glasses back on. They start to walk again and Tina says, "You think there were pictures on the roll of film?"

"Yeah," Jackson says. "That little tail end of the film wasn't sticking out, like it would for a new roll."

"How old is the film?"

"Really old. It says Kodachrome on the outside, and I looked it up online, and I think it's from the 1960s." His voice is steadier now, and Tina is glad they are talking about something related to Ro. She understands it will take a long time for Jackson to heal, but maybe this is a good starting point.

"The film is even older than you are," Jackson says.

Tina smiles; forty is ancient when talking about rolls of film, just middle-aged when talking about people. "Do you think it can still be developed? Or does film disintegrate or something when it gets old?"

Jackson shrugs. "I don't know."

"Let's get it developed."

"But it's not ours."

"I don't know who else we could give it to," says Tina. "So we either develop it or throw it away."

"Maybe there are secret pictures on it."

"Mrs. Goodson probably didn't even know that roll was in the camera case."

"Okay. But I still feel bad. I think I'm going to feel guilty forever."

"What about sad?" Tina says. "A big amount of sadness that you've never felt before, so it's hard to describe? And it leaves this feeling in your stomach that reminds you of feeling guilty?"

"Maybe," says Jackson. "Sad about what happened to Mrs. Goodson and sad that I'll never see her again. Or maybe I just haven't learned the words yet?"

Tina wishes there was no word—in any language—to describe the combination of horror and sadness and fear and pain Jackson must be experiencing. She wishes she knew a magic trick where she could snap her fingers and instantly make things better. She wishes Ro would step into the salon tomorrow and bring along a small trinket for Jackson. She wishes for a lot of things, none of them actually possible.

AT HOME, JACKSON gives Tina the roll of film he found in the camera case and also five rolls filled with pictures he took. Tina has no idea where to get film developed nowadays. When she was younger, every drugstore had film developing onsite. Now, she's unsure.

"Maybe the old film will be a nice way for us to remember Mrs. Goodson," Tina says. "We'll see another side of her, what she was like outside the salon."

"I'm glad it's color film."

"How do you know?"

"Kodachrome is color. Don't you want to see what color Mrs. Goodson's hair was? Before it turned white?"

"Oh," says Tina, and she's surprised because she's never thought about what color Ro's hair used to be. She only thought of Ro as someone old, but of course she was once young. Tina is disappointed in herself. She can't believe she never wondered about Ro's life before the mall, before the grouchiness, before her desire to divest herself of many of her husband's things by giving them to Jackson. Of course there was so much more to her, so many different versions of Ro over the years. Of course, of course. It's hard to remember sometimes that no one is only who they appear to be at the moment. It's hard to remember sometimes all that goes into a life, all the different versions of a person throughout the years, all the ways in which people are capable of changing.

That night, after Jackson goes to sleep, Tina searches on her computer. First she looks up summer camps. Maybe a few weeks away will be good for him. She looks up photography camps and magic camps, and they're all so expensive. She wonders how even families with two incomes can afford them. She looks up regular summer camps; perhaps sailing and swimming and making lanyards will be a nice break from Jackson's everyday life. But those camps are expensive too. She types "magic" into various search engines. She finds an article about the oldest magic shop in New York City and decides they'll take a trip down to the city on the train, and she'll let Jackson buy a few tricks from the store. She writes down the address of the store on a scrap of paper.

Tina also wants to buy something small, a gift Jackson can use right away. A few pages into her search leads to a website about Miracle Berries, which are supposed to change the taste of food from sour to sweet after a berry is eaten. She orders a package of freeze-dried berries. She has a hard time believing they'll work, but maybe it'll be an amusing little experiment.

Then Tina finds a company online that specializes in developing old rolls of film. They also develop 35 mm film, so she downloads a mailing label and puts all the rolls of film into a padded envelope. How did Jackson manage to fill five rolls without her noticing him taking pictures?

Tina is not tired and doesn't know how to occupy herself for the remaining hours before she drifts into sleep. She stares at her computer screen and realizes she hasn't watched any art videos since Ro's death. She hasn't felt like drawing. But she's curious about what Annie has been up to. She navigates to YouTube and sees Annie has uploaded a new video. In the small thumbnail, Tina can see Annie is still wearing her bright pink extensions. Tina clicks on the video, which is titled "New Hair, New Attitude!"

"Hi, guys!" Annie says, waving at the camera. Tina turns down the volume so as not to wake Jackson. "I wanted to do something different today. As you can see, I look different. I hope you love my hair as much as I do. It was done for me by Tina Huang at Sunshine Clips in Greenways Mall, and, you guys, you should totally go see her if you want your hair done because she's *amazing*! And, no, before anyone asks, we're not related, even though we're both Asian. I think she's Chinese too, but remember, not all Chinese people know each other, even if they live in the same city. I shouldn't have to say this, but some of the questions I get in the comments are so stupid, so it's better to say something now."

Tina isn't sure whether to feel flattered or appalled that Annie Amazing is shilling for her. She hopes no one thinks she paid Annie to advertise for her. Really, what does it matter? How much longer will the salon be in business? And will people really assume they're related because of their race? How stupid can people be?

"It's strange, you know, I always thought I knew what it means to be an artist, but then Tina did my hair and I sat there thinking she's an artist too. My hair was her canvas. An artist doesn't have to be someone who paints or draws or makes sculptures. Isn't there art in everyday life? Yesterday, I got this lemon cupcake at a little bakery, and it was beautiful with an ombré yellow frosting and I thought about the baker making all these different shades of yellow frosting. And not only did that cupcake look beautiful, it tasted great. So who's to say dessert isn't art? Just ask Wayne Thiebaud!" Then Annie laughs at her own joke, and Tina pauses the video, googles Wayne Thiebaud, and stares at his paintings of cakes and pies and parfaits and ice cream cones and feels a movement in her chest because she's stunned by their beauty. What does it mean that art—even art seen through the ugly glow of a laptop screen—can make her feel this way? She clicks the play button on Annie's video again.

"I guess I've been kind of snobby about what I think art is, and I want to open myself up to seeing art everywhere, you know? I think my new attitude sprang up when I got my hair done because I just feel so unlike myself. I want to be more open, different."

Tina thinks about the reinventions one can go through at seventeen, eighteen, nineteen. If a little pink in her hair can make Annie feel so different, what will happen once she moves out of her parents' house, meets new people in college, tries to make her way in a new town or city?

"Anyway, I'll wrap it up. But two things: look for art in your everyday life. It's everywhere. And go see Tina Huang at Sunshine Clips if you live in the Capital District. I know everyone is calling Greenways 'the murder mall,' and maybe that's true, but think about the people who work there, okay? Think about how they have to go there and deal with stuff and maybe think about giving them your business? So check out Tina Huang, who is a real artist!"

Tina closes the laptop, takes a deep breath. Why does the fact that Annie Amazing called her an artist—albeit referring to her styling skills—make Tina's head swirl and spin? Maybe it is because this is the nicest thing anyone has said about her in a long, long time.

A WEEK LATER, Tina finds a thick envelope in the mailbox. The return address is from the film developing company. She covers the envelope with a large Bed, Bath & Beyond coupon, hoping Jackson doesn't see it. She'll look through the photos first before deciding whether to show them to him.

Jackson prepares himself a bowl of mint chocolate chip ice cream with chocolate syrup, and Tina slips into the bathroom with the envelope. She sits on the closed toilet seat and uses a small pair of nail scissors to cut the envelope open. Inside are six smaller envelopes filled with photographs. How long has it been since she's gotten a roll of film developed? Maybe a decade, probably more. What a strange, nostalgic feeling to have the heft of developed photos in her hand. She ordered doubles of Ro's roll—she's not sure why—and she can tell which photos are from Ro's film because that envelope is twice as thick as the others.

She opens the flap and lets out a deep breath when she sees the images. In the first photograph, Ro is standing in a large garden next to a topiary shaped like a bird. Her blue shift dress with white cuffs and Vidal Sassoon–style bob make Tina think it's the early sixties. Ro's hair is the color of caramel. The sun is in Ro's eyes, but she's smiling and looks happy. There are more photos of the garden, Ro posing next to other topiaries, Ro posing next to pink and purple and yellow flowers, and then there's one of Big Ben; these photos must be of a trip Ro took to England. And then, the second-to-last photograph in the pile shows Ro with a man sitting at a table in front of two plates piled high with fish and chips. Next to one plate is a pint of dark beer, and next to the other is a glass of water. This man wears little round tortoiseshell glasses that remind Tina of Jackson's glasses. He is starting to bald, even though he's young with dark hair and an unwrinkled face. Both he and Ro grin at the camera and lean into each other, their shoulders touching. Tina is certain the man is Ro's husband, Lawrence. Tina flips to the last photo, and there's a peach blur of a finger in one corner, and Ro and Lawrence are no longer posing. Lawrence is lifting a thick wedge of potato to his mouth and Ro is turned, in profile, smiling at him, a loving expression on her face. "My God," says Tina because she is shocked at the tenderness. Ro was always kind to Jackson, but there was nothing soft or vulnerable about that kindness, just an efficient firmness, like a schoolmarm pleased her charges had memorized their multiplication tables. Tina thinks about how many decades must have passed since this photograph was taken, thinks about how this Ro could have never imagined what the end of her story would be. All that's left are articles about her death, nothing about her life. How could young Ro know that everything about her—her love, her vacations, her work, her friendships, her hobbies—all of those things would be erased, reducing her name to words used to identify the victim of a horrible, senseless crime?

IN THE KITCHEN Jackson is at the table eating his ice cream and reading another one of his books, this one with an otter wearing a Sherlock Holmes hat on the cover. Tina gives one copy of Ro's photographs—except for the last, candid shot—to Jackson. She wants to keep that photo—both copies of it—for herself because this photo feels private, like something Ro wouldn't want others to see. "Vacation pictures," Tina says. "They probably had other rolls from the same trip so they didn't miss them. But look at her hair. Look how pretty it was."

Jackson puts down his spoon, moves the ice cream bowl out of the way, takes the photographs, and looks through them silently. He holds the photos by the corners, and Tina wonders how he knows to do this. Has he ever touched a photograph before? When she was young, her father always chastised her about getting fingerprints on family photographs, telling her she wasn't careful enough. Had Jackson just been born careful?

"She looks like someone from a TV show," Jackson says, holding up one of the photographs.

"Who? A famous actress?" says Tina, looking at a photo of Ro standing in front of a fountain in Trafalgar Square, holding a large rectangular purse at her side.

"Just like someone who would have been on an old TV show."

"She looks happy, doesn't she?" Tina says, and Jackson nods. It's good, Tina thinks, for Jackson to have these photos. Maybe he will study them again and again, and this will be how he remembers Ro. Maybe in his mind he'll see young Ro with the caramel-colored hair and the large purse instead of Ro falling in the food court.

"Here are the photos you took." Tina gives Jackson the padded envelope.

"You want to see them?" Jackson asks, and Tina nods.

The first roll consists of photos of Frito, Kevin's dog, in the bookstore. Most of them feature her sleeping, but in the last few she's eating a bone-shaped treat. The second roll contains photographs of the mall, the insides and outsides of stores. There are some photographs of a group of architects that came to the mall a few months ago. Tina doesn't know what the management company that owns the mall has decided to do in light of the shooting. She suspects the entire place will be torn down, and after a while, after the memories of what happened have faded, they'll likely erect an office building. Offices can exist in spots where bad things happened. The third roll is made up of photographs taken outside, dandelions and worms and sparrows, the ordinary outdoor life in their backyard, many of the things Tina never takes the time to notice. The fourth and fifth rolls contain the photographs that interest Tina the most. They are pictures taken in the salon, photographs of some clients, a handful of Ro looking at the camera, her hand up, as if she's saying, "Hurry up now, just take the photo."

"Could I have one of these?" Tina says, and Jackson hands her a photo of Ro. She stares at it and asks, "Do you remember what she was saying when you took these?"

"She said she didn't like to have her picture taken. She said that if I gave her the camera she would take pictures of me, but why would I want that? I can just look in the mirror if I want to see myself."

Tina wonders if these are the only photographs of Ro taken in the last few decades.

"I took a lot of pictures of you," Jackson says, passing the photos to Tina.

She flips through them and notices she's not smiling when she's cutting or styling hair. She looks bored, like someone who is just trying to get through the day. Is this how she looks to her clients? To everyone in the outside world?

"I like this one," Jackson says. He holds up a photograph where he's caught Tina drawing at the reception desk. Tina can't see what she's drawing, but she can see it's on the back of a long receipt, probably one of those excessively long ones from CVS. Tina examines her face, and in this picture—this picture only—she wears an expression of concentration. She doesn't appear bored or sad or fed up. She looks content.

THE NEXT DAY, the Miracle Berries arrive. After they eat dinner, Tina holds up the bag and explains they are supposed to temporarily rewire your taste buds.

"No way," says Jackson.

"Want to test them out?" Tina says, and then she's annoyed at herself for not trying them first. If they didn't work, she could have sent them down the drain, and Jackson would never know about her late-night impulse purchase.

Tina goes to the refrigerator, takes a lemon out of the crisper drawer. She gets out the cutting board and a paring knife and slices the lemon into wedges. *Please work, please work*, she thinks, a silent invocation.

She slides a small plate with the lemon slices onto the table and sits down. She holds open the bag of berries to Jackson, and he takes one and puts it in his mouth. Tina takes one from the bag too, and they chew silently for a few seconds.

"Ready?" Tina says, and Jackson nods. They each pick up a lemon wedge, hold it in front of their mouths. "On the count of three?"

"One, two, three," Jackson says, and both Tina and Jackson shove the lemon wedges into their mouths. Tina looks at her son, whose teeth have been replaced by the wedge of lemon skin. It takes a moment until she tastes a burst of sweetness on her tongue. She sees Jackson's eyes widen in delight, and Tina feels grateful for this strange alchemy, this small bit of magic.

LATER THAT WEEK, Tina texts Maria and asks for Annie's phone number. Then she texts Annie, tells her she has some photographs of Ro she can use for her project. Annie texts back, saying she'll stop by the salon after school to pick them up. At three thirty, Annie shows up at the salon still wearing her pink extensions. They are well taken care of, and Tina is certain Annie carefully removes them each evening, cleans them, and then puts them back in every morning.

"Oh my God, these are great," says Annie, looking through the envelope of photos. "Where'd you find them?"

"My son had an old roll of film that once belonged to Ro," Tina says. "I thought the photos would help with your mural. There's a more recent one too."

Annie nods, stares for a while at the photograph of Ro that Jackson took, then says, "She wasn't in the CIA, was she?"

Tina pauses a moment, debating whether to forge on with her lie, then says, "No."

"And you made up the circus stuff too?"

Tina nods.

"I tried to research her, but there was nothing. I figured maybe the CIA stuff would be secret, but there should have been some record of her in the circus. And if she really did fall in front of an audience there would be newspaper articles."

"You're right," Tina says.

Annie shuffles through the photographs of long-ago Ro. Tina wonders whether Annie figured out her lies before or after she made the YouTube video promoting Tina's salon. Annie says, "Why did you lie to me?"

"I don't know," Tina says, even though she knows exactly what set her off.

"You know my videos, don't you? I looked over my notes and saw you used the name Rosalie Amazing, and I figured out you were probably making fun of me. I don't know why I didn't catch it before." Annie chews on her bottom lip, still unable to meet Tina's eyes.

Tina admits to seeing her videos. She feels awkward and guilty about her lies. She knows she acted like a child.

"Why are you giving me these?" asks Annie. "Why didn't you just let me work off the stories you'd told me about the circus and the CIA?"

"I guess I wanted your project to honor Ro, and I thought the photos would help," Tina says. "I think it would be nice for people to think of Ro as someone with a long and complicated life and not just a victim."

"What did I say that made you make up all that stuff?"

"I don't really remember," Tina lies.

Annie sighs. "Please? I'm trying to be different. Better."

Tina sees tears pooling in the corners of Annie's eyes. She is unsure whether it would be better to tell the truth or not, but she doesn't want to continue lying. "You said Ro was nothing after I said she never became a poet."

"Oh," says Annie, but confusion lingers on her face.

"You said that wanting to be something and not becoming that thing means someone is nothing."

"Oh, no, I didn't mean . . ." Annie says, her voice trailing off. "I mean, everyone is *something*."

"Right, we're all *something*," Tina says.

"You want to be an artist," Annie says, looking Tina in the eyes, and she says it with the usual Annie Amazing certainty. Tina doesn't say anything for a few seconds, and before she can respond, Annie says, "That's how you found my videos. The only people who watch them are people who look up how to draw or paint."

Tina shrugs noncommittally.

"And when I said Rosalie Goodson was nothing because she never became a poet, I hurt your feelings."

"I'm too old for hurt feelings," Tina says, although this is not true.

"Let me help you," Annie says. "I can teach you whatever you want to know about art. We can have a truce."

Tina imagines Annie trying to teach her, imagines Annie getting frustrated when her progress isn't up to par, imagines Annie slapping at her hand with a ruler, like an old-timey nun. Annie is not as annoying as Tina initially thought, but Tina guesses she would not be a patient, forgiving teacher.

"I'm sure you're busy with school," Tina says. "You don't owe me anything. Just honor Ro, and I'll be happy." If Annie wins an award for this project, if someone from the *Times Union* or Spectrum News covers the senior capstone show, then anyone who googles Ro's name might first stumble upon an image of Annie's painting, rather than the facts about how she died.

"I really want to pay you back for the hair and these photos."

Tina thinks, then says, "How about this? I want to get some art supplies, but I don't know where to start. I usually use scrap paper and one of those yellow pencils or a free pen from the bank when I draw. How about you help me pick out good materials to use if I want to get a little more serious about art?"

"Yes, of course!" Annie says. "I *love* shopping for art supplies. Do you know about the different hardnesses of pencil lead?"

"No," says Tina.

"Oh!" says Annie, clapping her hands together. "You're not going to believe the different types of marks you'll be able to make with different leads. And different types of paper will yield different results. Your mind is going to be blown by all the paper textures."

"Okay," says Tina, trying not to laugh at Annie's enthusiasm. "We have a deal." She reaches out, shakes Annie's hand, and this time she doesn't think of osmosis, of a transfer of Annie's skills, but instead imagines what her own hand might be capable of making.

May

The Witness

Maria wanted to go to the Humane Society for Giving Back Day. There, she could distract herself with animals—play fetch with a dog or dangle a toy mouse on a string in front of a kitten or refill hanging water bottles for hamsters—and ignore her classmates. The seniors had four options for Giving Back Day: the Humane Society, the food pantry, a retirement home, and Washington Park, where Maria is wearing thick black rubber gloves and picking up trash. The teachers assigned everyone randomly, which is why Annie, who hates animals, is at the Humane Society, probably faking an allergy to dander so she doesn't have to touch anything.

Maria moves up a hill and looks at the amphitheater below. No one is onstage, the rows of seats empty. When she was a kid, her parents brought her here to watch musicals in the summers, and it felt magical being outdoors as the sun set slowly, watching fireflies light up the park behind the playhouse while actors performed onstage. She wishes she could go back to those days, when it felt like wonderful things could unfold before her eyes. Now, Maria is doing everything she can to avoid her classmates who were also assigned clean-up duty in the park. She knows Garret Yo and Breck Winters each have a flask of alcohol stolen from their parents' liquor cabinets, and she knows there are plans to gather on the footbridge over Washington Park Lake at one thirty and return to school drunk. It's stupid, though, if they think fifty kids are going to be able to get drunk on two small flasks of liquor, which Garret and Breck proudly displayed on the bus ride to the park.

"Hey."

Maria turns and sees Chloe halfway up the dirt path on the hill, the garbage bag she's holding nearly full. Chloe reminds Maria of Santa, with that bulging bag slung over one shoulder, but Maria doesn't joke about this because she's not sure if she and Chloe are friends anymore.

"Hey," says Maria. She and Chloe have not had a real conversation in months. She wonders if Chloe sought her out or if she accidentally climbed halfway up this hill and was surprised—or maybe disappointed—to see Maria at the top.

"I think I got all of the trash in the entire park," says Chloe, dropping the bag on the ground in front of her. "Do you think we got the worst assignment? Everyone else gets to be inside in air-conditioning."

"At least it's not raining."

"That's right," says Chloe. "I forgot about this. Maria Sunshine."

If Chloe wants to insult her, she might as well leave Maria to clean this spot alone. But "Maria Sunshine" doesn't sound like an insult; it sounds almost like a compliment. "Why'd you come up here?" Maria asks.

"To look for trash."

Maria sees Chloe scanning the path, sees her tapping the fingers of her left hand against her thigh, and understands Chloe is filled with energy today, like she often is, and has likely been running around the park shoving garbage into her bag. This might be the first time she's stood still all afternoon.

"There were a few soda bottles up here, but I got them," says Maria. "I'm kind of hiding out for a few minutes."

"You want me to leave?" Chloe says.

Maria shakes her head. She wants to spend time with Chloe. What happened between them was weird, not a real falling out, just a break and a drift. It was over the movie Chloe was making, her insistence on trying to solve the mystery of who burned the theater supplies under the bleachers. Maria made herself scarce so she wouldn't have to deal with the movie. She threw herself into her relationship with Seth, took on extra hours at Chickety Chix, and told Chloe she needed time to work on college applications.

Chloe hefts the garbage bag back over her shoulder, makes her way up the hill, then lets it drop to the ground again. She rummages in her backpack and pulls out a sweating Nalgene bottle. Maria hears the ice cubes hit against each other as Chloe lifts it to her mouth. "You want some?"

Maria realizes she's very thirsty. She hadn't thought to bring water. "Yeah," she says. Chloe hands her the bottle and Maria takes a long sip. "Thanks." She looks into the bottle and sees several thin rounds of lemon. "You cut up a lemon to put in your water bottle?"

"I'm fancy like that. It's how I imagine all water is served in California." Chloe takes the bottle back, says, "I can't believe how far apart we'll be next year."

Chloe is going to NYU to study in their film and television program. Maria will be going to UCLA for acting and musical theater. Maria wants to tell Chloe they've been far away from each other for months now; just because they live in the same town, it doesn't mean there's a closeness between them anymore.

"Yeah, it'll be weird," Maria says. And then, because she feels like it's the polite thing to say, she adds, "I'm sure we'll see each other over breaks."

"Congrats on UCLA, by the way. I never said that, even though I saw your post on Instagram. That's totally impressive. I hope you ran to Mrs. Wilder the second you got your acceptance."

Maria is glad that even after all these months apart, Chloe is still sticking up for her. "I really didn't think I'd get in."

"Of course you got in. You're really good. Did you send in a video?"

"I went down to New York City one weekend. They had the auditions there."

"Screw Mrs. Wilder," Chloe says. She picks up a small rock, throws it down the hill, where it lands in a patch of grass. "One day you're going to be signing autographs and she's going to wait in line for hours and then when she gets to you, she'll try to take credit for your success and you'll be like, 'Security! Please take this mentally unstable woman away!'"

Maria laughs. "At first not getting a part this year really sucked, but then I kind of stopped caring about it." But Maria wondered often how her senior year might have unraveled differently had she gotten a role in *West Side Story*. She would have never punched the cast list in frustration, never met that boy in gray who destroyed so much. Chloe would not have suggested working together on the film about who burned the clothes and props. Everything would have been different. "Congratulations on NYU too." She liked Chloe's post on Instagram but hadn't left a comment, felt like it would be disingenuous since they hardly spoke anymore.

"Yeah, thanks. Hey, can I ask you something?" Chloe says, pulling her phone out of her pocket. "It took me way too long to figure it out, but this is about you, right?" She shows Maria a picture of the brick wall beneath the bleachers with the number and letters *4MR* spray painted on it. Maria can see some of the burned theater props in the foreground. "Wayne Scott Phillips destroyed all that stuff for you since you didn't get a big part in the musical, didn't he? How did I not get that 4MR meant 'For Maria Robles'?"

Maria doesn't want to talk about this. She is afraid Chloe wants to interview her so she can include a plotline in her *Burned Dreams* movie about the boy and Maria. She is afraid that once Chloe saw all those comments online saying Maria was the object of the boy's unrequited love, the film shifted its focus to examine whether Maria was somehow complicit in the shooting. She doesn't want to answer any questions about whether she thinks his bullet was meant for her that night. Maria feels certain it was, although she has not admitted this to anyone. She doesn't want to talk about how much guilt she feels every day when she wakes up and remembers Ro Goodson is dead. She has difficulty talking about the future, about college and what she wants to do there, because it feels like she's on borrowed time, that she was the one who was supposed to die that night. But maybe she owes Chloe some sort of explanation. "Yeah, it was him. I tried to talk him out of it. I didn't want him doing anything for me."

"Why didn't you tell me?"

"I don't know. I guess I didn't want to talk about it," Maria says. "I thought if I ignored him, nothing more would happen."

"But that day under the bleachers, you knew?"

"Yeah."

Chloe nods, plays with the drawstring on her garbage bag. "How could this kid have been in school with us all these years and no one knew he could do such terrible things?"

"I don't know."

"Goddamned three-named fucker. These psychos always have three names, don't they?"

"I should have told you he destroyed the theater props," says Maria, "but I didn't want it to come out in your movie. Are you still working on it?" She's dreading hearing about the movie. Maria feels twisted up inside, a sick and nauseous feeling. She wishes she had her own bottle of cold, lemony water to sip. She could drink a gallon right now without taking a breath.

Chloe sits on the ground. She looks up at Maria and says, "I never finished it."

Maria had been so certain Chloe was working on the movie all these months they weren't hanging out.

"I had nothing to say. I mean, beyond, 'Here, look, there's all this destroyed stuff.' None of the theater kids wanted to talk. They were being all melodramatic, even though everything burned was replaced. After the shooting, I put things together, how Wayne Scott Phillips was in love with you. But I didn't want to tell that story and drag you into things." Chloe pops back up to standing, leans against the tree again.

Maria feels like an idiot. She'd spent all those months avoiding Chloe, and for no reason. Of course Chloe wouldn't have gone through with the movie. "Maybe if I'd been honest with you at the beginning, other things wouldn't have happened. Or maybe I should have told the police who burned all that stuff, and they would have stopped him before he could do anything else."

"It's not your fault, if that's what you're getting at."

"It feels like it was, in a way. And I am sorry for not telling you. I know I ruined your movie."

"It's fine," says Chloe, waving away Maria's comments with her hand. "I made a movie about my grandma and am using it for my senior project and also submitted it with my college application. I'm sure the people reviewing my application were like, '*Another* grandma movie? Kids from the suburbs are *so* boring.'"

Maria laughs. She's missed Chloe, missed their easy camaraderie.

"The movie is so cheesy I can't even handle it, but it got me into college and it'll fulfill the senior project requirement."

Maria nods. "It'll be cool to see it."

Chloe rummages in her backpack, finds a pack of gum, pops a piece into her mouth. "You're doing something with Annie for the senior showcase, right?" She bends and cinches the yellow drawstring on her garbage bag.

"Yeah," says Maria.

"I saw the paintings in the art classroom. Mrs. Owens is super proud of the project. It's probably exciting for teachers when their students do something really good."

Annie's project has moved beyond a focus on Rosalie Goodson. It's now about gun violence in America. Annie painted watercolor portraits of one hundred people killed by gun violence in the last year. Mrs. Owens told Annie one hundred portraits was extremely ambitious, even ten would make the point, but Annie said the point was how prevalent gun violence is. Ten portraits wouldn't tell the full story.

The portraits will be printed on envelopes containing wildflower seeds and distributed during the senior showcase. While Annie distributes the envelopes, a slide of each portrait will play on-screen, and Maria will read a line from a poem she wrote about each person. The poems will be printed on the backs of the seed envelopes. At the end of their presentation, audience members will be urged to plant the seeds so something beautiful might bloom in memory of those who were lost. The title of the project is "What They Loved Best" because each poem speaks to what the person liked most in life. Rosalie Goodson's poem is about her garden, so in Maria's mind the project is mostly a tribute to Mrs. Goodson since all these flowers will, she hopes, spring from it. Maria is not sure she'll be able to get through the reading without crying about all the sad and senseless deaths. The fact that Annie's watercolors will be projected on a screen gives her some comfort that people will be looking at the portraits, not at her.

"It's a cool project," says Chloe. "And I had an idea."

Maria takes a deep breath. Another Chloe idea. Maria just wants to spend time with Chloe with no big ideas being foisted upon her.

"You ever hear of seed bombs?" Chloe says. She double-knots the tightened drawstring of the trash bag, then she ties a bow. "They're usually made by guerrilla gardeners."

Maria shakes her head.

"So people throw them in places, usually in cities, that could use something pretty. They throw them over fences into empty lots or drop them into planters. The seeds turn into flowers and the flowers attract bees and birds, which helps the whole ecosystem. When flowers start appearing, places that had been neglected are suddenly kind of beautiful."

"How big are seed bombs?" asks Maria.

"The size of ping-pong balls. You make them by mixing seeds, powdered clay, compost, and water. Then you let them dry and launch them. When it rains, the clay dissolves and the seeds germinate."

"That sounds cool," says Maria, "but we're giving out seed packets, so people can decide where they want to plant their wildflowers."

"Right, right," says Chloe, "and that's great, but it's also kind of passive, right? How many of those envelopes will end up in drawers and never get planted? I mean, sure, give out the envelopes because they're a cool idea, but I've been thinking how we can turn your idea into action. I thought it would be awesome to record a bunch of people launching seed bombs and shouting, 'Shoot seeds, not guns!' I could film it, and I bet we could make it go viral. And we could sell the seed bombs and donate money to an anti-gun-violence organization."

How is Chloe able to speak in full paragraphs without pausing for breath? Now Maria remembers how exhausting it is to be Chloe's friend, to be in the position of always having to agree with her ideas or face Chloe's immense disappointment. But is this actually a decent idea? It would be good for people beyond their high school to know about this project. It would be good too to make a donation and help out in some small way.

"I'd have to ask Annie," says Maria, and Chloe sighs.

"Where's she going to college? Somewhere in California?"

"She's going to Yale to study painting."

"From regular know-it-all to an *Ivy League* know-it-all," says Chloe, tilting her head back so her nose is high in the air. She sniffs hard, like some animal who smells the scent of food wafting in the breeze, and she looks so ridiculous that Maria can't help but laugh, even though Chloe is being mean.

"So what's going on with you and Seth?" says Chloe, and Maria knows this is because she can't stand to talk about Annie anymore because she has the misguided notion that Maria and Annie have become good friends. Chloe looks behind her, down toward the playhouse, as if she's waiting for a show to start on the quiet stage, and Maria can tell she doesn't want to make eye contact because she's worried Maria will say things are great with Seth, that he and Annie are all she needs in her life, and Chloe has become unnecessary.

"He's going to UAlbany next year to play lacrosse."

"You going to break up before you go to California?" says Chloe, twirling the cap off her Nalgene bottle again. This time she doesn't offer Maria a sip.

"I don't know. I don't really know anything anymore, you know?"

"Yeah," Chloe says. "Life is weird now and it's probably most weird for you. Wayne Scott Phillips pretty much ruined everything."

"I try not to say his name. That's part of our project. We want to say the names of the people who were killed, show their faces, make sure people remember them, not the ones who shot them."

Chloe slips her empty bottle into her backpack and hefts up her trash bag. "The whole project is kick-ass. So will you talk to Ivy League Annie and see if she wants to collaborate?"

Maria nods. She will propose this idea to Annie, and she hopes Annie will say yes because before high school ends, she wants to do something good and helpful and meaningful. Something that might help make the awfulness she's felt since Mrs. Goodson's death diminish a little, and maybe Chloe is the key to making this happen.

SOME DAYS AFTER school Maria goes to Bouncetown to hang out with Seth. He works there now that lacrosse season has ended, and it feels like an odd reversal for Maria to be the one hanging around and waiting while Seth works. But Maria doesn't want to work anymore, certainly not at Chickety Chix, definitely not at the mall. Bouncetown makes her feel claustrophobic, the place filled with inflated rubber structures for children to slide down or jump on or run through. The sound of the air inflating the slides and trampolines is constant and everything has the chemical odor of warm rubber and plastic. It's a place where Maria does not feel at peace, but since Seth spends most afternoons there, she joins him because she does not want to go home and deal with her family, does not want their pitying looks, does not want to answer their questions about whether she's okay.

Today there's a birthday party and Seth is running all over the place, making sure kids have taken their shoes off and no one has brought anything sharp onto the jumping areas. Maria has thought about sneaking in an X-Acto knife and walking through the room and stabbing everything, watching all of Bouncetown deflate. She doesn't know what to do about the emotions she's feeling, a swirl of anger and guilt and regret, and she thinks deflating everything in this place might give her a momentary sense of relief. Some afternoons she looks around at the kids squealing and laughing as they jump and thinks how absurd it is that the world just keeps going on, that everyone keeps doing silly things to stay entertained. It feels especially wrong that Maria is allowed to go on too. She keeps thinking she should have died that night. And since she didn't, what good is she doing by being alive? Spending her afternoons watching children jump up and down seems like a waste.

"Hey," says Seth, hovering above Maria, who is on a stool in the corner reading *The House on Mango Street* for her English class. "Can I ask you a huge favor? We're super short-staffed today. I need someone to help out with this Bounceball game."

"I don't know how to play Bounceball," says Maria.

"It's like regular football, just on a bouncy football field."

"I don't know how to play regular football."

"Don't worry about it," says Seth. "These kids are, like, six, so you just have to make sure no one gets hurt. But you have to put this on." He holds out a shirt with black-and-white vertical stripes, which is about four sizes too big for her.

Maria reaches for the shirt, feels the thin polyester fabric, brings it to her nose, and sniffs. She is relieved it mostly smells like detergent, with only a faint hint of sweat.

Seth leads Maria to a giant inflated green football field in the center of Bouncetown where two dozen little boys wait. They are split into teams, one wearing sleeveless red mesh jerseys over their regular clothes, and the other team wearing green ones.

"Just make sure the kids are following the rules. If they don't, blow the whistle, stop the game, and make the offender sit on the bench outside the field." Seth pulls an orange plastic whistle on a lanyard out of his pocket and hands it to her.

Maria stands in a corner of the inflated field and waits while Seth explains the instructions for Bounceball to the group of children gathered around him. She pulls the whistle on the lanyard over her head.

"Got it?" Seth shouts to the little boys, and they scream that they do. "Okay, go!" Seth blows a whistle and throws a Nerf football up in the air, and the boys explode with action, running all over the inflated field. The football lands but none of the boys possess enough dexterity to catch it. Several run toward it, and the bouncing field makes the ball roll right to Maria. She looks at Seth, and he gestures with his hands for her to pick it up, so she does, then she looks again at Seth to see what she should do next. Four little boys are gathered around her, looking up with expectant eyes. "Throw it," Seth mouths, and she pulls her arm back. The football flies through the air, hits the mesh wall that's on the other side of the field, and drops onto the green rubber beneath their feet.

Seth grabs the ball, tosses it up in the air, and once again, none of the boys are able to catch it. They tumble together on the inflated field, and finally one boy in a red jersey picks it up and starts running, and Seth yells, "The other way! You're running toward your own goal!"

Maria moves toward Seth, bouncing cautiously in her socked feet. Half of the boys are splayed on the field, giggling and letting their bodies move with the motion of the inflated field. Two boys in green jerseys are now fighting over the ball.

"What if we figure out something else to play? Something fun, but with no teams and not so many rules."

"The parents paid for a football game." Seth gestures toward a group of parents near the entrance to the inflated field.

"They don't know how to play! Look," Maria says, pointing at the field. Now more boys are lying flat on their backs, allowing the undulating floor to move them. The boys on the ground remind Maria of a war scene, a group of soldiers shot dead.

"We just have to ride out the timer," says Seth, "and then everyone can go eat cake and the parents can say their kids played football today."

Seth calls a time-out and explains the rules again. He points to the two foam goalposts, says it's important the boys not score on their own team. Then he puts the ball on the ground instead of throwing it in the air, and the two biggest boys fight over it. They grapple with the ball, then they start kicking each other while still holding on to the ball, and Maria looks at Seth to see if he's going to stop them, but he's just watching, as if what the boys are doing is perfectly acceptable. Then the bigger of the two, a chubby, red-faced boy with a crew cut, kneels with one hand still on the ball, forms the fingers of his other hand into a gun, points at the other boy, and screams, "Bang, you're dead!"

"No!" Maria yells. "No way!" She marches over to the boys, moving quickly, even though the ground is unsteady. She shoves the whistle in her mouth and blows again and again, the sound cutting sharply through the air.

"Chill, Maria," Seth says, jogging toward her, nearly toppling over because of all the boys making the floor bounce as they run over to see what's happening. "The parents are watching."

Seth's words barely register, and Maria grabs the crew cut boy's collar and shouts, "You're out of the game!" He resists, wails that she's mean, but she pulls his arm hard, even though he begins to yelp. She keeps blowing on the orange whistle until she's yanked him off the football field and onto the regular, cement ground, which feels hard and cold beneath her socked feet. She realizes everyone has fallen silent around her, but she doesn't care.

"Sit!" she orders the boy, pointing to a bench. He's snuffling and no longer looks anything like the brute he'd been just a few minutes before. The boy collapses cross-legged on the ground, instead of on the bench.

"All right, enough," says a parent with a pair of aviator sunglasses pushed up on his head, and Maria says, "No, it's *not* enough! He pretended to shoot another kid!" When she finishes speaking, she realizes she's been shouting, speaking louder than she has in months, and her throat feels raw.

"I think you're overreacting," says a woman in a blue-and-green plaid shirt.

Maria brings her hand to her chest and realizes she can barely breathe. "I'm not," she says, but suddenly she feels drained of energy and needs to sit down on the floor next to the little boy who is still crying, needs to put her head between her knees and try to catch her breath, and in the background she can hear Seth say, "Of course, yes, I understand, I'll make sure you get a full refund."

CHLOE POURS COMPOST, powdered clay, and wildflower seeds into a bucket. They are in Chloe's garage with a blue tarp underneath them so they don't get seed bomb ingredients everywhere. Maria uses the garden hose to add water to the bucket and Chloe reaches in and mixes everything with her hands. They talked all afternoon as they drove around town to get supplies, and they are still talking. A lot has happened in the past few weeks and it feels good to be able to rehash everything with Chloe. The day after she yelled at the boy at Bouncetown, Maria and Seth broke up. They agreed she needed time to sort herself out. Maria has started seeing a therapist every Thursday, which her parents had begged her to do since Ro's death. It's hard for her to tell a stranger about how she feels or to revisit what happened, but Dr. Eastland is helping her understand that she needs to process her emotions or else she'll explode again and again, like she did at Bouncetown.

"I guess this is what people mean when they say, 'a new chapter,'" Chloe says. "Like moving on from the past, right?"

"Yeah, but it just feels like a lot of things are changing all at once. Can I?" says Maria, pushing up her sleeves. She wants to say that she's glad one of the things that has happened recently is that she and Chloe are friends again, but it would be too sentimental to say out loud. Their friendship is the thing that feels most steady and certain in her life right now.

"All yours." Chloe pulls her hands, which are covered in compost and clay, out of the bucket. Maria plunges her hands into the mixture, which is surprisingly cold, but it feels good to mush everything around and feel the small, hard seeds and the moist clay and compost. They work quietly, rolling seed bombs and lining them up in neat rows until finally the tarp is almost covered.

They drag the hose out to the driveway, spray dirt off their hands, and head inside. Chloe's little brother, Christian, is in the kitchen spreading chocolate frosting on a tray of brownies. "Moooooove," says Chloe, and Christian steps to his left so Chloe and Maria can wash their hands again with dish soap in the sink.

Chloe turns toward Christian. "How did you not come get us and tell us there are brownies?" She reaches a dripping hand toward the tub of frosting, and Christian lifts it high in the air. He is fourteen and had a growth spurt since Maria last saw him. Now he's about half a foot taller than Chloe and looks suddenly grown up. Maria remembers when he was so tiny that there was a wooden stool with a train painted on it in the bathroom that he used to reach the sink.

"It's for school!" says Christian. "There's a bake sale tomorrow for the Robotics Club."

"Nerd," says Chloe, but Maria knows Chloe adores her brother, knows she will be sad to leave home for college because they spend so much time together. She wonders if Chloe chose to go to school in New York so she could still be close enough to come home on the weekends to see her family. Maria wonders whether she would have chosen to go to school closer to home too if the past year had been different, if she hadn't felt the need to escape this place.

"I'll get you the prototype for the seed bomb launcher soon," says Christian. Chloe asked Christian to make launchers because he's good at building things. "They're made out of paper towel tubes and rubber bands. You can probably throw the bombs farther than you can launch them."

"It's fine," says Chloe. "We just need something to use so we can shout, 'Shoot seeds, not guns!'"

"I heard you're going to California," says Christian, turning to Maria as he smooths the frosting on the brownies. "I want to go to Caltech."

"Yeah, I'll be in California."

"Maybe I'll see you out in L.A. in a few years," says Christian.

"Sure," says Maria. "I'll give you a tour. I should know my way around by then."

"Dude," says Chloe, "by the time you get to college, Maria is going to be famous. She'll probably be a regular on a TV show. She's not going to have time for a little dweeb from her hometown." She puts a bag of popcorn into the microwave, presses a button, and leans against the counter.

Maria smiles. This is something else she forgot about Chloe: her absolute certainty that Maria will succeed, even when Maria feels no confidence in her own abilities.

"Well, don't forget me when you become famous," Christian says. He hands the spatula and almost-empty tub of frosting to Chloe. Chloe takes a spoon from the cutlery drawer and passes the spoon and frosting to Maria.

"I won't forget you," says Maria, scraping the side of the frosting container and putting the spoon in her mouth. How can she forget Chloe and Christian and the place she came from, the place where she grew up? She has lived here for eighteen years and this town is part of her. She can go all the way across the country, she can try for a clean slate, but she knows all that has happened here will be impossible to forget.

MARIA AND ANNIE's project is the final presentation in the senior showcase. Maria stands at the podium and waits for Annie's first portrait to be projected on the screen. She sees Annie near the first row of seats holding a large wicker basket full of envelopes of wildflower seeds with her portraits and Maria's poems printed on them. Chloe has been in the lobby all night selling seed bombs.

Maria sees her parents and her sister, Julia, in the third row, and her dad smiles, gives her a thumbs-up. She sees her mother push her father's hand down, whisper to him, probably something about the serious mood of the presentation.

The lights in the auditorium darken and the first watercolor portrait appears, and it's so big on the screen, and Maria looks at the little girl's peach skin, the greens of the leaves behind her echoed on her cheeks and forehead. Maria will read the name of each person and one line from each poem. They've handed out a booklet with all one hundred poems in case anyone wants to read them all the way through. She looks down at her pile of notecards, in alphabetical order, and reads about Ava Ableson, age seven, killed in a school shooting, who loved her kitten very much. As Maria goes through the cards, her voice gets stronger. She is glad Annie fought for a hundred portraits.

After their presentation is over, everyone in the auditorium rises in a standing ovation. Maria is surprised to see some of her teachers crying. When the clapping quiets, Maria announces they will be shooting seed bombs outside in half an hour at the baseball field behind the school. She reminds them that Chloe is selling seed bombs for four dollars each in the lobby and all proceeds will go to anti-gun-violence charities.

In the hallway, there is a long, snaking line of people waiting to buy seed bombs. Next to Chloe's table, there's a display of the originals of Annie's portraits on the wall, and there are many people looking closely at the paintings. After Maria makes her way behind the table, Chloe whispers they've made almost $1,500.

Jackson and Tina are there, and Tina seems more interested in Annie's watercolor portraits than Maria's poems, staring intently at the display and asking Annie all sorts of questions about the materials she used. Jackson leaves his mother and comes to Maria.

"I'm going to read all of these," says Jackson, holding up the booklet of poems.

"They were sad to write," Maria says, "but it felt nice to memorialize these people too."

"I liked your presentation. The only thing that could have made it better would be releasing one hundred doves because doves are a symbol of peace."

"That would have been cool," says Maria. "Maybe I should have worn my dove costume."

Jackson laughs, shakes his head. "I'm going to get a real dove one day."

"Maybe you can get a hundred."

"When I grow up I'm going to get a horse trailer and fill it with a hundred doves," Jackson says. "I'll drive the doves all over the country for my magic shows."

"I can't wait to see your show," Maria says. "I'll be in the front row." She fills a brown paper bag with seed bombs and hands it to Jackson. "Can you do me a favor? Could you give these to Kevin at the bookstore? I know he lives next door to Mrs. Goodson's house, and I was hoping he could throw them around her property."

"My mom said someone bought her house, but they're not moving in until August."

"If he threw them now, the wildflowers can grow all summer."

"Okay, I'll ask him to throw them," says Jackson, taking the bag.

"You and your mom coming to launch seed bombs?" says Maria, and Jackson nods. She puts a few more into Jackson's bag.

"Do you think the school is going to let the flowers grow forever?" Jackson asks.

Maria is almost certain they'll be mowed down before school starts in the fall and the field is needed again. "I don't know," she says. "I hope so."

"It would be cool if the flowers are still here when I get to high school."

"That would be very cool," says Maria. She imagines the flowers blooming and growing wild and tall, imagines a colony of doves nesting in them, the area a peaceful sanctuary for anyone who wants to escape for a few moments, to shut out all that is loud and upsetting in the world around them.

FIFTEEN MINUTES LATER, the crowd walks through the halls and out the back door of the high school. Maria spies her family, but there are so many people here she can't get to them. Then Maria notices a local news crew in the parking lot, filming the event. The entire crowd—hundreds of people—walks slowly toward the baseball field, and Chloe begins a chant through a megaphone: "Shoot seeds, not guns!" Once the crowd is steadily chanting, Chloe records everything on her iPhone. Seth walks with the crowd holding a handful of seed bombs. Maria catches his eye, and he makes his way through the mass of people to walk with her.

"Hey," he says.

"Hey," Maria replies.

"This is pretty great."

"Yeah, it all came together." Maria gestures to the crowd, which is filled with parents and students and teachers. "Thanks for coming along." She thinks things will be okay between them, that their relationship is transforming into something new and different but good.

They arrive at the baseball field, and Maria's parents approach them, and Maria sees Seth's jaw tense. "Don't worry," Maria says. "I told them we're friends."

"Seth," says Maria's father, holding his hand out for a shake. Maria's mother gives him a hug. "This is pretty impressive work, huh?" says Maria's father.

"Yes, sir," Seth says, and Maria tries not to laugh. Seth has always been excessively formal and awkward around her parents.

"We're so proud," says her mother, and she draws Maria near, kisses the side of her head.

"Shoot seeds, not guns!" shouts Chloe through the megaphone again. Maria watches as people throw the seed bombs or shoot them from one of the dozens of launchers Christian made, hundreds of seed bombs arcing through the air and coming to rest in the outfield.

After the field clears out, Maria, Seth, Chloe, Annie, and Christian pack into Seth's green Volvo and drive to the hiking trails near the high school, where they've decided to throw all the remaining seed bombs. It's hard to believe that in a few months Maria will be thousands of miles away from everyone in this car. Right now her shoulders are touching Chloe's and Annie's in the back seat, and she wishes she could somehow hold on to this moment where everyone is so close by.

They park in the lot near the trailhead, Seth finds a flashlight in the glove compartment, and they get out of the car. Annie lifts a basket of seed bombs from the trunk and says, "Doesn't someone need to water the seedlings and then care for the flowers once they bloom?"

"They get watered by rain," says Chloe.

"That feels like leaving too much up to chance," says Annie. "What if we end up having a drought?"

Chloe plucks a seed bomb out of the basket and hurls it into the woods. "Have a little faith."

Christian says, "Here, I have launchers." He gives the flashlight to Seth and reaches into a plastic grocery bag and hands one to each of them.

They walk away from the car and stop near the trailhead. "Do you think we should launch the seeds here?" Seth says.

"This is a good spot," says Maria. She does not want to go any farther into the woods. She looks into the darkness beyond the trailhead and remembers the boy walking through the food court, appearing in the hallway when she punched the cast list, lounging on the couch in the props closet. For months now, every time she's been anywhere dark and shadowy, her heart pounds, wondering if someone will emerge from the darkness to terrorize her.

Maria waits as everyone loads their launchers, then she turns the flashlight's beam toward each person as they release their seed bombs. No one is talking, and in the distance, Maria can hear the repeated hoots of an owl. She holds the flashlight steady and wishes she could always bathe them in light, illuminate the way to ensure they are safe from what lurks in the dark.

June

New Tricks

The mall will be closing in a week. The remaining stock at Book Nook is 75 percent off, and anything that doesn't sell by Friday needs to be boxed and sent back to the chain's warehouse. The afternoon is quiet, almost no customers, which allows Kevin to read a book about constructing doghouses. There are fold-out blueprints in the back of the book, so he considers buying it. He wants to make Frito a nice house of her own.

In a month, they'll be moving to Pennsylvania. A teaching position at a small college an hour west of Philadelphia popped up on the academic job lists at the end of February—very late for a good job to appear—and Gwen applied in March and was hired in April. Everything happened so fast—the interview, the offer, the acceptance—and the past few months were a disorienting swirl. Kevin is glad to leave all this behind. He knows he needs a fresh start, especially after what happened to Ro. He can't help but think of her every time he walks past the food court, can't help feeling a chill when he thinks about how she died.

Kevin looks up from his book as Jackson Huang walks by the bookstore, and he lifts his hand to wave to the boy. He glances toward the salon, sees there are no customers, sees Tina at the reception desk sketching in an enormous pad of drawing paper. He averts his eyes from the food court and tries to busy himself rearranging the little bobbleheads of characters from *Game of Thrones* near the register. He tries to shake thoughts about Ro's death from his mind, but for the past three months he kept asking himself whether he could have done something to stop the shooting. What if he'd gone to the police after Maria told him about the boy at her high school? Would they have taken him seriously? What if he told them the boy liked to come into the store and flip through books about guns? Would they have investigated? Would they have been able to stop him? Was the fact Kevin said nothing, did nothing, a factor in Ro's death?

Kevin is glad that soon he will no longer have to come to the mall. He's grateful to have the distraction of moving and starting over. He's glad Gwen will have full-time work, glad she'll get to teach students how to write poetry. Her book will come out in October, and he imagines a party thrown for her at the college, an auditorium packed with students who are eager come to hear her read.

After she received her offer, Gwen wanted to negotiate a position for Kevin at the college, but he declined. "Let me finish my dissertation first," he said, even though he knew this would irritate her because this potential job was an opportunity he would have never gotten on his own. Pretending to work on his dissertation had been a good stalling technique for years, and continuing to pretend could buy him more time to figure out what he wants to do. He never wanted to teach and still doesn't.

"I can't negotiate later, I have to negotiate now before I sign the paperwork," Gwen insisted.

"Don't worry about me. I'll figure something out."

"All I do is worry about you," Gwen replied, and Kevin had nothing to say in response.

Kevin hears footsteps approach and looks up from the dog book and sees Gwen. She has never come to the store without the kids.

"Hey," he says. "Where are Sammy and Simone?"

"With my mom at the university library. She says it's pretty quiet since the summer session just started."

"What are you doing here?"

Gwen points to the 75 percent off sign. "You know I can't resist a book sale."

"You sure this is the best time to be buying new books? It'll just be more to pack."

Gwen sighs, turns to a picked-over shelf of cookbooks, plucks one about Moroccan food off the shelf, and flips through it. She leaves it open to a photo of a large jar of preserved lemons. "Living in that tiny house has made me want more and more and more. I want a house filled with books, shelves overflowing."

And here, finally, is the revelation about how stifling it's all been. "We can get a big place in Pennsylvania. You can have all the books you want."

"I'll have my own office at school too with bookshelves to fill. It's such a simple thing to want, isn't it? Your own space."

Kevin knows that adjuncts aren't given offices of their own. An office is more than a space; it's something symbolic, something that says she belongs. In the last eight years, Gwen's had conferences with students in hallways, next to the photocopier, in campus coffee shops, outside on the lawn between buildings. He understands what having an office means to her.

"I'm sorry about the tiny house," Kevin says. There's no room for a bookshelf in their space. The few books they have are stacked in the corners. Library books reside in a tote bag that travels to and from the library.

Gwen looks up from the cookbook. "Why are you sorry?"

"It was too small for us. And you spent so much time worrying about the kids."

"I worried about that other house we rented too. Didn't you

wonder why the rent was so cheap? Eight hundred dollars a month for an entire house! Something had to be wrong with that place."

"I thought it was so cheap because all the old Victorians on our street were haunted."

"You believed that?"

"I didn't believe it, but I thought everyone else did."

"Lead paint, black mold in the walls and under the floorboards. People renovating those houses would find so much bad stuff. I liked having a house that was brand new."

It never occurred to Kevin that there were good things about the tiny house. It felt so oppressive, so much like a vise squeezing and squeezing him. "I know you worried about the kids falling. You were obsessed with the idea."

"Well, without that worry, I wouldn't have my book," Gwen says.

She says it so matter-of-factly, as if it's something completely obvious. But is she right? Without the worry, without the preoccupation, would she have written a book about falling? Would she have won a book prize? Kevin thinks yes, probably. Something else would have inspired her. "I'm just glad the book worked out," he says.

"Speaking of the book," Gwen says, pointing to a big poster behind him. Gwen's face adorns it, the book's title, *Plunging from a Great Height*, below her face. "People coming into the store have to look at my giant face every day! I can't believe you never took it down."

"I didn't know what to do," Kevin says. "So I just left it up." The reading didn't happen because the shooting occurred that night. Kevin should have taken the poster down as soon as he was allowed back into the bookstore. Why had he left it up for so many months? Perhaps the poster is just more evidence of the stasis of his life; when he doesn't want to make a decision, he does nothing at all. It's a pattern affecting both little things and big things. Little things like the poster, big things like his dissertation. Not taking action when Maria mentioned her stalker felt at first like a little thing, something he shouldn't poke his nose into, but then swelled into something big and irreversible.

Gwen looks at the food court and watches the scattering of customers spread out across the tables. It's lunchtime, and the only people still coming to the mall are bargain hunters or employees. "Do you think about it? What happened here?" They have not talked much about Ro. It has been difficult to know what to say, how to process it. Gwen and Kevin told the twins only that Ro passed away. When they asked for more details, Gwen and Kevin could only repeat, "She was old." A lie by omission, but it was also the truth.

"It's hard not to think about it," Kevin says, jutting his chin toward the food court.

Kevin wasn't in the mall when it happened. He was on his way back to Book Nook after picking up snacks at Trader Joe's, when a text arrived saying any employees not at the mall should stay away because of an incident in the food court. He panicked, thinking Gwen and the kids and Joan might be there, might have gone early to get dinner in the food court, and in that moment, he understood what was meant by the term *heart-stopping fear*. He had no idea what the incident in the food court might be and worst-case scenarios pulsed through his mind. He called his family and felt grateful he caught them still at Joan's house. He raced home and watched the local news while the twins watched *Cars 3* and *Coco* on the TV in Joan's bedroom, a rare treat to spend an entire school night staring at a screen.

Finally, the kids went to bed in the guest bedroom, and by the time the eleven o'clock news came on the victim of the shooting had been identified. Joan, Gwen, and Kevin sat stunned and silent. Finally, Joan looked out the window at Ro's house and said, "Her bedroom. She forgot to turn off the light." Both Gwen and Joan began to weep—that single burning light the catalyst for their tears—and Kevin felt unsure of what to do or say. How could they harbor such compassion for someone who never treated them in a particularly neighborly way?

At that moment, he realized Ro was at the mall for Gwen's reading. She'd copied down the information on the poster. As he sat on the couch, feeling helpless as Joan and Gwen cried, he made a vow to never tell Gwen. He would protect her from ever thinking this horrible event was connected to her in any way.

"Let's take the poster down," Gwen says. She comes behind the counter, already reaching for a piece of tape on the corner. Gwen rolls up the poster and deposits it in the trash can under the register. Then she points to the photograph in the Moroccan cookbook of the preserved lemons. "How big do you think this jar is? Sixty-four ounces? Can you imagine having enough room in your kitchen for this?"

"So we're thinking big for the next place?" says Kevin. "Half gallon of preserved lemons on the counter big? What is that, like five bedrooms?"

"At least five," says Gwen. "And you would not believe the counter space."

"*Miles* of counter space," Kevin says, smiling.

Gwen removes a twenty-dollar bill from her wallet, pushes it across the counter. "Can you ring up the cookbook?" she says. Something has changed in her voice; she suddenly sounds serious.

Kevin rings up the cookbook with the discount plus an additional manager's discount and hands Gwen her change. "A bargain," he says, but she doesn't respond.

"Listen," she says, "I came because I wanted us to talk. Alone."

The store is completely empty except for him and Gwen. What does she want from him? Why is she acting so solemn?

"I got a call from the chair of the English department," she says. She tells Kevin one of the lecturers teaching first-year writing received a fellowship and would be leaving. The chair wanted to know if Kevin wanted the job—four classes a semester, all the same class—for a year.

If things work out, there might be an opportunity for renewal and the possibility for a permanent position.

"I'm not done with my dissertation—"

"It doesn't matter. People with a master's can teach that class."

"But we already talked about this. We agreed you wouldn't negotiate for me."

"I know, but this kind of fell into our laps. Maybe it's some sort of sign? Don't you think it would be fun to work in the same place? Kind of like grad school all over again."

"How did the chair even know I could teach that class?"

Gwen looks away for a moment then says, "I asked about possibilities before I signed my contract. I mentioned you."

"I told you not to."

"Why would I pretend you don't exist?"

Kevin wishes he could figure out a way to tell Gwen he doesn't want to teach. It should be a simple thing to admit, but the words are hard to form after so many years of keeping it a secret.

"Finish your dissertation while you teach these classes and then you can go on the job market. Having a year of teaching under your belt will be good. It'll prove you can hold down a full-time job."

"I can hold down a full-time job," Kevin says. "What do you think I've been doing here?"

Gwen says nothing, looks around the store, and Kevin can see her taking in the pawed-over shelves, the large section of toys and knick-knacks and notebooks with cute animals on the covers. He sells far more of these trinkets and toys than actual books.

"She wants an answer tomorrow. Just take the rest of the day to think it over, okay?"

"Okay," says Kevin, slipping the Moroccan cookbook into a bag. He wants to say no, but maybe he's stupid for resisting a safe path. He might not love having a career in academia, but how many people love their jobs? How many people get up in the morning glad for the work ahead of them? Maybe Gwen is right that this is some sort of sign, some huge stroke of luck. Saying no to this would be incredibly foolish. "Okay," he says again, "I'll think it over."

When Kevin gets home from work, Joan is in the tiny house sitting on the couch and Frito is wearing a pink tutu. Sammy is holding a Hula-Hoop several inches off the ground, and Simone is trying to coax Frito through it. "Come on, Fabulous Frittini!" shouts Simone.

"What's happening here?" Kevin says, setting his messenger bag by the door.

"Grandma bought Frito a tutu," Sammy says.

"Frittini!" says Simone. "That's her performing name."

Kevin looks at Joan, who says, "They were so good all day I told them I'd buy them a treat. I was thinking ice cream sundaes, but they wanted a costume for Frito."

"We're training her to do tricks," Simone says.

A few nights ago, the family was at Joan's house watching TV and the twins became enthralled by a pack of dogs dancing and leaping through hoops on a variety show called *Talent Abounds!* One of the dogs even carried a chocolate milkshake on a tray while walking on its hind legs. The twins got the idea that Frito is the type of dog capable of learning tricks. Kevin tried to teach them the saying *you can't teach an old dog new tricks*, but the twins were adamant that Frito was a genius and could still learn new things.

"How's it going?" says Kevin.

Simone is holding a treat between her thumb and pointer finger, moving her hand up and down to get the dog's attention, but Frito is planted on the ground, four legs splayed out, the tutu bisecting her midsection.

"Work in progress," says Joan.

"Go," says Sammy. "You don't even have to jump. Just step." He lowers the Hula-Hoop by about an inch. Frito doesn't move.

They all watch as Frito licks a back leg and tries to get something out from between her toes. Then she swivels her head, distracted by a squirrel outside, bounding from one tree to another.

"Frito, you need to just *try*," says Simone, and Kevin is struck by how much she sounds like Gwen. And then Kevin realizes she sounds like Gwen talking to *him*, encouraging him to finish his dissertation and get going on an academic career. "Just pay attention and try."

"Maybe she doesn't want this," Kevin says. "Maybe she's not meant to be a performing dog."

"But Grandma got her a tutu!" Simone says, as if buying a tutu is all that's necessary for a dog to perform the type of tricks that would cause a crowd to stand up and cheer. Simone crawls through the Hula-Hoop and holds the treat in front of Frito's face. Frito's tongue emerges and she laps up the treat. "Now move," Simone says, picking Frito up, moving her through the Hula-Hoop.

Kevin squats next to the couch. "Does Frito remind you of me?" he quietly asks Joan. He watches Simone pick up Frito once again and move her back through the Hula-Hoop, and he thinks of Gwen's offer to help with his dissertation. If he'd let her, she'd probably write the thing herself, just to do what needs to be done.

"What?" says Joan. Kevin sees Joan looking at the plump dog in a tutu licking her chops, then nosing around Simone's hands, searching for more treats.

"Nothing. Never mind," Kevin says. "Where's Gwen?"

"She went to Bertolli's to get a pizza for dinner," says Joan. "And I should head out. I've got book club tonight." She stands up from the couch, and Kevin rises too.

"Thanks for watching the kids today," Kevin says, walking Joan to the door. "And thanks for the tutu." He turns back and sees that

Sammy is trying to get Frito to step through the hoop again, but she's not interested; she's still looking for more treats, still hopeful Simone might have another hidden away.

"Come on, Frittini!" yells Simone. "You can do it!"

"Yeah, you can do it!" echoes Sammy. "Try, try, try!"

"Guys," says Kevin, "dogs can hear way better than humans can. You don't have to scream."

"This trick isn't even that hard," says Simone, "so why won't she do it?"

"Just be a good dog!" says Sammy. "Just move!" He pushes Frito's rear with one hand, but instead of moving, she collapses on the ground.

"Believe it or not, they had perfect library manners," Joan says. "They kept their voices down all day."

"You must possess some magical powers because these two are not known for their library voices," Kevin says.

"Well," says Joan, "the promise of a treat at the end of the day works wonders."

"Here, treat," says Simone, sighing and extracting another treat from her pocket and feeding it to Frito.

Joan opens the front door and says, "She's a good dog, Kevin. She'll figure out what she wants to do, whether it's going through that hoop or not. I trust that she'll sort things out." Before Kevin can respond, Joan is across the lawn and disappears into her house.

LATER, AFTER THE pizza has been eaten, after Kevin has read the possum story to the children for maybe the nine hundredth time, Gwen puts up the baby gate at the entrance to the loft. Kevin grabs two IPAs from their small refrigerator, Frito follows them through the door, and they go outside and sit on the bottom step.

"Are you going to miss this place?" Gwen says. She takes a sip of beer and scratches Frito on the head.

Someone bought the tiny house and will be coming at the end of the month to haul it away. Amazingly, Kevin made money on this sale; he's being paid almost three times what he spent on materials.

"Yeah, I'll miss it. I've been in this town for eleven years now." He'll miss Joan, and he still misses Earl, even though it's been almost three years since he passed. Joan has always been a part of the twins' lives. How will it feel to move away? To leave her? They will only be five hours away, but that is an enormous difference from a walk across a not-so-big lawn.

"I've lived in this town my whole life," says Gwen, although it's not something she needs to say. They both know it. "It's going to be strange going somewhere new, a place where I don't know anyone. And I worry about my mom being all alone here."

"She has friends," Kevin says. She's got her book club, her colleagues from the library, old friends who come for brunch on weekends. He hopes the people who move into the Goodson house will be good neighbors to her. "She'll be okay. And remember, we'll have that giant house, so whenever she retires, she can come live with us." Kevin takes a long swig of his beer. He knows they are not out here to talk about Joan. They are out here because Gwen needs an answer.

Frito heads onto the lawn and trots off toward the fireflies lighting up the bushes. She returns with a tennis ball.

"I can't," Kevin says, tossing the ball back into the darkness. Frito chases after it.

"The job?" Gwen says.

Kevin nods and takes a deep breath. "I don't want the job. I don't want to finish my dissertation. I've been trying to convince myself that I should, but I don't want a PhD. I don't have any use for one. I don't want to keep writing about literature, and I don't want to teach."

"Then what do you want to do?" Gwen sets her empty beer bottle on a step. Kevin can tell she's trying to keep her voice steady. She sounds like she does when the twins have done something unruly in public, when she wants them to understand her disappointment without raising her voice.

"I don't know. I've been dragging my feet because I can't figure out what else to do. I'm sorry if it'll be embarrassing for you to tell your chair that I don't want the job."

"I'm not embarrassed, but I don't understand."

Frito returns with the tennis ball and Gwen takes the ball out of her mouth and throws it. She throws it hard and far, over onto the Goodsons' lawn. Frito's tags clank as she takes off after it.

"Why not just finish? Haven't you been working toward this for so many years?" Gwen asks.

But he hasn't. Maybe at first, when he first started graduate school, but he's known now for years that this isn't what he wanted to do. But there was that dream of Gwen's, both of them teaching at the same school, then one day their kids as students at the school, so he allowed things to drag on. Maybe he never thought she'd find a job—not because she wasn't good enough but because teaching jobs were so hard to get—so the dream could exist as a fantasy. But now things are real—a job for Gwen, the possibility of a job for him—and if he doesn't stop things, he might fall into a life he doesn't want. "I'm done," he says. "It's not what I want anymore."

"So you just quit?" Gwen says. "After all this time?"

"I'm tired of not making decisions," Kevin says. "Of doing nothing."

"Finishing would be doing something."

"I don't want to."

"You sound like the twins," Gwen says. "I don't want to eat broccoli. I don't want to go to sleep. I don't want to read this book tonight."

Kevin sighs. So Gwen is angry. Of course she is. He's been lying to her for years, pretending they want the same thing, pretending that her fantasy could coalesce into reality.

Frito returns, and Kevin feels too tired to throw the ball again, but

Gwen stands up, takes the tennis ball out of her mouth, and throws it hard again, nearly all the way across the Goodsons' lawn.

"I've been thinking a lot about how not making decisions is a big problem for me." Kevin tells Gwen about Maria, about how she came to talk to him about the boy stalking her and how he did nothing. And how he's thought about that every day since the shooting, wondering if he could have changed the outcome.

"Oh, Kevin," Gwen says, sitting down again. Her voice has softened. She picks up her beer, which is empty, and Kevin hands his almost-empty bottle to her. "That's not your fault."

Kevin shrugs. He didn't shoot the gun, but maybe if he could rewind time, take some sort of action, Ro would still be here, peering down at them, judging them for drinking beer or talking too loudly or throwing a tennis ball onto her pristine lawn.

"I just don't want to teach," Kevin says.

"So what's the next step, then?"

"I don't know," says Kevin. What else can he say? That he has no plan? That deciding to tell Gwen he's letting go of the life he once thought he wanted feels like enough for now? "I'll get us another beer," he says, buying himself a few minutes to gather his thoughts, although he wishes he could disappear for a while, could hide somewhere until he has an answer.

He goes back into the house, careful not to wake the children, and grabs two more beers from the refrigerator.

Outside, the stars are bright, and Kevin remembers his father always said that when the sky is dark and clear and the stars are shining, it means the weather will be nice the next day.

Gwen says, "I've always been working toward this job. I don't think I could have gotten through those years of adjuncting, of being underpaid and treated like shit by so many schools, if I didn't think I was working toward something. So it's hard for me to wrap my head around you not knowing what you want. But it'll sink in. I just need a little time."

"I guess you had a good role model in your dad," Kevin says, and then he worries that he sounds like he's feeling sorry for himself, for having a dad that worked in a cubicle at a boring office job, who died of a heart attack in his forties, for having a life with only his mother that was sad and lonely and quiet.

"I guess," says Gwen. "In both of my parents. They were very goal-oriented." Frito returns and this time Gwen takes the ball from her mouth and throws it more gently onto Joan's lawn. Then she says, "That's why I liked you. You felt different from the life I grew up with."

"For not having goals?" He tries to make a joke of it, but Gwen doesn't laugh. Kevin thinks the conversation is shifting, but he's not quite sure where it is going.

"For not always working toward a finish line. For doing things that are unexpected. Like the tiny house. Like the costumes at the bookstore. I never knew who you'd be when I brought the twins to see you."

"So you're fine with not knowing my next step?" He thinks about the possibilities he's already contemplated: mall Santa, goose poop cleaner, beekeeper, tiny house builder, professor. All of them feel wrong.

"Well, maybe *fine* is too generous. But I think we'll be okay."

"I think so too," Kevin says. He feels a lightness in his chest because, after all this time, he's finally told Gwen the truth. He hears the jingle of Frito's collar in the distance and wonders what she's doing over on Ro's lawn. They are silent as they drink their cold beers and listen to the sounds of crickets and the occasional car driving down the street.

THE FAMILY BRINGS flowers to the Albany Rural Cemetery each month. When they visit Earl's grave, they place the flowers next to the headstone. They don't stay for long. But one cool day in the spring, when his family was gathered around Earl's grave, Kevin noticed the hills and paths and plenty of space for walking and exploring. He thought of how quiet the cemetery is, how no one bothers you there, how everyone goes about their business in peace.

Since that day, Kevin has come to the cemetery three or four times a week with Frito, and they spend an hour walking, exploring the old gravestones, some of them tilted and about to fall flat on the ground, looking at the antiquated names like Erasmus and Fidelia and Adalbert. Kevin likes the sounds of birds and chipmunks. He knows it's a sad place, but it's also become a sanctuary, a place he can think.

He and Frito walk up a grassy path and stop at Chester A. Arthur's grave. Kevin looks up at the bronze winged angel sculpture. The angel—oxidized green with time—is laying a palm frond on top of Arthur's granite sarcophagus. There's something calming to Kevin about her looming figure, about how she's perpetually standing guard.

He admires the craftsmanship of the statue. It's strange to think a cemetery might have nearly as much art as a museum. He thinks about how well things used to be made—there's plenty of evidence of this artistry all over the cemetery, from the statues to the mausoleums to the carved lambs on the gravestones of children—but Frito grows impatient and tugs on her leash. "Okay, okay," Kevin says. Frito is usually content to follow Kevin, so it's strange that she wants to lead the way. Kevin thinks she might be on the trail of a squirrel, but he hasn't heard any rustling in the leaves. Frito pulls and pulls, and she leads Kevin to a headstone under a large oak tree. There are acorns all over the ground near this headstone, which is not as weather-worn as the others near it. Kevin looks at the name carved into the stone: *Rosalie Goodson*.

"Would you look at that," Kevin says. Frito sniffs around the headstone, and Kevin holds the leash tightly and watches as she explores. Is it possible that Frito knows this is Ro's grave? Or maybe there's a simpler and more reasonable explanation; maybe she's just attracted to the relative newness of this grave, to the recently upturned soil around it.

After a few seconds of sniffing, Frito settles down between Ro's headstone and the older headstone next to it. Kevin sees it belongs to Lawrence Goodson, Ro's husband. The dates on the headstone reveal he died over twenty years ago. Joan never talked much about him, only mentioned that he was a nice man, a friend of Earl's. Kevin remembers Joan once saying Ro couldn't be that terrible, after all, if someone as kind as Lawrence married her.

Kevin allows Frito's leash to go slack. He'll let her rest here for a few minutes. They are in the shade of the oak tree, but the day is warming up, and Kevin wipes sweat from his brow. He brushes away a few leaves from Ro's headstone. Now that several months have passed since her death, he feels more sorry for her than angry. He doesn't think there was a funeral, doesn't think she had any close family. He is unsure if anyone mourned her.

Kevin stares at Ro's headstone and allows himself to think about something he tried to push out of his mind. A week after the shooting, a police officer came to Book Nook. She showed Kevin a business-size envelope sealed in a plastic evidence bag. "KEVIN" was written in neat but shaky capital letters on the envelope. The officer said the envelope, which was located in the purse Ro was carrying the night she was shot, contained a thousand dollars in cash. The police checked and Kevin was the only person working at the mall with that first name. "Have you seen this envelope before?" the officer asked, and Kevin shook his head. She asked if Kevin was expecting to see her that evening and he told her that normally Ro didn't come to the mall in the evenings but she might have been headed to Gwen's book party. "Would there be any reason for her to bring you money?" asked the officer. Kevin shook his head again.

Why in the world would Ro give him money? It is a mystery that went with Ro to the grave. The officer explained that since there was no last name on the envelope, and no clear reason why Ro would give Kevin the money, that it, along with her other belongings, would likely go to Ro's next of kin. "Of course," Kevin said, because nothing else felt appropriate to say. And even if the money was meant for him, he wouldn't feel comfortable taking it. How could he take money from someone who never accepted his family?

But now that Ro is gone, now that she is no longer peering down at his family from her bedroom window, Kevin can think of her more objectively, study her like a character in one of the novels he dissected in school. Kevin remembers teaching Introduction to Literature, and how he spoke to his students about round and flat characters. For so long, he thought of Ro as flat, as someone representing only bigotry. But what if that envelope of money was a peace offering? What if she'd wanted to help his family in some way? Kevin told his students that round characters are capable of change and surprise. Perhaps Ro was more complex than he'd ever considered. She might not have been a good person, but maybe she was capable of some small moments of goodness.

"All right, Frito," Kevin says, giving the leash a gentle tug. "Let's walk."

Frito blinks and rises slowly. For a moment, her legs are wobbly, but she regains her balance and begins to walk.

"Good girl," Kevin says. He wonders how many more years they have of walking together. Kevin and Frito walk slowly to Earl's grave. Kevin always stops here for a few minutes, always wishes for some sort of ghost or angel to appear, to help steer him in the right direction, to give him the advice he needs to move forward. Today they listen to the leaves on the trees rustle in the warm wind. But of course nothing and no one appears, and Frito gets restless, and then Kevin knows it is time to go.

On the last day of June, a U-Haul truck and a dumpster appear in Ro's driveway. A gray-haired man in khaki shorts and a yellow T-shirt emerges from the U-Haul and enters Ro's house using a key. Kevin watches him from a small window in the tiny house. The man must be here to clean the house, to take everything he wants and trash the rest. Kevin is alone at home; Gwen took the twins to the town pool. Frito is fast asleep under the kitchen table. The mall is closed. In a few weeks, they will travel to Pennsylvania to look for a house to rent and then they'll come back and pack up their tiny house and also dredge out all the things stored in Joan's attic and basement. But for now, there's a lull. Kevin has nothing better to do than spy on this man next door.

For an hour, the man goes in and out of the house, tossing things into the dumpster and hauling boxes into the back of the U-Haul. By midmorning, he is drenched in sweat, his shirt plastered to his back. Kevin wonders why this man is alone. He looks to be in his fifties, certainly old enough to throw out his back with all that lifting. Kevin takes a glass and fills it with water from the sink and heads outside.

"Hey there," Kevin says. "I'm Kevin. I live next door."

The man hops down from the back of the truck. Kevin holds out the glass of water and the man drains it. "Thanks. David." He extends a hand for a shake. "The water in the house has been turned off."

Kevin says, "Let me get you more," as David hands the glass back to him. He returns to the tiny house, finds the big pitcher that Gwen uses to make iced tea, fills it with cold water, and brings that and the filled glass back out.

David has a strange expression on his face as he notices the tiny house. Kevin is certain David will ask about it, will want to know how it's possible to live in such a small space, but instead David drains the second glass of water then says, "I'm glad Aunt Ro had kind neighbors."

It takes a moment for Kevin to realize David is speaking about him. He supposes he's kind enough to offer a thirsty man some water, but he'd never been particularly kind to Ro. "You're her nephew?" Ro had never spoken about any relatives.

"My mother was her cousin. We weren't really close, only saw her maybe ten times in my life at stuff like weddings and funerals. But our family is small, and I'm the closest relative, so it's up to me to clean the house out. I don't think I realized what a task it would be. I should have hired some service, but I thought it was something I should do myself."

"Can I offer you a hand?" says Kevin.

"Oh, that's too much to ask."

"I wouldn't mind." It will be good for him to do something physical, and besides, he's curious about Ro's house. He can't imagine what it looks like inside.

David nods, then says, "My aunt, was her life here okay? I should have visited, especially after Uncle Lawrence died. But that was twenty years ago and my kids were toddlers and the drive from Bethesda is six hours, and I just never made it. I should have."

"Life gets busy," Kevin says. "I'm sure she understood."

"Maybe," says David. "It feels strange. I regret not getting to know her. And then, you know, the way she died, it was all so terrible. I'm glad my mom's no longer around. It would have devastated her to know Aunt Ro died in such a violent way."

"Were your mom and Ro close?"

"When they were younger, before my mom's family moved to Maryland when she was a teenager. She always said Ro was complicated and difficult, but her heart was in the right place."

Kevin wants to give David something he can hold on to, some small fact about Ro that might offer him a bit of comfort. "I had beehives in the yard for a few months, and one day my son tried to pull out one of the frames to get honey and was stung all over. Ro took good care of him. She gave him ice and some cream to put on the stings."

"It's nice when neighbors look out for each other," David says. He brings his wrist to his forehead to wipe away sweat. "Hey," he says, "how old is your son?"

"Six. I have a daughter too. They're twins."

"Let me show you something," David says.

He leads them into the house, and Kevin looks at the disassembled living room, sees a wooden coffee table and a painting of mountains and trees over a brick fireplace. Then his eyes go to the bookshelf, and there is Earl's first book of poetry lying on top of it, as if someone had just plucked it out and was planning to read it. Kevin is stunned that this book is something Ro possessed.

"This way," says David, leading Kevin to the basement stairs. "Watch your step."

At the bottom of the stairs, David flips on a light switch and one bare bulb on the ceiling flickers on. Two others remain darkened. "My guess is she didn't come down here much, but look." He holds his hands out, palms up, and Kevin sees the most elaborate train layout he's ever seen in his life. It is probably twice the size of the living room of the tiny house, with a small and detailed downtown filled with shops and cars and miniature people. There is a train station with benches and a ticket agent, a park with swings and a slide and a duck pond and a carousel, even two churches and a synagogue. There is a diner and, oddly, there are three Chinese restaurants, all on the same block. There is a bakery with a sign in the window that reads, BEST CHEESECAKE IN TOWN! and next door to it an ophthalmologist's office. There is a neighborhood full of houses, and there are tiny figures mowing the lawn and painting the shutters and raking leaves. Past the town there are mountains and there is a tunnel through one of the mountains for a train to travel through. There is a forest filled with pine trees and a large, shining lake at the forest's edge. Two large boats with white cloth sails float in the lake.

"Kind of amazing, isn't it?" David says. "I think my Uncle Lawrence put it together."

Kevin can't believe this tiny, elaborate world existed right next door in Ro's basement. What is more miraculous—this train layout or the fact that Ro owned Earl's first book? Kevin is not sure.

"Maybe your kids might want it? I think you'd probably have to do some repairs since everything is so old, but what do you think?"

Kevin lets his eyes wander around the layout and notices more and more small objects and people and even animals. He sees blue mailboxes and red fire hydrants. He sees deer in the forest and geese in the park. There are flowers in front of the houses in the residential section of town, and he recognizes miniature versions of many of the flowers and plants from Ro's garden. There is a home that looks just like Ro's house; the only difference is that this house has a lemon tree in its yard. A woman with sandy hair holding a wicker basket overflowing with flowers is heading into the house. Sammy and Simone would be delighted to have all of this, to imagine their way into the lives of all the small people occupying this town. Kevin will need to call the movers and ask them to bring a larger truck so they can pack all of this—the trains and restaurants and mountains and benches and people, so, so many tiny little people scurrying all over the town. He imagines their full and busy new lives in Pennsylvania, a giant jar of preserved lemons on the kitchen counter, this small, elaborate world in the basement, and he says, "Yes, we'd love it."

PART III

Later

Say Hello

As he waits to go onstage, Jackson is reminded of a time long ago when he stood near the curtains before a performance, that time with Maria too. That was over a decade ago, at his elementary school talent show, and the tricks he performed were small and quiet, what he was capable of doing as a nine-year-old. And Maria—who is so beautiful and kind and now, so famous—agreed to help him then, just as she agreed to be his assistant today. Jackson cannot believe he is on this large stage in New York City, in the semifinals of *Talent Abounds!* The theater seats two thousand, the biggest crowd, by far, Jackson has ever performed for. He is the only magician in the competition now, the only one remaining of the three magicians that America voted through to the quarterfinals. It is the middle of the summer before Jackson's sophomore year of college, and even though he's registered for classes for the fall, he's unsure of whether he'll return. The winner is crowned in September, after classes have started.

Maria leans in close to Jackson and whispers, "I love them," as she points to a screen showing the act currently onstage. There is Joey, who is around Jackson's age, with his dog, Wally, a border collie trained to jump through hoops, walk backward, jump rope, and do flips in the air.

"Do you think they'll win?" Jackson asks, and Maria laughs and says, "Depends on whether America likes dogs or magic better. Or child singers. Why are there always so many child singers on this show?"

There are too many of them, running around backstage, warbling their warm-up exercises, and Jackson does his best to avoid them.

"Border collies are really smart," Jackson says, pointing at the screen where the dog is doing a handstand on his front paws. "They're the easiest dogs to train. They always win the agility competitions in dog shows."

"I didn't know that," says Maria. "My dog is very dumb. Maybe the next one should be a border collie."

Maria owns a Pomeranian with a tongue that lolls out. In paparazzi photos, Maria is always carrying the dog, and Jackson is unsure if the dog is able to walk, or if it's been so damaged by overbreeding that the ability to walk has been bred out in favor of cuteness. Sometimes the dog is carried by Maria's boyfriend. Jackson googled him. He is a regular person, not an actor, a skinny guy with thick-framed glasses who works as an animator for Disney.

It is perhaps a cheap move to have Maria as his assistant; Jackson knows this. He knows he'll probably get a lot of votes from her fans, most of whom likely don't care at all about magic. Right now Jackson can barely look at Maria because she is so beautiful, someone you'd see only on TV or a movie screen, not in real life. She is wearing a red dress, which is short and tight, and shiny silver heels, and her hair is twirled up on her head, and she looks every bit the famous actress. Jackson squeezes his eyes shut and then opens them quickly, as if doing so will wake him from this dream, an absurd dream of being on this large stage, of having Maria Robles as his assistant once again. He thinks of the last time they were onstage together; she was dressed as a dove in an oversized white sweatsuit and orange socks, and he wore an old vest that belonged to his mother. Now he's in black slacks and a black button-down and his hair is tall and spiky. His mother showed him how to use mousse and gel—not too much, so it looks as if there's nothing in his hair—to make it stand up in this gravity-defying way, as if it too is performing a feat of magic.

Maria currently stars as Hope Springs, a young cardiologist who's survived heart problems of her own—both medical and romantic—on *Choosing Hope*, the most popular drama on television. *Choosing Hope* is on the same channel as *Talent Abounds!*, so of course the producers were delighted when Jackson mentioned Maria's involvement in tonight's show. A few weeks ago, after he made it to the quarterfinals, Jackson nervously sent a direct message to Maria. He didn't think she'd respond. He assumed she got thousands of messages a day. He wrote, "I don't know if you remember me, but a long time ago you were my assistant for a magic show. You were a dove." Two minutes later, she wrote back, "Of course I remember you. Life is good? What are you up to?" And he wrote back and told her yes, life is very good, he is in college in Boston, a biology major, and after he graduates he wants to go to veterinary school. He told her about the magic, which was only supposed to be a hobby, something he practiced in front of a mirror at home or at kids' birthday parties, and how *Talent Abounds!* was an unexpected surprise. He asked if maybe, just maybe, she might be willing to come to New York and help him out for this one show. He doesn't write this, but he knows she has an apartment on the Upper West Side, and she flies across the country all the time, so maybe this wasn't that big of an ask. "Yes," Maria responded immediately, "let's get the band back together!"

And so here she is, standing right next to him, and it feels unreal. Jackson and Maria stare at one of the screens backstage and watch Joey and Wally the Collie. Joey scrambles up a tall tower and puts on a wig of long blond hair made of yellow yarn. He leans out the window, flings the yellow yarn braid out the window of the tower. He is Rapunzel. Wally scrambles up the braid, leaps into the window of the tower to save Joey, and the crowd cheers.

"Do you remember Kevin? He worked in the mall," Jackson says.

Maria pauses, scrunches up her eyes. "I don't know," she says. "What did he look like?"

"He had a big orange beard. And then he shaved it off."

"Oh, right, him. The bookstore guy. He would dress up and read to kids. He was nice, easy to talk to."

"He breeds and trains border collies now. So if you want, I can put you in touch if you want to get a second dog. A smarter one."

"A smarter dog would be really, really nice," Maria says.

After Jackson exchanged messages with Maria, he started googling other people from his past, seeing what became of them. When he googled Kevin, he found a page for his business, based on a large farm in Pennsylvania. The website featured a picture of Kevin and his wife and their teenage twins, whom Jackson vaguely remembers. Kevin's hair is gray now, and he looks happy in all the photos on the website. His wife is a poet who has won a lot of awards. It seems strange, Jackson thinks, to list his wife's awards on a website about breeding and training dogs, but maybe Kevin is so proud he can't help but brag. There are also photographs of Kevin's kids training several of their border collies and competing at dog shows and some of Kevin's mother-in-law, who retired from her job as a librarian and now helps the family train dogs.

Feeling buoyed by Maria's response to his message, Jackson decided to send Kevin an e-mail at the address listed on his website, and a day later a response appeared. "Those days at the mall seem so long ago!" Kevin wrote. "They seem like a completely different life." Jackson agreed; all those afternoons sitting in the empty salon, reading books and doing homework, waiting for his mother to finish her work for the day feel so different from his current life, which was packed from morning to night when he was in school and packed and busy in a different way now that he's on *Talent Abounds!* Jackson told Kevin about his aspirations to be a vet, and Kevin wrote that if he ever wanted to, he could come work with the dogs. And so there's this possibility, a way to work hands-on with animals, so if magic does not pan out—and Jackson understands it most likely won't—then there's this thing he can do, something practical. It's strange, Jackson thinks, how things loop around, how people from your past can come back into your life—even someone as famous as Maria—and say hello again.

Joey and Wally the Collie run off the stage to much applause, and Maria reaches out a hand to pet the dog, says, "Wally! Great job!" Joey comes to a complete stop, staring at Maria. "You too," Maria adds.

"You're here," says Joey.

Jackson smiles because it is the sort of thing he would say, something obvious and true, but not really worth saying. He's getting better at talking, at being confident, and he credits magic with helping him overcome his shyness. When he's onstage, he feels like someone else, like someone who knows all the right things to say. Being on *Talent Abounds!* has been good for him.

"You're on in one minute," says the stage manager, holding up his pointer finger. Jackson nods, checks his watch, looks where the second hand is. He knows no one wears this kind of watch anymore, the kind that needs to be wound every morning. But the watch was given to him long ago by his friend Mrs. Goodson. It belonged to her husband, and Jackson has worn it almost every day since Mrs. Goodson died. It's special to him, and on days when he forgets to put it on, he feels like something is missing.

"People are going to be so surprised when they see you," Jackson says.

"People are going to be so surprised by your trick. I can't believe how good you are, Jackson. You're really, really good."

Jackson feels his face warm, embarrassed by this praise. "Do you have the gun?"

Maria nods, points to the small pouch around her waist that houses the prop. It took a lot to convince Maria to shoot it. It's a trick gun, releases only noise and smoke, and only shoots hollow wax bullets that heat up and melt once the trigger is pulled. But it looks real. Maria asked if there was any other way to do this trick, but Jackson said no. He has wanted to perform the bullet catch for years. He wants to put his own spin on the trick, wants to change it in a way that feels significant. And maybe, he hopes, this can help them both with what they witnessed all those years ago.

Jackson nods at Maria, and they step out onto the stage. The crowd starts cheering, delighted by Maria's presence. Is this what it's like to be popular? Just the fact of your presence is enough, just you being here—not doing anything—is enough. The clapping gets louder in a swell, and then all four of the judges rise. They are receiving a standing ovation even though they have not performed yet. Maria smiles at him, acts as if this is all a big surprise, but Jackson wonders if this is what her life is like all the time. Sometimes people recognize him on the street and tell him they like his tricks, say they hope he wins the show. But that's nothing like this, an entire auditorium on their feet.

Jackson scans the audience for his mother. It's hard to see because of all the lights shining onstage, but his mother is in the row right behind the judges, and the judges are lit from above and the front, so his mother is bathed in light. She is in art school in Manhattan; she got a special scholarship for adult students and she, like Jackson, is a sophomore. Jackson and his mother talk on the phone every week, compare their classes, complain about homework. His mother says it's weird being a fifty-year-old sophomore, but she minds it less than she thought she would. She tells him her classmates can't believe it when she tells them how old she is. Jackson thinks she still looks young, because she's only got a few strands of white hair, because her skin is still smooth and clear. "Asian don't raisin, Mom," Jackson tells her, and she laughs, curses his memory, says he's never forgotten a single thing she ever said.

She still cuts hair on the weekends to earn some money, but she's going into debt to pay tuition because she wants to dedicate herself to school. Jackson suspects his mother waited so long to go to college because she was always taking care of him, because she wouldn't ever put herself first. If he wins *Talent Abounds!*, if he wins the $1,000,000 prize, he will pay for her tuition, and he'll pay the rent on an apartment with enough space to set up her easel and paints, and she can move out of her tiny place in Queens. But even if he doesn't win, she seems happier than he ever remembers her being, and that's worth something too.

Finally, the British judge, Oliver, turns to the crowd and shushes them. "Jackson has an act to do!" he declares. It takes almost a minute—Jackson knows because he sneaks glances at his watch—for the clapping to quiet down.

The judges sit, and then Brittany, the young judge who rose to fame on a dancing competition show, looks at Maria and says, "It's an honor. A true, true honor."

Brittany is known for being melodramatic, and Jackson glances at his mother and sees she's grinning, trying not to laugh.

"It's an honor for *me* being Jackson's assistant. He's an amazing magician," Maria says.

"And how did you two come to know each other?" asks Gail, who is about Jackson's mother's age, who decades ago used to be as successful in acting as Maria is now, but for the last decade has served only as a judge on a variety of reality shows.

"We're old friends from long ago," Maria says and Jackson thinks that if it hadn't been for the mall, they never would have met. How strange that the mall—such an ordinary place—could bring people together who might not have otherwise crossed paths.

"Well, onward!" says Mort, a short, bald comedian with a lisp who no one thinks is particularly funny anymore. Jackson likes Mort, though, because he laughs extra loudly every time a comedian performs on the show, whether or not the comedian is funny. And Mort is good at moving things along, at saying "Onward!" when there's been too much chatter, too much idle time onstage.

Jackson turns to the audience and describes the bullet catch. He holds up a small aluminum cup and tells the audience Maria will shoot a bullet from across the stage and he'll catch it in the cup in his mouth. They'll hear the bullet rattling in the cup, unless it shoots through it and into his throat.

"This trick sounds extremely dangerous," says Oliver, and Jackson says, "It's the most dangerous trick in the world. Throughout history magicians have died performing it."

"We've got our medics on standby!" declares Mort, and two figures step out of the curtains to the back of the stage.

Jackson walks to stage right and holds up the aluminum cup, which is the size of a shot glass. Maria walks to the other side of the stage, turns to face the audience, then slowly withdraws the gun from a pouch strapped to her waist. The lights dim and images of a starry night sky appear on the screen behind them. Spotlights illuminate only Jackson and Maria; the stars fade and the rest of the stage is bathed in black. Eerie music plays. Maria lifts the gun so it's pointed right at Jackson. He puts the cup in his mouth, holds it between his teeth. The volume of the music lowers until there's only silence. No one in the theater is talking or rustling; they are all paying attention. Maria holds both hands out in front of her, steadying the gun. Jackson quickly blinks twice, the signal that it's time.

Maria pulls the trigger and a booming sound fills the theater. It's not the sound of a gunshot, but rather the sound of flapping wings. A cloud of smoke emerges from the barrel of the gun and from out of the smoke one hundred doves appear, wings flapping, white feathers illuminated by the spotlight above. All the doves flap and flap, in flight, and arrange themselves. It takes a few moments for the audience to recognize what has happened: the doves have come together to form the shape of a heart, a white, beating heart at the center of the stage.

Jackson can hear *oohs* and *aahs* coming from the audience. The sound of flapping wings fills the theater. Jackson knows this heart is cheesy, but can't something be cheesy and spectacular too? He plucks the cup out of his mouth. Maria turns toward the audience and shows that her hands are empty. She unbuckles the pouch from her waist and it too is empty. The gun disappeared into the cloud of smoke a few moments after it was shot.

Jackson walks in front of the heart of birds and holds up the empty metal cup. Then he tilts it toward the birds, and one by one, they fly into the cup, which isn't even big enough to hold one bird. Within a minute all one hundred doves are gone. The audience gasps, unaware Jackson's trick is performed with holograms and projections.

Once the birds have disappeared, Jackson again tilts the cup to show it's empty. He covers it completely with both hands, and when he lifts the hand on top, the cup is gone and one last dove remains. This is his one and only dove, Harry, named, of course, after Houdini. Harry lives with Jackson in his off-campus apartment. Jackson filmed Harry many times to create the images projected onstage, layered multiple recordings of his flapping wings, and no one but his mother, Maria, and the stage techs know the secret behind his magic.

Harry stands patiently on Jackson's palm, and Jackson raises his hand and blows gently on the bird, who takes off and lands on Mort's right shoulder. The audience jumps to their feet, clapping loudly, and for a moment it feels as if everyone in the theater believes magic is real.

Even if he doesn't get to the next round, this feels like enough. Jackson looks at his mother in the first row and remembers the talent show in the elementary school auditorium when she clapped so loudly for him, even though his tricks were small and no one else cared about them. He remembers that oversize vest with the floral embroidery on the back. He remembers feeling small and stupid until he heard his mother's applause cutting through the silence.

He thinks about those quiet afternoons in Sunshine Clips, his mother sketching with a free pen from the bank on the back of long CVS receipts, him reading books in an empty stylist's chair—and mostly those chairs were empty, and mostly their afternoons were quiet—Mrs. Goodson the only regular customer. Everything feels full now: there is such a din of noise in this room, and back at his mother's apartment there are canvases propped against every wall, the oil paint on them slowly drying, the rooms filled with color and light. He thinks about how they have come a long way from those days at the mall, those quiet afternoons of folding black capes under flickering fluorescent lights, of glancing into the hallway at that WET FLOOR sign in the same spot for over a year because no one ever fixed the leaky roof. Jackson looks at his mother smiling and clapping, and he thinks how, in so many ways, their lives turned out to be spectacular.

KARIN LIN-GREENBERG is a Chinese American award-winning writer whose debut collection, *Faulty Predictions*, received the Flannery O'Connor Award for Short Fiction. Her second collection, *Vanished*, was the winner of the Prairie Schooner Raz-Shumaker Book Prize in Fiction. Her story "The Sweeper of Hair," the basis of this novel's opening chapter, was a finalist for the Nelson Algren Literary Award and was published in the *Chicago Tribune*. Lin-Greenberg is an associate professor in the English Department at Siena College in upstate New York. Find out more at karinlingreenberg.com.

Acknowledgments

Thank you to Jess Errera and Kathy Schneider for their wonderful advice and expert guidance; I'm lucky to work with you both. Thank you too to the team at the Jane Rotrosen Agency for their support of this novel. Thank you to Jenny Alton for believing in this book and for asking the right questions about the characters and plot that sent me down a productive path of revision. Enormous thanks to Dan Smetanka for the insightful edits that made this a better book. I'm grateful to Laura Berry, Rachel Fershleiser, Megan Fishmann, and everyone else at Counterpoint for all you have done for this book. Thank you to Nicole Caputo and Jaya Miceli for the beautiful cover.

Thank you to Premila Reddy, without whom this book would not exist out in the world. Thank you to Helen Fuller for reading a draft and lending her expertise on nine-year-olds. Thank you to Christine Sneed for providing valuable feedback early on that helped me figure out the characters in this novel. Thank you to my family, especially my brother, Erik Lin-Greenberg, for his enthusiastic support. And thank you to Jeff Janssens for, among many other things, always being my first and most encouraging reader.